DELIVER THYSELF FROM EVIL

Rand Corle

ISBN:
ISBN-13: 978-0615805719
ISBN-10: 061580571X

CONTENTS

1 - AN ACT OF DEFIANCE

Michael Long stood nearly motionless, his body slightly bent toward the delicate task before him, his fingers wrapped carefully around the heavy brass knob attached to the front door. The door was closing slowly, inch by painful inch, but this was a process that could not be rushed. He leaned in further and pressed his ear against the wood, listening closely for any sound of movement from inside. The bolt touched the strike-plate with a faint 'click', and Michael froze just for an instant, his heart pounding in his ears. A momentary shiver of fear ran up his spine. Was the noise loud enough for his mother to hear? Don't be stupid, he told himself, of course she didn't hear it. But he could not be absolutely certain of that. Edith Long was known for her ability to hear sounds completely inaudible to others, and if she caught him sneaking out of the house he was going to be in big trouble.

Last night before he fell asleep, Michael had considered all the risks of what he planned. There was no point in going over them again now, and this was no time for cold feet. He took a quick breath, gave another easy tug, and the latch settled softly into the jamb.

It was the summer of 1963. The sun, high in a cloudless sky, marked the hour as shortly after noon. Heat waves already danced above the sloping brick drive that led off toward the highway at the foot of the hill. The broad, open lawn, immaculately kept and well watered, was so brightly lit that the grass looked almost silver-gray rather than the lush green that was its color in softer light. There was some relief from the heat on the covered porch where a swirling,

1

irregular breeze kept the air moving. But the boy did not notice the heat and had no intention of staying on the porch.

With the front door closed Michael turned, took the tall front steps with a single gigantic leap, and hit the ground running. In a flash he was around the corner of the house and into the garden behind it. A mixed stand of cedar and oak on the west side of the garden was his first objective. A few dozen yards into the trees and he was no longer visible from the house. Glancing back to make sure he could not be seen, he abruptly changed directions.

He ran across a broad, grassy clearing, forced his way through a dogwood thicket on the other side, and finally came to the tall brick fence that surrounded the house and grounds. A ten-foot-high fence is no obstacle for a determined boy, and he made short work of the barrier as he scrambled up a nearby tree, leaped onto the fence's wide top, then onto a tree on the other side and back to the ground again. The chance of immediate discovery was gone, but the boy pushed on rapidly, eager to put distance between himself and what lay behind.

Beyond the fence stretched a broad area of thickly forested hills and swampy lowlands bisected by a small river valley. Michael's father owned the land, an irregularly shaped tract that he used for hunting and fishing on those rare occasions when he had the time for it, but the boy and his father never came here together. In the woods Michael was always alone, and most of the time he preferred it that way.

A few people thought the boy was misunderstood. Most, with neither kindness nor understanding, thought him abnormal. But if the word 'abnormal' is taken to mean 'not normal' both opinions were quite correct. Michael was unusually quiet and unusually self-contained for his age. He had no real friends and sought none, preferring the companionship of a good book to playing with the neighborhood kids. In school, where he could be heard to speak most often, his quick mind alienated his peers fully as often as it astonished his teachers.

His mother often had occasion to call him disobedient, and when she was really angry, a number of other terms even less complementary. He had no desire to anger his mother. All he wanted was the time and the freedom to discover the world in his own way, but his mother had other ideas. Children needed structure and guidance, and with extraordinary determination, she provided both.

When she told him the day before that he had better be on time for his next lesson or there would be hell to pay, he knew she meant it. She didn't exactly use the phrase "hell to pay" but she didn't have to. He knew from long experience what it meant to break one of his mother's rules, and on this particular summer afternoon he was frankly determined to pay hell whatever price it required.

About a quarter mile beyond the fence he came to a low rise and slowed his pace. On the other side of the rise the ground sloped steeply downward into the river valley. He veered to his left into a gully that ran from near the top of the rise to the valley floor and half slid-half ran to the bottom. The ground near the river was spongy but dry this time of year. He picked his way through the trees and undergrowth and paused briefly at the river bank to select the best way of getting to the other side.

When the snow melted in the spring the little stream became a torrent that spilled from its banks and covered the entire valley with rushing water. But now the river flowed peacefully on its winding course beneath a solid canopy of leaves. The sandy stream bed was strewn with rocks that ranged from small pebbles to large boulders rising well above the water line. The boy crossed by leaping from boulder to boulder and quickly climbed the opposite bank and the steep hill beyond.

A half-mile past the river valley the woods ended abruptly at the edge of a large, sloping meadow, and Michael stepped into the light. This was the western edge of his father's land, the place he usually stopped to rest when he came out here.

Several feet in front of him a bushy-tailed grey squirrel, startled by the boy's unexpected appearance, froze for a heartbeat and eyed him suspiciously from its perch on an old, weed-covered plow. A look of mild amusement flickered across the boy's face. He recognized the animal from its tail, which was unnaturally bent to one side, a relic of some forgotten skirmish in its battle for survival. The squirrel was often around to greet him, and the lad always looked forward to the encounter. He slowly raised his hand and said softly, "Hey there, buddy. How's it going?" The squirrel's tail gave a nervous twitch in response. Sometimes the boy brought it little tidbits of food, and it waited for a moment to see if any would appear. But there was no food today, the boy having left in too much of a rush to visit the kitchen first, and the squirrel did not wait long.

Its endless quest for food allowed for no wasted time. Suddenly the squirrel's tail gave another twitch, and it jumped from the plow into the tall grass, off to forage beneath the giant cottonwoods that grew near the field's edge.

As he watched the squirrel disappear another slight smile could be seen to flicker across the boy's face. Then, pulling a big red bandana from the back pocket of his jeans, he wiped the sweat from his forehead. The sunlight fell hot on his skin, and the glare caused him to shade his eyes with his open palm as he walked over to the plow. There was an orphan ash tree struggling with limited success to grow through the plow's hitch assembly. Under it, he found a spot that was partially out of the sun, and sat down to rest.

It was one of those rare Minnesota afternoons when the sky was a crystalline blue from horizon to zenith. The meadow lay luminous in the late July sun, and the air had a quality of quivering transparency peculiar to the driest and hottest of high summer days. Trees, rocks, even blades of grass appeared to shimmer in the rising heat but somehow remained clear and distinct even as they seemed to move. An intermittent breeze from the southwest carried the remote songs of meadow larks and the sweet smell of fresh-cut hay curing in the sun. The tall grasses on the fence row swayed gently in the restless air, speaking in arid whispers.

High in the sky an eagle circled, its lazy wings stretched wide to catch the rising air. It saw the boy but ignored him, its sharp eyes fastened instead on the almost imperceptible movement in the grass not far from the boy that betrayed the location of a bull snake. The boy noticed the snake too. His eyes couldn't match the eagle's, but his ears caught the unmistakable hiss of scales on dry grass. From the sound he knew the snake was twenty to thirty feet away and large, perhaps as much as four feet long. It had to be a bull snake because it was the only species in this region large enough to make the sound he heard, and it must be hunting the squirrel or one of its cousins. He hoped the snake would fail even though he knew it had to kill to live. He didn't like the thought of the squirrel being crushed to death in the coils of a snake. The boy felt a sense of connection with the squirrel and the other wildlife of these woods and meadows. There were predators in his world too, and like the squirrel he kept them at bay through self-reliance and singular purpose.

The child was small in stature for an eleven-year-old, a little over four feet tall and fence-rail thin. His eyes were of a somewhat indeterminate color. People did not remember the color of his eyes, but rather the direct, penetrating way he had of observing the world about him. His high forehead was partially hidden by a shock of unruly brown hair. His manner was alert, his brow perpetually furrowed by an enduring quest to understand everything. His mouth was calm and serious, and when he paused to think he had the subconscious habit of drawing his cheeks in slightly, making him appear just as surly and difficult as his mother believed him to be.

There was another characteristic feature in his manner that waxed and waned in direct correlation to the physical proximity of his mother. When he left the house, the feature had been sharply evident. Now it was almost gone. The feature can best be described as vigilance, the kind of vigilance born of an acute awareness that bad things can happen, and that one had better be ready when they do.

As his breathing slowed, his face began to relax. He did not think about it, but he was beginning to feel better than when he left the house. The world always seemed brighter and more benevolent out here, and what the world gave him, the boy subconsciously reflected back.

He felt a sudden impatience to push on and rising to his feet he started across the field at a brisk trot. The meadow hay lay cut and neatly raked, and he lifted his arms wide and leaped each straight windrow as he came to it as though he planned to soar rather than jump. If his mother had seen him in this moment she certainly would have had to look twice to recognize him. In the short span of time it took to catch his breath his face had gone through a remarkable transformation. In place of vigilance there was a look of simple joy and easy, careless serenity, a look so common to boys his age and so foreign to the personality the lad showed in front of others. The wrinkled brow had disappeared almost entirely, and for the moment so had the seriousness, abandoned at the brink of this sunny land and the summer afternoon he would enjoy as long as he could make it last.

On the other side of the field Michael carefully worked his way through a tangle of rusty barbed wire and plunged into a tall thicket that grew upon the steep hillside beyond. His path took him up and around the hill until he finally broke through to a small patch of open ground near the summit. From this vantage point he could look far into the distance in every direction except toward home.

Breathing hard and sweating heavily from the climb the boy again pulled out his bandana and sat down facing toward the west. Far away a train whistle blew. He shaded his eyes and squinted at the horizon, trying to find the source of the sound. The railroad passed no more than thirty feet from the base of the hill, its right-of-way flanked by a busy country highway. Vehicles of every shape and description rushed back and forth constantly, and long trains rumbled by at least every half hour.

He loved this place as he loved no other. He loved it because it was both the loneliest and the busiest spot he knew. Here on this hill he was connected to the hustle and bustle of human life, yet he stood apart from it, free to think his private thoughts and dream his secret dreams uninterrupted, but always accompanied by the ubiquitous, impersonally stimulating din of a multitude of human purposes that were not his own. He knew there were people in the world who went where they pleased and did what they wanted. Someday he would do the same.

As he watched the traffic pass beneath his feet his thoughts focused on a topic that was often on his mind of late. He wanted more than he wanted anything else to walk down the hill and stand beside the road with his thumb stuck out. Someone would stop and give him a ride. He'd seen hitchhikers do it many times. It didn't matter where he went after that as long as it was away from here. It was not yet time he knew, but he was determined to do it one day— to quit this place, to fly away like the larks and the robins when the air turned cold and the leaves began to fall—except that he would not return again in the spring. When he left he would never return. This is why he came back again and again to this lookout high on the hill, to dream of the day he could leave it forever.

He had been on the hill perhaps an hour when he heard a voice calling him from far away. From the sound of it, Danny didn't seem very happy about looking for him. As he got closer the boy heard his older half-brother more clearly. "Michael! Goddamn it, Michael, where the hell are you?"

He could hide, Michael thought, but that would only postpone the inevitable. Sooner or later he would have to return to the house, so it might as well be now. He got up quickly and started down the hill at an angle, away from the sound of Danny's voice. Danny was almost as familiar with the woods as Michael was, but nobody, not even Danny, knew of the lookout on the hill, and Michael wanted to keep it that way. He circled back avoiding the meadow to get behind his brother, and not until he was well away from the lookout did he respond.

"Danny, I'm over here," he called.

Danny turned, swore again and changed directions.

When he drew close Danny spoke angrily, "Damn it, I've been looking for you for half the day, kid. I've seen you out this way before, but Christ, this is half-way to the next county."

Michael smirked at the exaggeration. "Come on, Danny. It's not *that* far. What do you want?"

"What do you think I want, you little shit? Did you think you were going to get away with this? The bitch is mad as hell, and she wants you back at the house right now. You know she's going to kill you for this."

The bitch is what Danny called his stepmother. Dan Long's first child was a bastard, labeled so in the callous custom of the age for having exhibited the inexcusable judgment of choosing parents who were not married. Danny had been born out of wedlock to the part-time housekeeper who worked for Dan's parents. At his father's insistence, the boy came to live in the Long household after his mother died of cancer when Danny was six.

Even though there were several years between Danny's birth and Edith Long's marriage to Michael's father, Edith resented the boy almost as deeply as she resented Dan's insistence that the boy come to live with them. It wasn't that she blamed Danny personally for events he could not possibly have controlled; she just did not suffer sinners easily. The child was a product of sin, a constant reminder of his father's lack of Christian virtue. She would have hotly denied that she treated him different from Michael, but the truth was that Danny was already an angry and headstrong child when he came to live in the big house at the edge of town, and Edith's somewhat draconian child-rearing methods only made him more so.

Edith was a born-again Christian, come to her faith not in childhood, but shortly after she discovered that her husband was not quite the man she thought she married. There was something both comforting and irresistibly compelling in the unbending message and the harsh demands religion placed upon her life. It gave her the moral and emotional anchor she had always sought, and until the moment she accepted Christ as her savior, had never found.

When Michael Long was very small, he genuinely enjoyed his mother's Bible lessons, and he believed the stories she read to him. His mother said the Bible was a true account of actual events, and he had no reason to doubt her. The stories were fascinating, full of great and heroic characters who did wonderful things. He vowed that he would do great things too one day, just like the people in the Bible stories.

He didn't remember exactly when he began to doubt, but by the time he reached the age of nine or ten the stories somehow began to lose their luster. They didn't seem real anymore. If these were actual stories of real events, then there were a lot of questions that needed answers. But his mother believed faith was the only path to knowledge, and that meant logical questions with regard to religion were not only unnecessary, they were downright sacrilegious.

She told Michael often that he would understand everything in good time, and at first he accepted that. But as his mind developed, no understanding came to him, only more doubts and questions that she failed to answer. He could have kept his mouth shut and just accepted his mother's words at face value, but he was far too independent for that. To Michael, what was true and what wasn't mattered a great deal, and if things didn't make sense he insisted on clarification. As a result the lessons gradually became a test of wills and a source of confrontation rather than the entertainment and solace they were in the beginning.

Yesterday, when his mother was talking about the Great Flood and Noah's ark, Michael had listened quietly until she got to the part about a sample of every living thing marching into the ark to be saved. He'd heard the story dozens of times, and there were many things about it that troubled him. This time he interrupted to ask, "If every animal was put into the ark, what happened to the dinosaurs?"

His mother looked at him sharply and then demanded, "Where did you read about dinosaurs?"

"They're pretty hard to miss, Mom. All you have to do is read the science section in the newspaper. It's no big secret."

His mother sighed heavily. It was both a sign of exasperation and a warning not to try her patience. It was becoming harder and harder to protect him from this kind of worldly corruption, but even worse, the boy seemed to seek it out rather than try to avoid it as she warned him to. She knew the question was no accident. Undoubtedly, he had been reading about dinosaurs. He read about them because the subject interested him, and that worried her more than anything else.

When her son first started asking questions she looked upon them as evidence of keen interest. They were a useful diversion that allowed her to expand upon the lesson she was teaching. But she soon came to regard Michael's frequent interruptions as her personal cross to bear. The questions were endless, and for the most part unanswerable. But the fact that her responses didn't satisfy the boy caused her neither to question her beliefs nor to modify her teaching methods. It just made her angry, and the more difficult and persistent the questions were, the angrier she became.

She knew it was futile to explain, but she tried anyway because that's what good Christian mothers were supposed to do. She always did her best to use verbal correction before employing other means.

"There were no dinosaurs, Michael," she said with an air of finality, "and you ought to know that. There is no mention of dinosaurs in the Bible and there are none alive today, so they never existed. They are a figment of man's imagination."

"Then where did all the bones come from?"

She could think of no ready answer that included a Biblical reference, so she made one up. "God allowed Satan to put bones in the ground to test our faith." The Bible didn't say that of course, but given the premise that the Bible was the inerrant word of an omnipotent creator, and the fact that dinosaur bones did indeed exist, she thought it explained things quite nicely.

There were a number of further questions that occurred to Michael at this point, but the notion that dinosaur bones were not really animal bones but mysterious supernatural artifacts seemed rather silly. "Why would God do a stupid thing like that?"

"Michael, that's enough! Do you expect the creator of the universe to drop by and explain everything to you? Use your mind. Reason it through."

"That isn't reason, Mom. It's just stupid."

"Michael, that's it! I will not have you questioning me like this. Do you think I'm lying? The Holy Spirit has revealed God's truth to me!"

"Okay. When is he going to reveal it to me?"

"That will be enough, young man! You are being needlessly difficult and uncooperative, and if you keep this up I will have no choice but to give you a proper beating. Is that what you want?"

"No Mother, I want to understand."

"I'll give you understanding in a minute if you don't stop this foolishness."

It was an undisguised threat calculated to silence him through intimidation, and Michael deeply resented such attempts. With his mother it always came down to threats.

"What's that supposed to mean, Mom? Do you think beating me up again will make you right?"

The remark pushed Edith over the edge. She grabbed Michael by the arm and dragged him off to the bathroom to wash his mouth out with soap for his impudence. Then she gave him five hard blows with the stick she always kept handy for these occasions and pushed him up the stairs to his bedroom.

Her last words to him before she shoved him roughly into his room were: "…and I am sick and tired of you coming in late for your Bible lesson, young man. Tomorrow you *will* be on time and you *will* keep your mouth shut and listen!"

He was late sometimes, but being late wasn't the real issue and Michael knew it. She wasn't angry because he was late. She was angry because he had the audacity to insist upon asking questions she could not answer.

The bedroom door slammed in Michael's face, and Edith's angry steps receded to the end of the hall and tromped back down the stairs. Michael turned to face his room and stood for a moment, staring into the air. Well, if he was going to be beaten whether he showed up or not, he might as well spend his time doing something he actually enjoyed. With an angry shrug he resolved to do something he had never before had the courage to do. Tomorrow he was going to skip the goddamn lesson entirely.

By contemporary standards Edith Long was sufficiently educated and of reasonably sound mind regarding secular concerns. But she was absolutely steadfast in her refusal to apply her intellect to questions of religion, and utterly intolerant of those who did. She did not think herself unreasonable. She believed she could reason with the best of them, but only up to the boundaries of her faith. At some point you had to *believe*, and thinking about things that required the guidance of faith just got you into trouble.

Unlike her parents' church, her adult beliefs required an unbending literal adherence to the Bible's every pronouncement. Every word of every chapter of every book in the Bible was the *truth*. No exceptions. Yes, there were certain passages that seemed to be at odds with each other and with known fact, and those she couldn't successfully rationalize into agreement she dismissed as 'mysteries' that were simply beyond her understanding—mysteries that her intellect could not possibly resolve without her faith to guide it.

If truth be told, the state of Edith's marriage had a lot to do with her choice of faith. The union of Dan and Edith Long had been a disaster almost from the beginning, and there was more than a little spite in the occasion of Edith's epiphany. Michael's father hated it when people preached, and Edith, perfectly aware of her husband's distaste, discovered the ideal excuse to preach all the time. But while it was true that Edith's rebirth in Christ gave her a convenient weapon in her ongoing war with Dan, her actual motivation was irrelevant. The effect on the family was the same whether her conversion was sincere or not. An unhappy marriage became hell-on-earth.

Dan didn't object to religion as such, but he had strong objections to Edith's version. In his adult life Dan had been to church precisely once: to get married, an experience he did not recall with fondness. Although he thought of himself as a Christian, he viewed Edith's somewhat medieval beliefs as way too much of a good thing.

For a time Dan fought his wife's aggressive sermonizing and tried to refute it, but what he regarded as his modern 'humanistic' Christian views were no match for her unbendingly harsh ones, particularly when all of the humanism was due to influences entirely outside of Christianity.

Even if Dan had known the Bible well, which he did not, he could not have defended his beliefs using its authority. Most of what he thought of as his religious beliefs simply were not in the Bible. There was no Biblical reference supporting religious 'humanism,' or anything that even remotely resembled it, unless one were willing to bend the meaning of the text out of all recognition. Actually, Dan could not have defined religious humanism were he asked to do so. It was such an amorphous and question-begging term. His 'religion' actually came from many sources. From the Bible he lifted a few favorite passages that sounded wise to him, and without rhyme or reason labeled the rest parable, legend and metaphor. But as he soon discovered, he could not arbitrarily reject part of the Bible as factual truth and expect to win an argument with someone who arbitrarily accepted all of it. Edith could site scriptural authority to support nearly every scrap of nonsense she uttered, and Dan, while he counted himself a believer, was hamstrung by the baseless conviction that the Bible only meant exactly what it said some of the time. When denying the literal accuracy of any part of the Bible, he called it all into question. Either it was authoritative or it wasn't. If it was then Edith was right, and if it wasn't, his beliefs were as much nonsense as Edith's were.

Dan asked Edith to marry him not because he loved her but because she was pregnant with Michael. He still felt a disquieting sense of guilt over the way he had acted the last time this happened, and he told himself he could learn to love her. But that was a long time ago, and now he could not remember the last time he and his wife had even exchanged a kind word with each other. It was bad enough when they fought, but Edith's endless preaching was just too much. Finally he reached a breaking point, and in a moment of weakness he allowed Edith complete control over the rearing of Michael as a means of getting her to shut up and leave him alone.

One afternoon after a particularly bitter dispute over what kind of religious training the children should have, Dan and Edith came to an agreement. Edith would stop trying to convert her husband and leave Danny alone. In return, Michael would be given to his mother to bring up as she pleased without interference. That was how Michael came under the exclusive influence of his mother, sacrificed like the Biblical fatted calf on the altar of his father's discomfort and his mother's zeal.

At the time it seemed to be the only acceptable solution short of divorce, and Dan thought nothing of what the arraignment would do to Michael. Although he was not consciously aware of it, his second son served as a symbol for his miserable home life. Every time he thought of the kid he thought of Edith's pregnancy and his marriage and became irritated. Let Edith have him, he thought. The child was her mistake. Let her deal with it. The boy seemed happy with his mother, at least at first, and that was good enough.

Dan regarded the agreement as more-or-less permanent, but Edith had no intention of keeping her word. Until God revealed a better way to break down her husband it was simply the expedient thing to do, and it had the advantage of extracting Michael more-or-less permanently from his father's clutches. The bargain held for a week or two and then collapsed over some dispute that nobody could remember. The endless arguments resumed, but the family division stayed in place. Danny hated his stepmother as much as Dan did, and if given a choice he would always choose his father. Michael, who was five years old at the time and still loved both of his parents without reservation, was not allowed a choice. He did not understand what had happened, but eventually he learned to live with it.

Edith's authority on child-rearing was the same as it was for every other subject. The Bible said, "Train up a child in the way he should go: and when he is old, he will not depart from it." It was her sacred duty to train Michael up in the way God commanded, and that is exactly what she intended to do.

But as Michael's young mind began to develop, it became more and more difficult for Edith to answer his doubts and questions in a manner that satisfied him, and gradually she began to rely on force to keep him in line. She didn't want to hurt the boy, but she could not afford to lose control. For the sake of his immortal soul he had to be harnessed by whatever means was required. So the more Michael questioned her teaching the more severe became his punishment. Spankings with an open palm became spankings with a stick. The spankings evolved into beatings. The beatings gradually grew in duration and intensity and the implements of punishment became heavier.

As Michael and Danny drew near the house, fear began to force its way into Michael's mind. It was time to pay for his afternoon of freedom, and he knew the price would be high. He should run away, he thought. He should just turn around and run away and never come back. But he knew with a bitter sense of inevitability that he wouldn't do it.

His mother always stopped when he begged forgiveness and said he was sorry, but the cost of begging carried its own price, and Michael hated giving in. He knew a real man would stand up and fight for what he knew was right. A real man would never give in no matter what the cost, just like his dad when he was in the war. His dad was a hero, with the medals to prove it. Michael wanted to be brave like his dad, but he was old enough to know that courage wasn't something you found on a shelf or borrowed from somebody else. Courage came from inside you. He had no idea how it got there, but if it wasn't in you when you needed it, there was no point in looking elsewhere.

Michael wanted to fight back, but he already knew that would only make it worse. He wanted to run away from home, but he knew he was not yet ready to make his way in the world alone. So today, like so many days before, he was going to be beaten until he begged for his mother's forgiveness. He would hang on for as long as he could stand it, but he knew he was going to break eventually. He always did.

2 - SUFFER NOT THE CHILD

Edith Long sat ram-rod straight, jaw set, hands folded stiffly over the Bible in her lap. Her eyes, hard and narrowed with anger, stared at the door at the other end of the room as though envisioning the forthcoming appearance of an object of intense displeasure.

The plain, wooden rocker upon which she sat moved back and forth in a steady, precise rhythm propelled by her feet pushing down against the floor to rock backward and then pivoting up to allow herself to rock forward. She had been at it for some time, rocking back and forth in a slow, steady rhythm, her muscles making little movement except for those required to make her feet pivot at the ankle.

As was her custom, Edith refused to look for the boy when he failed to show up on time. The Lord would bring him to her eventually. Instead she spent the half hour normally allocated for Michael's daily moral and religious education reading Biblical passages on obedience and punishment. He was often late for his lesson, and he was always punished for it. She hated it when Michael disobeyed almost as much as she hated being forced to punish him.

Being late was one thing. Missing a lesson entirely was unprecedented, and as the hour of one-thirty passed Edith vowed that she would have something special for Michael when he returned. Two o'clock came and went and Edith, getting angrier by the minute, decided it was time to act. She found Danny and bribed him with the promise of a twenty-dollar bill if he found his brother and brought him back to the house. Satisfied that Danny was properly motivated and would do as she asked, she returned to the sun room to wait.

Lately Michael seemed to bring out the worst in her. She knew she sometimes lost control and went a bit too far, so it was a good thing the Lord approved of her methods and motives and forgave her if she occasionally stepped over the line with her son. Disobedience required the application of the stick to keep it from becoming a habit. She had a duty to discipline the child when he strayed no matter what it did to her peace of mind.

The room where Edith sat was called the sunroom, but there was no immediately obvious reason for the name. It was actually a four-season porch. Built by her husband, it wrapped around two sides of the house at a level six inches lower than the main floor. It had its own outside entrance facing west that Michael often used in the summertime when he came in to have his Bible lesson. Windows formed a solid line around the outward facing walls of the room, but as usual they were all tightly covered. Only a few inconsequential afternoon rays penetrated here and there through cracks in the wooden shutters. Edith preferred the shutters closed. The darkness helped her concentration when she dwelt upon the Mind of God.

On one wall a large bookcase rose high into the gloom, its shelves packed with the paraphernalia of Edith's faith. She was an avid reader, and the bookcase contained her entire library of hundreds of devotionals, Bible commentaries and scriptural studies, all of them reviewed and pre-approved by the elders of her church. The walls were otherwise bare except for a needlepoint nativity that occupied an honored spot directly opposite Edith's reading chair. The needlepoint was the product of a church charity auction, made by Edith herself and purchased at the auction for a price far higher than it should have commanded. It was poorly done. As a piece of decorative art it was practically worthless, but the piece served as Edith's constant reminder of the wonderful work she and her church were doing for the less fortunate children of God, and in this light the flaws were practically unnoticeable.

Edith's high-backed rocker was a family heirloom, carried to Minnesota in a covered wagon and handed down from mother to daughter until it reached Edith after her mother died. The chair was simply and expertly built of the finest oak and as solid as the day it was made. Its finish was speckled and darkened with age but it never squeaked despite being used almost daily for nearly a century. Beside the chair was a table of comparable vintage that held a brass reading lamp equipped with a single sixty-watt light bulb. The lamp was the room's only illumination.

Edith's beloved King James Bible lay in her lap. It was her most prized possession, a gift from the members of her congregation in grateful recognition of her tireless charity work. The Bible was a marvel of decorative art, beautifully bound in leather, with delicate, gold-edged leaves, an ornate typeface, and margin illustrations that mimicked a style popular in monasteries a thousand years before. She rarely read it. The typeface gave her a headache and she had other Bibles, but its mere presence made her feel closer to God.

Edith's eyes flickered toward her wrist watch and then back to the door at the end of the room. It was almost three p.m., half the afternoon wasted, gone forever. There was no excuse for this, no conceivable mitigation, no possible misunderstanding. The thought never crossed her mind that Michael might have an acceptable reason for missing his lesson, that he might be hurt or detained for some other reason. He was not supposed to have left his room in the first place, yet he had been gone from the house at least since one p.m. to his mother's certain knowledge. If he was hurt it was God's punishment for disobedience, and she could do nothing about that.

Does he want to make me angry? she thought. Does he want to be punished? Doesn't he understand what he's in for when I get my hands on him? He knows how angry I can get, yet he goes out of his way to provoke me. Edith's jaw muscles worked in frustration. Well this time the child is going to learn once and for all what it meant to disobey his mother!

The outside door opened suddenly and sunlight streamed into the room framing the area where Edith sat. She looked up and her jaw, already thrust forward, jutted out even more aggressively as Michael followed Danny through the door. Michael hesitated just for an instant when he saw his mother's ominous glare, and the screen door struck him in the back, urging him the rest of the way inside.

"Shut the door," Edith snapped. Michael turned around in confusion. The screen door was already closed.

"The other door, Michael. Shut the outside door! Do it now!" Michael turned and pushed the main door closed. The room darkened again.

Edith was seventy pounds heavier than the day she was married, but the weight made her look massive rather than fat. The gloom seemed to accentuate the hard, masculine lines on her face as she rose slowly to her feet. She knew the effect her physical presence would have on Michael and she used it, crossing the dimness with measured, deliberate menace to tower over him.

She stopped within inches of her son, forcing him to bend his head back to face her. Suppressing an almost unbearable urge to look away, Michael bore her gaze evenly, waiting for her to speak.

"Where have you been?" she demanded.

"Out walking," Michael answered. The tremor in his voice was slight, but Edith recognized it as a weakness she could exploit.

"All afternoon? Out walking all afternoon? You missed your lesson completely! This is unacceptable, absolutely unacceptable!"

She waited a moment for a further response but none came. "Well? What do you have to say for yourself?" she barked.

"Nothing."

"Nothing? *Nothing?* We'll see about that! I am finished with your sinful disobedience, Michael. It ends now. You are going to learn respect for God and your elders once and for all."

Danny interrupted her. "Hey, what about my twenty bucks?"

Edith turned her angry eyes on Danny and snapped, "You'll get your money when we're finished here."

Michael glanced at Danny but said nothing. He was not surprised that his brother was going to be paid for finding him, Danny would not have done his stepmother's bidding at all without some form of payment, and it made no difference. Eventual punishment was inevitable.

"Get over here, Michael!" Edith turned, gesturing angrily for him to follow as she walked back toward her chair. Danny could see that his brother was shaking. He knew Michael was afraid, and he had good reason to be. Edith looked as though she might explode at any moment. The fool really stepped in it this time, Danny thought. If Michael would just get in his thick head what it took to get along in the world, he wouldn't run into problems like this, but he always had to do things the hard way. The little shit really pissed him off. He had to be such a goddamn martyr all the time.

Danny didn't have to attend Bible lessons, and being under his father's protection, he had no reason to fear his stepmother's wrath. But he knew what he would do in Michael's position. He would nod his head in agreement, keep his mouth shut and give the old biddy the finger when she wasn't looking. You had to pick your battles. A half-hour of Edith's babble wasn't all that big a deal if it bought you freedom the rest of the day. You couldn't argue with her. It was pointless, and dangerous, as Michael ought to have figured out by now. Danny had tried several times to give Michael the benefit of his older, wiser experience. When the beatings first started he'd even tried to help the pitiful little idiot a couple of times, until Edith complained to Dan and his father told him in no uncertain terms not to get between Michael and his mother. He felt sorry for Michael in a distant way, but the distance was growing. There was no denying that Michael brought this on himself, and Danny was sick of the whole situation. Michael just wouldn't listen to reason, and it was foolish to help those who refused to be helped.

One of Edith's favorite Bible verses was Proverbs 13:24. "He who spareth the rod hateth his son: but he that loveth him correcteth him betimes." The verse was the source of the popular phrase: "Spare the rod and spoil the child." Like every other verse in the Bible, Edith took it very seriously. There were three heavy sticks leaning against the wall behind the rocker, each designed for ascending levels of God's loving correction. Today she chose the largest.

Edith turned back and glared down at her son again. She held the instrument of his punishment firmly in her right hand and smacked it against her left palm once as if to emphasize what lay in store. This time Michael did look away, his face blank, his eyes vacant as he struggled to make the room disappear. Maybe if he made himself go numb it wouldn't be as bad.

"This is going to hurt me more than it does you," she said as she hefted the stick.

Michael still did not look at his mother, but his eyes suddenly came into focus and his mouth tightened into a grim line of determination. "This is going to hurt me more than it does you," he mimicked the words derisively in his mind. What a goddamn lie! Thank you, Mother. Thank you for reminding me how much I hate you.

It was her face that betrayed her. Edith's face held not the slightest hint of pain or sorrow but rather an entirely unholy eagerness to inflict both on Michael. She grabbed his arm and gave it a cruel twist as she pulled him toward the familiar spot near one end of the room. She turned him roughly so he was facing the wall. "Now, let's see how long you have nothing to say," she said thickly. Then she stepped back, raised the stick, and brought it down hard on her son's shoulder.

His legs buckled, and Michael collapsed to his knees. The rush of breath that escaped his mouth was a stifled cry of pain.

Edith raised the stick and held it above her head. "Still nothing to say?" she demanded.

Michael was silent.

The stick slammed down on the other shoulder. A low groan got past his clenched teeth, and Michael's anger ignited anew as he berated himself for his weakness. Edith heard the noise and paused again.

"I don't want to hurt you, Michael. You can stop this."

Michael said nothing, his jaw clenched shut against the pain and his eyes wide open, focused on the wall before him.

The stick rose again. Another blow landed followed by another pause. Michael used the moment to rise to his feet. He glanced back at her, hoping she was finished, knowing she was not. The stick was already moving again. He turned away, hearing her grunt with effort as she swung. Thud! The stick connected with his upper back. "Confess your sins, child!" Another silent pause and then… "This is the price you pay for disobedience, young man." Thud.

The blows were aimed mostly at Michael's back, ribs and shoulders, places where evidence of a beating would be covered with clothing. But it wasn't enough. Michael wasn't talking. He was not giving in. In frustration, Edith changed tactics. Suddenly the stick struck Michael's neck at the base of his skull. He went to his knees again and pitched forward, stunned by the blow. His nose struck the wall and began to bleed.

"Stand up," Edith snapped. "Michael, stand up and take your medicine!"

Michael struggled to regain his feet, one hand on the wall and the other pinching his nose to stop the bleeding. His body was trembling violently now, partly in shock, partly in fear, partly in anger. He did not deserve this! Whatever he did, whoever he may have offended, he did not deserve this. And if there was a God of justice as his mother claimed there was, if there was a God who actually cared for the soul of Michael Long, he would strike this evil woman down where she stood!

She raised the stick again. "Why do you make me do this, Michael? Speak child! Confess your sins!"

Michael *was* speaking, but the voice was only inside his head. "God, make her stop!" screamed the voice. "Please God, make her stop!" It was a prayer in form only. He knew from long experience that God would not answer. If there was a God he was on Edith's side. There was only one way to stop her. He opened his mouth to give her what she wanted but nothing came out. His mouth wouldn't form the words. The pain was almost too much to bear, but letting her win was worse. How he hated her! Not because she beat him but because she made him afraid, and that made him hate himself. Only cowards were afraid.

"Don't let her win." It was the voice inside his head again. "Don't let her win. Don't let her win." The words repeated over and over like a mantra, a plea to his dying courage.

"Say something, Michael. Ask God's forgiveness!" The stick whistled through the air again. Thud.

Was he beginning to feel better? How could that be? Was it numbness or wishful thinking or was it real? Maybe it was the anger he felt building inside him. It seemed to take his mind off the pain. Let it grow, he thought. Let it fill you. Let it protect you. Yes, the agony was fading, forced into the background by something more powerful. He realized suddenly that as long as he was angry she could not break him. Let the anger grow! Let it take over!

The pain faded into sensory background noise. It wasn't real anymore, not like the blood running over his lips and down his chin. The blood became a focal point and a buttress for his defiance, incontestable proof that he could endure the worst his mother could do to him. The salty taste on his lips anchored the fury rising from deep in his gut. The fear and pain became as smoke that ripped apart and vanished in a hurricane of rage.

Michael suddenly realized he was on the floor. Expecting his mother to strike again, he glanced upward and caught Danny gazing down at him from several feet away, a mixture of pity and revulsion in his twisted smile. Michael grimaced, offended by the pity far more than the revulsion. He tried to get up—to tell Danny to get the hell out of the room if he couldn't take it—but his muscles were not working.

Danny observed his brother's struggle for a moment and then with an almost imperceptible shake of his head he turned his back and left. The money could wait. He didn't have to watch this.

Michael's eyes focused on Edith. She was glaring down at him, the stick still raised, but it wasn't moving anymore. He didn't know why she stopped and he couldn't remember when, but he wanted to mock her, to show her he wasn't broken. He managed one word, a word he heard his father and Danny use many times when speaking of Edith, a word he'd never had the courage to use to her face until now. "Bitch," he said. It sounded like a croak rather than a word and he barely heard it himself. But he could tell by the look on her face that she understood him. For a moment he thought she would start in again but she dropped the stick instead.

She was used to that word from her husband, but her own son, her beloved Michael, had just called her a bitch. She could not believe he would do that. Abruptly she turned and left the room.

Edith felt betrayed. Oh, how could she bear this terrible burden The Lord had thrust upon her? Michael's resistance was so strong. He seemed to care nothing for her, or for God. She tried to do her best by him, and he repaid her with disobedience, insults and disrespect. She did not want to beat her son, but God demanded submission. She had to do it. She had to force Michael's obedience. As the only righteous influence in Michael's life the weight of discipline fell on her and her alone. How she wished her husband would accept the Lord. It was so hard bearing this burden on her own, so difficult to bring up a child in Christ with his father steeped in sin.

Edith did not return to check on her son. She knew God required Michael to pay for his disobedience in full measure. She must not help him now.

Michael lay still on the floor for several minutes, his eyes closed. He hurt almost too much to breathe, but it didn't matter. He replayed the final moments in his mind. "Bitch." He heard himself say it again. It felt good, more than worth the price of the beating. "Go to hell, you fucking bitch." He mumbled the words aloud as he rolled over onto his stomach and struggled to his knees.

From the kitchen Edith heard Michael dragging himself up the stairs. If he could get to his room alone he probably wasn't hurt too badly. She decided to wait until he had time to contemplate his misdeeds before she went to talk to him. She was in her chair reading when her husband came home an hour later. Michael heard the car in the driveway and he heard the sound of the front door opening, but he could not hear the conversation as his father stopped to talk to Edith.

"Where's Danny?" Dan asked idly.

Edith looked up from her Bible. "I have no idea where your son is. Mine is in his room."

He hadn't asked about Michael, and something in the way she said that made him take notice.

"In his room? What's he doing in his room with an hour of daylight left?"

"Contemplating the wages of sin."

"Did you hit him again, Edith? Good Lord, what's the matter with you woman? Can't you control him without hitting him?"

"Daniel, I will not have you taking the Lord's name in vain in my presence. You can go straight to Hell if you want, but I am going to teach that boy the path to righteousness even if it kills him. I try to reason with him and he gives me sass. I try to beat some sense into him, and he just goes out and disobeys me all over again. It's as though he's possessed by the Devil."

"Maybe if you eased up and just let him be a boy for once."

"You mean let him grow up like all the other little hooligans in this neighborhood? Not on your life. My son will not turn out as you did."

"There's nothing wrong with the way I turned out."

"Do you think I'm going to let Michael become another libertine sinner who can't keep his thing in his pants? He's going to amount to something, Daniel, in spite of you."

Dan had heard this before, and he didn't like it. He moved a step into the room, glaring at his wife. "Just exactly what the hell does that mean, 'in spite of me?' I haven't had anything to do with him in years. Whatever he turns out to be is your doing, and if you don't stop beating him he'll turn into a criminal. Good God, woman!

All I want is a little respect, but you just can't stop bitching. If it wasn't for me you wouldn't have a rag to your name."

There was that word again! Edith rose from her chair to face her husband. "You've certainly taught him how to treat his mother with disrespect, and your money means nothing one way or another. I am not concerned with anything as tawdry as the treasures of this earth. I am getting a boy's soul ready for Heaven! That is my only mission."

"How's he going to eat in the meantime? Are *you* going to provide food and a roof over his head? Not damn likely! If you're so sure that God will provide, why don't you just take your son and get the hell out of here."

"But God *is* providing, Daniel, through you. You let me bring up my son the way I see fit and stay away from him and everything will be fine. I don't want you contaminating his mind with your foul mouth and your pagan ideas."

"Hell, I'm not around him enough to give him a cold let alone contaminate his mind. Any ideas he has are either yours or his own, and I'll have respect in my own house, woman. You remember that."

It was twilight when Edith finally came upstairs to see how Michael was doing. She was a completely different person now. Her face held a look of kind concern as she bent to see if he was awake. She carried a plate of food saved from supper as a peace offering.

"Take it away. I don't want anything from you," Michael said.

Edith sat down beside him anyway and set the plate of food on the floor. "I just don't know what I am going to do with you," she sighed. "I try to teach you the way that you should go, and you have nothing to do with it. I just don't know what to do. God help me, I don't." Her voice was filled with sorrow as she reached out to tenderly stroke his hair. Michael jerked his head aside at her touch, but she moved her hand to touch him again. "I try to provide you with a loving, structured home," she was saying. "I try to teach you the truth of God's Holy Word, and you give me nothing but attitude. What has gotten hold of you, Michael?"

"Did Dad ask about me?" Michael said. "Does he know what happened? Where is he?"

"Don't you worry about Dad, you worry about me," Her eyes flashed a reminder of the beating. "Now I want to know what's gotten into you."

"What's the use of talking about it?" Michael asked. "Just go away and leave me alone." He had no energy for this. What had gotten into him was what his mother did not want to hear.

"Someday you will understand, dear," she soothed. "The Lord came to me in a dream and promised me that you will understand. You will become a great witness for God someday, my son. He has promised me this."

"What if I don't want to witness for God?" Michael asked angrily. "It's *my* life."

"No, it's *God's* life. I have placed you in the hands of the Lord. In time He will tell you what to do. You will feel His Truth in your heart. Just be patient, and you will understand." She patted his shoulder affectionately, oblivious to the pain the gesture caused him, and then she smoothed his hair back and tried to plant a tender kiss on his forehead. Michael pushed her away, but she ignored his resistance and forced the kiss on him anyway. She rose to turn out the light. "God loves you, Michael. Get some sleep now," she said as she walked out of the room.

Michael reached painfully down to the plate of food his mother had left lying beside his bed and shoved it away as hard as he could. The plate slid violently across the hardwood floor, struck a wall several feet away and shattered, scattering food and pieces of glass everywhere. Edith heard the crash and hesitated for a moment at the top of the stairs. She could guess what had caused the noise but would not react now to this latest act of rebellion. She would deal with it tomorrow.

Michael turned slowly over, pulling the bed sheet up over his shoulder as he did so. He did not think he had any broken bones this time. The pain wasn't localized. Every molecule in his body seemed to hurt equally. He tried to sleep, but sleep would not come. Finally he turned over and opened his eyes. He looked out the window, trying to make out stars or the moon—anything far away—but the yard light on the garage, hovering over the scene like a searchlight on a guard tower, cut off his vision both above and at the edge of the lawn, and drew a curtain, black and featureless, between himself and the rest of the world.

He turned away from the window and glanced toward the ceiling. His mother said she could see God when her gaze turned upward, but Michael saw nothing but endless gloom. When the grandfather clock in the entrance hall struck midnight his eyes were still open, staring into the darkness.

3 - THE TREE OF KNOWLEDGE

In the beginning the city of Mansfield, Minnesota was nothing more than a few tents pitched at the railhead of the Saint Paul & Pacific railroad. In 1869 the road that was to become the main line of the Great Northern two decades later was pushing west from the Mississippi River. The tents provided shelter at the site of a well dug by the railroad to supply water for workers and steam locomotives. The town was first called DeHavalin, named after one of the railroad's investors. DeHavalin, Minnesota was incorporated in 1870, among the first of the many hundreds of towns and cities that grew along and near a route that eventually stretched more than sixteen-hundred miles from St. Paul to Seattle, Washington.

The house that the Long family lived in was built in 1895 on the highest knoll of a fifty acre plot of rolling grass and woodland that overlooked the railroad. At the time the site was more than two miles from the city limits, but the city grew in the ensuing years and now the house stood at the very edge of town. It was a massive brick edifice, almost a mansion by the standards of the time and place, designed in a simplified Victorian style that reflected the tastes of its owner. The wood that was used came from the virgin oak and pine that grew near the site. A brick foundry constructed especially for the purpose provided the facade.

The house's builder and first occupant, William R. Mansfield, was a railroad worker who quit the road in 1875 to become a general store owner and later a banker. The Mansfield fortune and the economic prosperity of the region grew together. For nearly forty years the Mansfield Bank was the primary source of the community's growth capital, and when he died in 1927, the city fathers renamed the town in his honor.

The house went through a succession of owners after William Mansfield died. When Dan Long bought the place in 1952, it was in foreclosure and its glory days were long past. But Dan's eye for potential saw through the dilapidated condition of the big old edifice, and recognized the gem underneath. He loved Victorian architecture, and he spared no expense in returning the house to all of its former opulence. He installed virtually every available modern convenience, and restored the place from top to bottom. When he was finished the house was even grander than the day the Mansfield family moved in. The old foundry was repaired and fired again, and a high brick fence was added to mark the border of the estate. The driveway, lined with the great oak trees planted by the original owner, was paved with brick for the full quarter mile of its length, and an imposing wrought iron gate was installed at the entrance to the grounds.

Michael's bedroom was on the second floor, a large corner room with high-windowed dormers facing south and east. A reading chair and a bookcase occupied the east dormer. The bookcase was the twin to the one in the sun room below. It was filled with a similar assortment of religious reading materials but geared toward a youthful mind. The enormous collection was made up of simplified and expurgated versions of Bible stories with lots of colorful pictures, nature books that taught nothing about nature but featured glowingly emotional commentary on the wonders of God's handiwork, and insipidly moralistic juvenile fiction. It was his mother's idea of what was proper reading material for a growing boy. The books bored Michael to death, and he hated it when his mother made him read them. He wanted to get rid of the books, but that was out of the question. They greeted him every morning when he woke up, a daily reminder of his mother's domination and control.

The rising sun was just beginning to light the room when Michael's body jerked and he opened his eyes with a start. He was trembling, his skin covered with cold sweat, and the bedclothes were lying on the floor.

It was the dream that awakened him. The details varied but the dream always featured a feeling of being abandoned in a place where mortal danger lurked around every corner. When he was younger, Michael sometimes awakened from the dream crying.

Eventually he learned to allow himself to become aware of his surroundings before reacting to the emotions that the dream summoned. The crying stopped, but not the dreams.

A sense of panic and betrayal stuck with him despite his efforts to push them away. He tried to breathe deeply, struggling to regain control, and yesterday's events leaped into focus prodded by a stabbing pain in his back. For the first time since awakening he became fully aware that every bone and muscle in his body ached. Strangely, the pain helped him gain control. The dream was fading, overcome by more immediate concerns. He was fully awake now and becoming calmer. He carefully turned onto his back and looked down at himself. There were several large angry-looking welts on his shoulders and torso and one spot on his back that felt like the skin was broken. There was even a bruise on his right leg, and he did not remember being hit there.

"Jeez," he muttered to himself as he let his head fall back on his pillow. Getting up was going to be agony. Yet he had no intention of staying in bed no matter how badly he felt. He had things to do. There were always things to do.

He worked his way to the edge of the bed and let his legs hang over the side. The plate of food from last night still lay scattered about across the room. He got slowly to his feet, limped over to it and kicked a few of the pieces with his toe. The anger from last night was still with him and despite any possible consequences he had no intention of cleaning it up. If his mother found it before the housekeeper got to it then so be it. It took a greater effort to get himself ready for the day than it had to get up off the floor last night, but he eventually found himself in the kitchen, washed and clothed.

It was Saturday morning and Michael was the first one in the house out of bed. In the summer he rarely slept beyond the crack of dawn and in the winter he was always up hours before sunrise. It was a habit born partly of an abiding impatience to get on with the business of growing up, and partly of a desire to live as much of his life as he could outside the range of his mother's stick. Edith would not be up for hours yet, and until then he was free to do as he pleased without having to worry about where she was and whether she would approve of what he was doing. He made himself a quick breakfast and then went outside and limped to the large two-story carriage house and stable that stood several yards behind the garage.

The building hadn't been used for its original purpose in decades. It was a storage location now, only rarely visited by others, but to Michael it served a very important purpose. When he was very young he came here often to hide from his mother or escape the shouting when his parents fought, and by the time he was five he knew every musty corner. The structure was in excellent repair and well maintained on the outside, Dan Long would have allowed nothing less, but inside it was a dusty, disorganized, cobwebbed clutter.

The place escaped a good cleaning out when the Long family moved in. Dan spent far more money than he planned on the estate's remodeling, and since he had no immediate plans to use the carriage house, he just had his contractor make sure that the structure was sound and the exterior in good repair. The contents, an accumulation of many decades and numerous owners, was left untouched. The building was filled with all sorts of fascinating, discarded and forgotten objects, from old gardening equipment and strangely shaped tools with incomprehensible functions, to boxes filled with the ancient bric-a-brac of lives lived long before Michael was born. He could amuse himself for hours going through the boxes just to see what they contained. There were old wooden toys. There were cooking utensils and curious knick-knacks of every shape and description. There were old clothes, musty books and family albums filled with fading pictures of people and places Michael had never heard of.

Once he found a journal belonging to somebody named Aaron Mansfield, its final entry dated March 22, 1918. Previous entries seemed to indicate that the writer was fifteen when the last notation was made. The journal fascinated him because Aaron seemed to have a very positive relationship with his parents. It was a concept so foreign to his own experience that he could hardly believe it was real. Nothing bad ever seemed to happen. He tried, but couldn't imagine what growing up like that would be like.

But it was the books that fascinated him most. The books were difficult to read at first. He didn't always understand the words, and the pages were damaged by age and mold, but they were Michael's first introduction to the world outside of his mother's firm mental control.

When he first found them, he was afraid to read them. He wanted to read, and he wanted to do what his mother told him was right. He could not do both. The books were not on his allowed reading list, but he knew if he let his mother inspect them she would throw them away, and he couldn't bring himself to let that happen. He would read a few pages and then stop, feeling guilty despite his deep desire to read on. Michael already took it as axiomatic that it was good to *know* things, but his mother's disapproving specter hung over him every time he opened a book that contained something worth learning.

This was not like reading the Bible. These books made sense to him. He could see how what he was reading fit in with what he had already discovered and experienced on his own. There were no conflicts that required blind acceptance, only those that required that he use his mind to understand and resolve.

As befitting an entrance guarding a pile of junk, the side door to the carriage house wasn't locked. Michael worked the latch and the door opened with a groan. Once divided by stalls and partitions for horses, carriages and equipment, the ground floor was now open from one end to the other. Although the windows were filmed with grime the room was fairly well lit. A narrow pathway wound through the rummage to a stairway near the center of the structure that led to the second level.

Michael climbed the stairs and threaded his way through another dusty maze to a large pile of rags behind a stack of wooden containers against the far wall. He knelt, pulled a metal box from under the rags and sat down on an old leather chair that stood in a nearby corner next to a window. Despite its obvious age, the box was clean and in good repair. Michael opened it, removed the contents carefully, and placed the box on the floor beside him.

In his hands he held three books, two of them from the local public library. One was a book of essays by a famous science writer. The second was a thick volume by a leading paleontologist that covered much of the current knowledge regarding dinosaurs and their evolution, and the third, a book he found at the bottom of one of the wooden chests in the carriage house, described (among other things) how to build a telescope from items found around the house. It didn't take him long to discover that the device described in the telescope book was little more than a toy, but it gave him an idea. He would build one, one that was not a toy. He was saving his allowance, and soon there would be enough to purchase the kit he had seen advertised in the Edmund Scientific catalogue. He kept this particular book in the box because it described several other devices he wanted to build.

Michael kept many secrets from his mother, but the old books and the contents of the metal box were the secrets he guarded most carefully. They were symbols as well as knowledge. These were his window to the outside world, his defense, his defiance, and his greatest source of pleasure. In the carriage house he learned of dinosaurs and a host of other subjects his mother did not approve of. There was little left in the carriage house books he had not read, so now, completely behind Edith's back, he went to the library on a regular basis to select books that interested him. He would bring them home to read and study. Then he would take them back and get more.

He had discovered the library at the age of ten. It was an absolutely fascinating place, books were everywhere and new knowledge could be found on every shelf. His fourth grade teacher, who was impressed by Michael's active thirst to know, urged him to seek the answers to his many questions there. Michael was afraid that his mother might find out if he went to the library, but as with the old books in the carriage house, eventually his desire to learn got the better of him.

Mrs. Smith, the county librarian, noticed him come in the door one Saturday morning and stand several feet from the check-out counter. She walked over to him and asked if she could help him find something. He glanced at her but said nothing. He looked as though he could not make up his mind if he wanted to speak or run away.

From his size she guessed he was around seven or eight-years-old, but his face looked older and more serious than any child's face ought to look. His eyes were intelligent and very direct, but somehow wary, a quality she found immediately engaging. She got the impression that his stern mouth and angry brow were camouflage. He isn't really stern or angry, Mrs. Smith thought. He's protecting himself. He wants to be a child, but he doesn't dare…someone is abusing this boy. The thought popped into her head unbidden. It was not the last time the notion would occur to her.

"Did you come to find a book to read?" she asked.

Michael said nothing.

"Can you tell me your name?" she encouraged.

"It's Michael," he said. "Michael Long."

"Hello, Michael. I'm very glad to meet you. My name is Mrs. Smith. Now that we know each other, can I help you find a book?"

"Maybe," said Michael. "I haven't decided yet."

"Well, I'm going to be right in that room over there, and if there is anything I can do to help please feel free to ask. In the meantime, you are welcome to look around and see if you can find something of interest. If you find a book, come see me, and I'll issue a library card."

She walked into her office and sat down, but she left her door open. She was curious to see what this boy would do.

Michael stood without moving for another full minute. Then his mouth firmed and he seemed to make a decision. He walked over to her door. "My teacher told me that you had books on every subject. Do you have any books on trains?"

"Yes, of course, we have many books on trains. Do you have something special in mind?"

"I guess not. I live by the railroad tracks, and I see trains all the time. I want to know about trains—modern trains with big diesel engines."

"Would you mind telling me your age, Michael?"

"Why? Does it make a difference how old I am?"

"No. It's only that I need to judge the level of your education in order to recommend reading material."

"I don't want any kids' books. I want to read the real thing."

"Do you think you can handle adult reading material?"

"I can handle anything I need to," said Michael.

Mrs. Smith chuckled doubtfully. "Well, let's see what we have. Come with me."

Since Mansfield owed its existence to the railroad, the library had a number of excellent books covering both the history and technology of railroading. Mrs. Smith first took Michael to the pre-teen section. He removed a couple of the books from the shelf and glanced at them then turned to Mrs. Smith and said with disgust, "Where are the *real* books?"

"These *are* real books, and they are written for children about your age," said Mrs. Smith.

"Come on. I came here to find something worth reading," said Michael. "Show me the real books."

Against her better judgment, Mrs. Smith led him to the technology section, and Michael picked out a fairly large volume on the design and construction of diesel-electric engines. She tried again to get him to chose something less advanced, but he would have none of it. Finally she gave up. She issued him a library card and cautioned him to be sure to return the book within the two-week loan period. She watched him leave, thinking he might look at the pictures but the reading material was obviously way above his level. Three days later he was back, asking for more books.

"You didn't read your book in three days did you?" she asked Michael dubiously.

"Why would I bring it back if I hadn't read it?"

"I thought maybe you found it too difficult and wanted something simpler."

"Look," said Michael, "I'm smart enough to figure out what I can read and what I can't. I'll let you know if I have any questions."

Mrs. Smith's smile contained both pleasure and amusement. "Okay, I guess I'll take your word for it," she said. "What would you like to try next?"

That first day in the library, Michael was not sure he dared to do what he wanted very badly to do. "Knowledge" in the secular sense was not in Edith Long's lexicon. One might use automobiles and other modern conveniences, but taking the time to understand them got in the way of a soul's quest for paradise.

His mother insisted that God was watching and would cast his soul into hell for the sin of seeking knowledge. For a long time he wondered why God would do such a thing. What was wrong with learning about the world God created? He could find no logical answer, and in the end he decided that his mother was wrong. God would not want him to remain ignorant. By the time he showed up at the library it wasn't God that made him hesitate, it was his mother. If she ever found out what he was doing, he knew she would go absolutely crazy.

Michael read until almost lunch time, then knowing his father would probably be in the kitchen, he put the books away and went back to the house. Edith and Danny were still in bed. Edith never got up before noon. Danny was usually out well past midnight on Friday nights and slept in on Saturday. Dan always spent Saturday morning in the kitchen reading the city newspaper as he drank his coffee. It wasn't that Michael had anything in particular to say to his father. He just wondered if his dad was aware that he had been beaten again yesterday.

From the time he was old enough to know that Dan Long was his father and what that implied, until he was old enough to comprehend that his relationship with his dad wasn't normal, Dan had been Michael's hero. Michael now understood that his father had no desire to be his son's hero, but he had no one else to turn to for help.

Michael blamed himself for not having the courage to somehow put a stop to the beatings himself, but he didn't blame himself for being beaten. The responsibility for that lay with the person holding the stick. Although he always had a hard time figuring out exactly what Dan was thinking, he was certain that his father did not share his opinion. Michael tried to start conversations about the abuse a few times, but on each occasion Dan either ignored him, berated him for letting it happen, or was completely indifferent.

Michael no longer mentioned the beatings directly. He'd learned that was the wrong thing to do, but he always sought out the company of his father after Edith abused him, perhaps subconsciously hoping that this might be the time that Dan would finally do something.

Dan Long did not approve of weakness, and thus, neither did Michael. The boy wanted help, but he wanted his father's acceptance even more. He gladly would have suffered the abuse if that meant his father would at least acknowledge his battle, so he tried to hide the evidence even while he hoped his father would notice.

As he approached the house Michael realized he was walking with a limp and had bruises that might be noticed. He buttoned his shirt to cover the marks on his neck and tried to stop limping on his damaged leg. As he entered the house, his posture was straight and his walk as purposeful and as rapid as he could manage to make it.

But he could not entirely hide the fact that his movements were limited and stiff.

Dan was indeed sitting at the kitchen table reading the paper. He glanced up when Michael first walked into the kitchen then went back to his reading. A second later he looked up again and demanded, "What's the matter with you, Michael?"

"I'm okay, Dad. Why do you ask?"

"You don't look good. Was that licking your mother gave you yesterday a little too much for you? I heard about it."

It was the wrong thing to say. The comment was actually intended to be sympathetic, but Michael took the words as a personal criticism.

Too much for him? Had his father been there? Had he seen what happened? Far from being too much for him, Michael had taken it like a man! Dan should have been proud of his son. He should have praised him for remaining strong. Instead, once again, his courage and stamina where being questioned by the one person whose approval Michael wanted more than any other. He wondered if his father had the slightest idea what he was going through. Michael was never beaten when Dan was around, but Danny had witnessed some of the beatings, including the one yesterday. Surely he must have told his father something about them.

Damn it, what the hell does he want from me, thought Michael. What's good enough for him? He was getting angry all over again. Michael remembered how Dan jeered at him the last time he mentioned a beating, how he was told that a spanking was the price of being a mamma's boy. Coming from his father the comment was devastating.

Dan was sure Edith was incapable of any real brutality, and he thought the reports he got from Danny were ridiculously exaggerated. Danny had a tendency to embellish the truth, particularly if he could vilify his stepmother in doing so. He understood Michael's complaints to mean that the boy did not like being spanked for being naughty. He advised his son to take his punishment or stop doing things to get punished. Although he held an extremely low opinion of his wife, Dan did not think of spankings as child abuse. It was the type of punishment well within the accepted norm. He remembered how he used to howl in pain when his mother beat him with her big wooden mixing spoon. It was a ritual he and his mother went through every time Dan got into trouble, and in his youth Dan was in trouble often. He didn't agree with Edith's reasons for taking a stick to the boy and he often chided her for striking her son when she claimed to be filled with God's love, especially when they were arguing, but he understood the necessity of physical discipline to drive a lesson home.

Michael's frustration at the situation boiled over. He wondered why he bothered to talk to his father. It did no good. To hell with him! He could take care of himself. "Hey, I'm just fine, Dad," he said with disgust, "You just sit there, read your goddamn paper, and let the world go on without you. I'll be gone in a second, and you can forget I was even here."

Dan gazed at his son for a moment, wondering what he said to provoke a response like that. This was just the kind of smart-mouth talk that got under his skin, and Michael should know it. "That'll be enough, boy. I just asked a simple question. If you can't give me a civil answer then keep your mouth shut."

"I didn't think you were really interested. I see I was right." Michael said angrily, refusing to admit that he was bitterly disappointed.

Dan noted the anger and filed it away in his baggage compartment. "Get out of here before you get into real trouble," he growled.

Michael turned away, and Dan caught a glimpse of what looked like a bruise on the back of his son's neck. Michael's collar didn't cover it completely. The boy looked pale too, and he seemed to be walking very stiffly. But if he was going to lip off just for being asked a simple question he could damn well stew in it. His son was developing an attitude that Dan couldn't stand for more than a few minutes at a time. It was a good thing he was Edith's problem or Dan might have gotten in a few licks himself. If the boy was going to lip off like that, he could just suffer through whatever the problem was without his father's help.

Michael wasn't hungry anymore. He turned and left the house, the limp creeping back into his walk. His conversations with his father never seemed to last for more than a few seconds and never seemed to end well. There was no reason that today should be any different.

He walked back to the carriage house, climbed the stairs and sat down on the old leather chair. After awhile he hung his head and began to cry.

4 - NEITHER LOVE NOR HONOR

She knew they whispered behind her back that she was easy. She never actually heard anybody say it, but she knew. It was never the men, they all liked her. It was the women. She could tell who they were by the way they looked at her, that odd mixture of envy and contempt in their eyes, the look that turned to jealousy and fear when she flirted with their husbands and boyfriends. But Edith Amundson was not easy. She was a realist. She did whatever it took to get what she wanted.

In 1949 Edith became the first person in her family to graduate from high school. If she had applied herself she could have graduated at the top of her class, but grades were never important. She had no plans for college. Instead she took a position in a local hardware store as a clerk and accountant. Normally that was a man's job, but it paid far better than the other jobs available to young women, and as usual, Edith got what she wanted. She worked out a deal with her new boss to live in the furnished apartment above the store and paid the rent with her body when his wife was out of town. As far as Edith was concerned the arrangement was temporary and strictly financial. Her only romantic goal was to marry rich. The goal acquired a name when Dan Long came home from the Korean War.

Dan was the only son of a local businessman and a decorated veteran, twice wounded in the months following the Inchon invasion. The second wound at Chosen Reservoir earned him five months in the hospital and a medical discharge. He had a long, ragged scar on his face from a Chinese bayonet and three small chunks of shrapnel in his leg that forced him to walk without properly bending one knee. He spoke only reluctantly of his war experiences, not from an inability to face them, but from a desire to save himself the boredom of retelling stories he was tired of telling. The two Purple Hearts and the Silver Star in his bedroom drawer hadn't seen the light of day since his welcome-home celebration.

Dan took over the family's lumber and real estate business when his father died a few months after Dan got home. Mike Long was a moderately successful small-town businessman, but he was slowing down and the business hadn't grown in several years. Dan changed all that with a business plan that took advantage of the company's considerable cash reserves to move aggressively on new opportunities as Dan recognized them. He kept the core business but branched out into retail and manufacturing, and Long Enterprises began to grow as never before.

Dan had a ruggedly handsome look about him and a calm, friendly, self-assured manner that seemed to draw women like a magnate draws metal. He could have married almost any eligible girl in town, and more than one did her best to land him. A war hero with a promising business career didn't come along every day. He wanted to marry and settle down, but he was understandably leery of the many women who threw themselves at him. Edith succeeded where the others failed because she was much too focused to let emotion get in the way of her objective. She did not love Dan, but she wanted him more than she had ever wanted anything in her life. She wanted him for the security, comfort and status she knew he would provide, and she was beautiful enough, smart enough and dishonest enough to make love immaterial.

Everybody in town knew who Dan was. But by the time they finally met, Edith knew a great deal more about Dan than the average man on the street. She knew what he liked to do to have fun. She knew what his favorite foods were and what kind of movies he watched. She knew approximately what he was worth and what he spent his money on. She knew who his friends were, and she knew his political opinions. She even knew Dan had a son from a previous relationship, and that was more than his son knew.

Edith planned with great care, gathering information methodically over a period of several weeks, and in the end she even knew the day and time Dan Long was going to meet his future wife. Dan always walked the three blocks between his office and Jensen's

Diner at lunch time. She decided that's when she would accidentally bump into him.

Dan had an important business meeting coming up in a few hours, and his mind was focused on that rather than his immediate surroundings when a pair of exquisitely shaped female legs entered his range of vision. The legs were so perfect that his concentration slipped just for a moment. He observed their sculptured shape appreciatively, glanced up to briefly apprise the woman they belonged to, and kept walking.

Edith thought for a second that he hadn't noticed her. But then he stopped and looked again, this time frankly staring. Edith's thrill of triumph did not show. She gave him a practiced 'aloof-yet-mildly-interested' glance and walked serenely past him and into a drug store several doors further on. Ten days later they just happened to meet again near the diner. This time Dan stopped and asked her to have lunch with him. She refused, but let him spend twenty minutes talking her out of her phone number. It wasn't long before they were being seen regularly together.

Dan's interest in Edith began with her gorgeous face and world-class figure, but it certainly didn't end there. Edith knew how to make men want her, and it didn't take long for Dan to want her very badly. Edith could act sexy and clever and kind and loving and passionate on cue, but she didn't know how to *be* any of those things. She did not normally feel the emotions she projected, especially if they were positive ones, and she was clever only when criticizing the ideas of others. To Edith, emotions and ideas were things other people had that made them vulnerable. She was afraid of being vulnerable and accustomed to using the weaknesses of others to control them.

The first time Dan asked her to go to bed with him she gave him a chaste no. The second time he asked, she said no again and then let him seduce her against her will. It was an act worthy of Oscar consideration, calculated to simulate helplessness before an overpowering sexual desire. The performance was so good she almost believed it herself for awhile. In the weeks that followed their first night in bed Edith projected the image of a woman hopelessly in love. Dan was completely taken in, and Edith simply let events sweep along to their inevitable conclusion. But she felt none of the emotions she so artfully portrayed except the satisfaction she felt

41

when she discovered she was pregnant. She knew this was the weapon that would give her everything she wanted.

Late one night fairly early in their relationship Dan confessed to Edith that he had a son born out of wedlock. Edith did not return the confidence by admitting that she already knew it. Instead she let Dan tell her the story as he wanted to tell it. People gave up far more information than they realized when confessing a secret sin.

"There is something I have to tell you," he said, caressing her shoulder.

She rolled onto her side and looked back at him. "What?"

"I have a son."

Now she turned around to look at him directly. "What?" Her voice and her eyes conveyed only astonishment and open curiosity, not the damning judgment he knew he deserved.

"I want you to know that I am the father of a boy. He is living here in town, but he doesn't know who his father is."

"Why haven't you told him?"

"His mother doesn't want him to know."

"Tell me her name."

"Gracie. Gracie Calloway."

She already knew the name, but she didn't want Dan to know she knew. He would not have guessed how she knew because he did not understand that these things had a way of becoming common knowledge among women in small towns.

"Why didn't you marry her?"

"I asked but she said she wouldn't marry a man who didn't love her."

Oh, the stupid little trollop! Edith didn't say the words out loud but the inner contempt she felt for the girl was almost physical. She ruthlessly suppressed the outward manifestation of her actual feelings and exclaimed sympathetically, "Oh Dan, it must be terrible for you!"

Dan looked at her. Was she being sarcastic? He thought for a moment that he could hear it in her voice. No, it isn't possible. She isn't like that, he decided. He was certain that Edith was an honorable woman and would understand the girl's motive as Dan understood it. While he did not feel love, he felt admiration for the independence and pride that seemed to be evident in Gracie's actions.

To his great regret, Dan would eventually come to learn that Edith knew little of independence and nothing of pride and admiration, but she knew a great deal about how to use the guilt of others as a weapon. She did not have to be in Dan's bed to recognize his sense of guilt when it came to this particular topic. She could have smelled it a mile away, and in the end it was this guilt, not love, that became the primary reason that Dan and Edith were married.

There was, however, one detail that Edith missed. She did not realize how difficult it would be to keep up the act. It was inevitable that the façade would begin to fall away eventually, but events would conspire to make it happen sooner rather than later. She remembered it as though it was yesterday. Eight months pregnant, and the son-of-a-bitch came home and told her that there would soon be a little boy coming to live with them on a permanent basis.

"What are you saying, Dan?" she had asked him. She could not believe it.

"His mother is dying of cancer, and he has nowhere to go," Dan told her. "I am the boy's father. There are no relatives other than me, and he needs a home. I cannot abandon him."

"Why not? You did it once before. Why is it different this time?"

"I will not send my son to be a ward of the state, not when I have the means to take care of him. I have learned a few things since I left him to his mother. I will not fail him now."

"What about me? What about *our* child? Have you thought about what this is going to do to us?"

"He is only a boy, Edith. I think I can manage to take care of the three of you without any trouble."

"You do not understand, Daniel. I will not have that child in my house. He was born in sin and no good will come from keeping him here."

"We were not married when you got pregnant, Edith."

"That is entirely different. You love me! You married me!"

"That's true, but it doesn't matter to Danny. He needs a home and I plan to give him one."

"Danny? His name is Danny?" She had never asked the boy's name. Until now the detail hadn't interested her.

"His name is Daniel. His mother named him after me."

"Oh, for God's sake! You are going to pay for this, Dan."

The fact that the boy was Dan's son and a bastard meant nothing to Edith on a moral level. At the time she was not religious and 'sin' was a word she used only to invoke guilt in others. In truth, Edith did not want this simply because it was not her idea. It introduced an enormous element of uncertainty in her life. She needed control—she had to have it—and she was completely unprepared for anything as life-changing as this.

Edith used every trick she knew to get her husband to change his mind but to no avail, and shortly after Michael was born little Daniel Calloway, late of a trailer house on the wrong side of the railroad tracks, moved into a bedroom across the hall from the nursery. In due time the boy's name was officially changed to Daniel Long.

Edith eventually calmed down, but that did not mean she accepted the arraignment. It only meant she learned to tolerate it, and only to the extent that she no longer made a spectacle of herself over it. From this point forward the outward Edith began to change. Her alluring sweetness, the joy she seemed to take in Dan's company, her concern for his well-being, her eagerness in bed, all began to evaporate. In public she maintained appearances, but in private Dan began to see the real Edith, and he didn't much care for what he saw. Where once he could do no wrong, suddenly he could do nothing right.

Edith's carping complaints about Dan's every action became a daily feature of married life, and somewhere around their third anniversary Dan gave up trying to make it work. If Edith would not provide him with human companionship and a moment's peace, he would find it elsewhere. One night he stopped at a bar instead of going home after work. One thing led to another, and he wound up in bed with one of his old girlfriends.

Edith was waiting at the front door when he got home the next morning. She demanded to know where he'd been, and Dan simply told her. He didn't promise not to do it again, and she didn't ask him not to. If he was getting it somewhere else, she wouldn't have to give it to him. But as Edith had predicted, there was indeed a price to be paid, on both sides as it turned out. That very afternoon, Dan took off his wedding ring and stuck it in the drawer with his other war medals. The marriage was over.

Edith didn't care that the relationship was dead. In a very real sense it had never been alive. She did not want to be in love, she wanted to be married. So she went on pretending in public that she loved her husband, and for the first time in her life she knew the emotion of hatred as an unwavering conscious companion. She told herself that Dan was the object of that hatred, but there was a much deeper, unacknowledged component to it. What she hated most of all was the fact that reality was not what she wished it to be, and much more importantly, neither was she.

Edith refused to leave her husband when he asked her if she wanted a divorce. That would have meant the recognition of that deeper hatred. Instead she began to eat, drink and smoke too much. Her once slim and beautiful body became heavy, and her perfect face grew lined and hard. In time she came to believe that her life, like her marriage, was over. And then on a cool October day in 1957 the Savior came calling.

It wasn't God at the door, of course, but rather a skinny, odd-looking woman of early middle age and a somber young boy who looked as though he wanted very badly to be somewhere else. The woman's hair was pulled into a severe bun, and her dress was at least two sizes larger and a decade older than she was. She wore no makeup unless one counted the broad, toothy smile plastered on her face. Her eyes were curiously empty, as though every last ounce of her personality had drained into her grin. Tightly clasped to the woman's breast was a large, black, leather-bound Bible, heavy enough to cause her to lean back slightly in order to maintain her balance. The boy's burden seemed even weightier, an enormous knapsack stuffed with religious tracts that he dragged along the ground like a ball and chain.

Neither specimen looked at all god-like, but Edith would have slammed the door in terror if they had, and in the long run it didn't matter. She didn't need God so much as she needed an excuse for what she'd let herself become. The woman in the ill-fitting dress was eager to give her one.

It was one-thirty in the afternoon, and Edith Long stood before her callers in a nightie and an open bathrobe, half-drunk, her hair in curlers, her fifth martini in one hand and her tenth cigarette in the other. She looked like a barfly trying unsuccessfully to cope simultaneously with a hangover and a bad hair day.

"What do you want?" She demanded with a gravelly sneer.

The odd-looking woman never missed a beat. She took note of neither the state of Edith's person nor her evident hostility. The woman had been trained since childhood to think only holy thoughts.

"Hello," she bubbled cheerfully, "we want to share with you the good news of Christ's love."

"Damn! Really?" Edith snorted in contempt at the woman's puerile enthusiasm and took another drag on her cigarette. She was reminded of the cocker spaniel she'd had as a child—the animal uncritically slobbered love on everyone—but for some reason she suppressed the impulse to voice the observation. Maybe it was the lost, lonely look of the boy that struck a chord with her. He looked exactly like she felt inside. Or perhaps it was the woman's smile, which seemed to bestow universal approval upon everything and everyone. Maybe here was a person who would truly understand and accept her. She never could put her finger on the real reason, but after a moment's hesitation she thought—what the hell—and invited them into the house.

The sales pitch was devastatingly simple: Your sins are forgiven. Turn your life over to Christ, and you will find peace. It was a creed that struck Edith at the core of her soul. All she had to do was believe, and her faults would transform into virtues, her ignorance would become wisdom, and her self-loathing would light the way to eternal life. It didn't matter who you were, what you had done, or how many times you did it. The only thing that mattered was that you believed in God's saving grace and were truly repentant. The shear enormity of the pain this had the potential to wipe from her heart was breathtaking.

So it came to pass that Edith Long prostrated herself before God, searched out every last ounce of sincerity in her soul, and begged the Lord's forgiveness for her many sins.

Suddenly what could only be a miracle occurred. The righteous light of the Savior's redemption seemed to fill her, and an enormous weight seemed to lift from her shoulders. Her soul, once dark and empty, overflowed with the light of God's love and acceptance, and for the first time in her adult memory she felt a profound sense of safety and peace.

She knew beyond all doubt that this was the Master's work. This feeling had to be the work of the Lord, because…well, because the alternative was just too pathetic to contemplate.

If Edith Long had died in that moment she would have died a happy, virtuous, Christian woman. But alas, she lived on, a sinner saved but a sinner still. In time it became woefully clear, especially to her immediate family, that God did not remove the flaws in Edith's personality when he forgave them. The "born-again" Edith was no more righteous than Edith the lost sinner. Only now, God provided unlimited forgiveness no matter what she did.

*   *   *

Edith descended the stairs from her bedroom shortly after noon. Danny was off somewhere. Neither parent kept track of the seventeen-year-old's comings and goings. Michael was supposed to be in his room studying for his one o'clock Bible lesson. He wasn't, but Edith didn't bother to check on him. She'd find him and punish him if he didn't show up on time.

Dan always spent Saturday afternoons in his study, smoking and catching up on his business reading. But when he heard Edith come downstairs, he went to find her. She was seated in her chair in the sunroom browsing a church bulletin.

"You wanted something?" She drew the words out disdainfully.

"I talked to Michael this morning," he said.

"Yes?" She turned the page.

"Yes. And the conversation was more interesting for what wasn't said than what was. I noticed he was walking funny when he came into the kitchen, and I asked him if you hurt him yesterday."

"Why should you be interested in my son's pain?"

"Physical abuse always interests me, especially when you are doing the abusing."

"It doesn't seem to be a problem when you abuse me."

"Cut the crap, Edith. I've never hurt you and you know it."

"Not physically. There are other forms of abuse."

"Yes, and I can attest that you know how to use them all yourself. Let's get to the point. When I asked Michael if he was hurt he denied it but he was obviously lying. His shirt was buttoned up, but I caught a glimpse of a bruise on his neck, a very ugly bruise. What does the rest of his body look like, Edith? What did you do to him yesterday?"

"I punished him for his sinful disobedience. I will always do whatever it takes to bring my son up in righteousness."

"If what I saw on his neck was the result of your righteousness, then you have no idea what the word means. Even though you don't have the guts to try it when I'm around, I happen to know that this is not the first time you have beaten him like this and I want it stopped." (He still didn't believe Danny's reports, but it was always best to go at Edith with all guns blazing.)

Now Edith rose to her feet and faced her husband. "Who are you to judge me? You are nothing but a pagan hypocrite. You are the one who told me that you didn't care what happened to Michael. You are the one who gave him to me. You are the one who said you didn't have time for him. Do you think he doesn't know that?"

At this point Edith decided it was time to lie. She sent a prayer for forgiveness winging toward Heaven and then said, "Do you think he doesn't hate you for it? Why do you suppose he wouldn't tell you what happened yesterday? It was because, deep down, he knows which parent is best for him. He knows which parent really cares, and he knows that he gets punished only when he deserves it."

The sentence that leaped out at Dan, as Edith knew it would, was the assertion that Michael hated him. Dan was a well-liked man who took his standing seriously. He resented Michael but thought he hid the emotion well, and aside from the obvious exception that was his wife, he didn't like the idea of someone feeling hatred toward him.

"What do you mean, he hates me? He doesn't act like it. If he hated me you'd think he would stay away from me but he doesn't. He's always pestering me. I think you're lying to me, Edith."

Of course she was lying. With deliberate calculation she was lying. These were desperate times requiring desperate measures. She knew she was losing her grip on Michael, and she wanted no interference from Dan. That would only make the boy that much harder to control.

"Lying is a sin, and I would never mislead you about this, Daniel." (It's for the greater good, she told herself. God will understand.) "I know Michael hates you because he has told me so directly. I have counseled him to be more forgiving, but he has refused to be moved and I can't say that I blame him. Michael can't possibly miss the difference between how you treat Danny and how you treat him. You worship the ground Danny walks on and you have no time for his brother. Why shouldn't he hate you?"

Dan was getting angry with himself for letting Edith get the upper hand. He was vulnerable here, and he knew it. Maybe there was a kernel of truth in what Edith was saying. He didn't have much time for the boy. In fact, since they split up the kids, he had almost no time at all. He could see how Michael might resent that. Maybe he really did hate his father. If he did then Dan was wasting his time. But he didn't want to let Edith get the better of him.

"You just be careful from now on, Edith," he said. "What you are doing is wrong, and you are going to cause irreparable harm to Michael if it continues. I will not have you disgracing this household."

"This household? Now we get to the real issue. I knew you had an ulterior motive. What you really mean is that you are afraid how I discipline my son will reflect poorly on you. I thought you said you were concerned about Michael. You don't care even a little what happens to him, do you? You know nothing about that boy, Daniel. He's more difficult than you can imagine. He defies me at every turn even though he knows what he'll get for doing it. For his own good he must be brought to heal by whatever means necessary. With God's Grace I will handle his discipline appropriately. Your approval has not been sought and is not required."

Michael had never been told why his father had no time for him. He asked his mother once why Dad wouldn't play with him and spent all of his free time with Danny. Edith lied on that occasion as well. Her response was that Dan didn't like little kids much, but it was nothing personal. When he grew up like Danny his dad might have time for him, if he was a good boy. She did not tell Michael that his parents had an agreement that his father would stay away from him. It was much later when he finally learned about that.

Dan retreated to his study to mull over Edith's words. He clearly remembered the occasion when he told Edith she could have Michael to bring up as she saw fit. He told her he didn't want Michael and had never wanted him. He said it because he didn't want Edith to think she was getting anything he valued, but he also said it because it was true.

How was he supposed to be a father to this kid? He didn't act, or even look, like the son of Dan Long. In every important respect he *wasn't* the son of Dan Long. He was Edith's boy and that was it. He admitted to himself that he felt guilty over the way he treated Michael, but he eased the guilt by telling himself he couldn't be blamed for it. He wasn't responsible for the way the boy was turning out.

Dan had been a star athlete in high school, and Danny followed in his father's footsteps. Everybody said that Danny was destined to become the greatest athlete in the history of Mansfield High. What could a maladjusted little misfit like Michael offer in the face of that?

While Dan massaged his guilt in the study, the boy in the carriage house stopped crying and raised his head. For a long while he sat immobile, thinking.

Remarkably, Michael's self-respect was still essentially intact despite the way he was treated, its preservation based on the one thing neither parent could touch: his mind. His experience told him that he had a capable mind, and he could rely on it. No amount of mistreatment would change that. This quality of his character was his primary line of self-defense. Without it, his parents would have destroyed him. He knew he was small and weak. But he also knew he could think. He had a good mind, and if he used it, he was convinced he could take care of himself.

In Michael's mind there were only two options. He could run away, or he could stay and fight. Things simply could not go on as they were. He wasn't ready to leave home. Edith's universe, the universe she raised Michael to believe existed, was a frightening place, steeped in evil and ruled by a God itching to rip him to shreds at the slightest provocation. It was one thing to question and then to doubt, but quite another to act with confidence against long-held childhood beliefs. Intellectually, Michael was leaving his mother's beliefs behind, but emotionally the process took time. Not believing in a vengeful God did not mean he immediately thought the universe was a safe place to live. It was easier to face the evil he knew he could cope with. The dangerous world outside would have to wait.

He remembered very well the time he overheard his father telling Danny that it was always best to face danger rather than run from it. "If you run," his father lectured, "you always leave your back exposed. Facing your enemy is almost always the safest course."

"What if you just hide so your enemy can't find you?" Danny asked.

"You can do that, and sometimes it's necessary to survive to fight another day, but don't make a habit of it. A life spent living in fear that you might be found isn't worth living."

Now he understood the words as he had never understood them before. The enemy was large and powerful and Michael was small and weak and alone, but he was through being a coward. He was done living in fear. His face became hard with determination. His decision was made. It was almost one o'clock and he knew Edith was in the sun room waiting for him. He rose to his feet. Today he would not keep her waiting.

She knew he'd be on time. She had no doubt that the beating she gave him yesterday was sufficient to teach him once and for all to mind his mother. She was sorry he had to be hurt but if he finally learned his lesson it would be worth it.

She heard a hand on the outside doorknob and looking up from her Bible, her eyes widened with the anticipated triumph of Michael's submission. The door opened and Michael stood at the threshold.

"I see that you have decided to be on time," Edith said with caustic severity. "Have you finally learned then?"

Michael remained in the open doorway. "Yes, Mother," he said. "I have finally learned. I came to tell you that the Bible lessons are over."

"*What?*"

"And I will not go to church anymore either."

"You'll do what I tell you, or you'll earn another beating!"

"You won't find it so easy next time."

"What do you mean by that?"

"I mean I will fight you the next time."

"I am your mother! You have no right to defy me! Your soul will be forfeit! You will go to Hell!"

"I've been there, Mother. Don't you remember? You took me yesterday. It doesn't scare me anymore."

Michael turned and stepped away from the door. It swung shut and the room darkened again.

Edith sat in disbelief. Had she heard him correctly? Did she hear him threaten to fight her? This could not be permitted! She leaped to her feet, rushed to the door and jerked it open. Sunlight flooded into the room and she squinted at the brightness, trying to see where Michael was. He was already several yards down the path that led into the garden.

"Come back here right now!" she commanded.

Michael acted as though he hadn't heard her and kept walking.

"Michael, you come back here!"

Michael stopped and turned around. "No," he said simply. He turned and kept walking.

Edith was infuriated. How dare he defy her like this? She stepped outside, the screen door slammed behind her and she started after Michael. He heard the door close and turned around to face her. Edith didn't have her stick. In the rush to go after Michael she completely forgot it. She came at him with her bare hands, and Michael waited for her. When she got closer she shouted at him, pointing back at the house, "I want you back inside right now!"

"No."

She reached her hand out to take him by the shoulder. He pulled away. She went after him again. This time when she reached for him, he grabbed her arm. Before she could react, he bit her as hard as he could. Edith screamed and jerked away, staring in horror at the bloody bite mark just above her wrist.

"You evil, evil child!" she exclaimed. "Is this how you repay my efforts? With violence?"

"Leave me alone."

"No, Michael, I will not. I will always do what I know is best for you, even if it is against your wishes."

Michael didn't answer. He turned back to the garden path and Edith let him go.

It was a momentary set-back. She knew God was testing her resolve. She would pass the test.

5 - THE PRICE OF FREEDOM

The beatings stopped when Michael bit his mother's wrist. The shock of his first physical resistance seemed to force Edith to pause and think about what she was doing, even if only to consider other ways to control him. But for the time being he was free to go where he pleased and do what he pleased on his own schedule. There was no church to go to, no Bible lessons to attend.

For several weeks Edith left him pretty much alone. She hadn't given up. She was more determined than ever, just waiting for the Lord to tell her what to do next.

Summer ended and school began. Edith suddenly took to leaving little notes to Michael around the house that contained fragments of Bible verses: "Vengeance is mine; I will repay", "the wrath of God cometh on the children of disobedience", "and he shall rule them with a rod of iron", "The wages of sin is death", "he that believeth not the Son shall not see life, but the wrath of God abideth on him."

It was an attempt at intimidation of another kind. If the rod didn't scare Michael anymore, then God would have to threaten him more directly. These were warnings that God's wrath still awaited the unrepentant soul. The significance of the fact that it was not God, but Edith herself who left the notes, entirely escaped her. That's how God got things done, by acting through his earthly disciples. She was God's tool, a vessel of His Will.

Michael had begun to doubt Edith's loving and brutal Lord of the Universe long ago and the notes had no effect. If there was a God, why would he waste his time incompetently fiddling with the lives of beings he could remake or destroy on a whim?

When the notes failed to work, Edith enlisted the help of her pastor to try and talk some sense into the boy. She did not tell him that the Reverend Gideon Pratt was coming to visit because she was afraid he would disappear if she did. Her fear was based on a complete misunderstanding of her son's state of mind. Having finally confronted an evil and won a victory, Michael was eager for another fight.

The good Reverend showed up one Sunday afternoon after church, and he and Edith ambushed Michael together in the family room. To Edith's everlasting regret and embarrassment Michael did most of the talking. He asked only one question, "Why should I believe you?" and then dismantled the Reverend's evasive and wholly inadequate answer in contemptuously pointed detail. Reverend Pratt left the premises with neither his dignity nor his charitable spirit intact.

Then one day without warning, when Edith had done nothing new for weeks, she stopped making Michael's meals and told the housekeeper to stop washing his clothes and making his bed. She told Michael if he refused to serve The Lord, she would see to it that *he* was not served.

Dan and Danny were unaware of what was going on. They didn't spend much time at home, and Michael didn't communicate with them when they were around. Dan spent as little time as possible in the house in order to avoid contact with his wife, and Danny always did what he felt like doing. That rarely included being home except to sleep, or change his clothes after practice. When Michael was hungry he made peanut butter sandwiches. His mother had the housekeeper stop buying peanut butter and bread to put more pressure on him, so he learned to eat whatever was available. He could usually find something, even if it was just a can of vegetables.

When Edith put a lock on the pantry door and emptied the refrigerator of almost everything edible, Michael started hoarding his allowance to buy soda-pop and candy bars. Then Edith refused to give him his allowance. Now she had him, she thought. Now he would be forced to give in or starve.

*   *   *

Michael tried to concentrate but his empty stomach kept interfering and finally he gave up. He wasn't the only student ignoring his assignment, but he was the only student making no effort to hide it. The book he was supposed to be reading lay unopened on the top of his desk while he stared out the window, his elbow resting on the book and his chin resting on his open palm. He was completely unaware that he had the undivided attention of his teacher.

Deborah Johnson was excited when she learned that Michael Long would be among her students that fall. He had a reputation as a bright and well-behaved boy who was always prepared. Her concern for Michael's behavior began when he started missing his homework assignments in the first weeks of the session.

Now, nearly two months into the school year, she could find little in his behavior to lend credence to the positive reports she heard from his previous teachers. His test scores were still at the top of the class but he seemed listless, edgy, and borderline uncooperative when asked to participate. She didn't understand it, but she was determined to get to the bottom of it. She knew Michael hadn't read anything for the past twenty minutes, so she decided to find out why.

"Michael, come up here for a moment, please," she said.

Michael turned his head toward her and then rose from his chair and walked slowly to the front of the room.

"Yes, Miss Johnson?" he asked.

"I want to know why you aren't reading. There is going to be a quiz on this, and I know you haven't read a thing."

"Yes, that's true."

"What is the matter with you, Michael? All the reports I've gotten say you used to be a model student. What's going on?"

"Nothing."

"You don't act like this at home do you? Your parents must be really concerned if you do."

Michael looked at her without expression. "How I act is nobody's business."

Miss Johnson was not accustomed to hearing a statement like this from a twelve-year-old.

"Oh, really?" she asked. "And I suppose it's none of my business either."

"If you want. I'm not hurting anybody. I just want to be left alone."

Deborah pursed her lips in frustration. "I don't think I like your attitude, young man."

"Okay."

"I don't understand this at all, Michael. Why are you so angry?"

"Am I angry?"

"Yes, you're angry! And you're making me angry."

"I can't help that."

"Are you in some kind of trouble at home?"

"Not really."

"Well, something is going on. I want to know what it is. Maybe I can help."

"I won't tell you."

"Why not?"

"Just stay out of it. I don't need your help."

"No, I think I'm going to have a talk with your parents about this."

Michael snorted in disgust. "Oh, that'll be productive."

"I don't understand what's going on inside your head, young man, but I do know that your parents deserve your respect."

"Really? How do you know that?"

"Michael *what* has gotten into you?"

"I better get back to my desk and start studying, Miss Johnson. Like you said, there's going to be a test in a few minutes, and I don't want to waste any more time. Can I go now?"

Michael didn't wait to be dismissed. He turned and walked back to his desk. Miss Johnson let him go. She could have pursued the subject more forcefully, but she sensed the uselessness of trying. Michael wasn't going to talk, and she was not the kind of person who would attempt to coerce the truth out of him. She watched curiously as Michael sat down and at last took up the assignment he should have been reading all along. There were seven minutes left in the reading period. Michael laid down his book with two minutes to spare.

Miss Johnson passed out the papers for her customary short essay quiz and waited while the students took the test. The bell rang for the lunch hour just as the papers were being passed to the front of the room. As the students filed out Miss Johnson gathered up the papers, returned to her desk and went through the pile until she found Michael's sheet. She was expecting to find that he had written almost nothing, but every answer was complete and precisely correct.

As she walked toward the teacher's lounge to have lunch, Deborah carried Michael's test paper with her. Her friend and confidant Sandy Thorbold was sitting at one of the tables. Deb walked over to join her.

"I thought you said that Michael Long was one of the best students you ever had," Deborah said as she sat down.

"He was."

"Well, something's wrong. He's becoming very strange and difficult. He sat for twenty minutes doing nothing this morning when he should have been reading. When I asked him what was wrong, he as much as told me to mind my own business."

"Are you sure that's what he meant?"

"Of course I'm sure."

"Well, how did he do on the test?"

"Look for yourself." Deborah tossed the paper across the table.

Sandy noted the perfect score. "Well, no problem there at least."

"And that was after reading for less than ten minutes. Either he read the assignment earlier on his own, or he's an incredibly fast reader. It isn't his ability and his test scores, it's everything else. He seems to be developing a terrible attitude, and I didn't realize how bad it was until I spoke to him today."

"It's probably nothing, Deb. Kids go through this kind of thing all the time. It's just a part of growing up. He'll get over it."

"I don't know about that. He seems very angry with his parents about something."

Sandy chuckled. "You don't know his parents very well, do you?"

"It isn't funny, Sandy. Michael is acting *very* strangely. It's as if he has something on his mind that's more important than school work."

"And exactly how does that make him different from most other students in your class?"

"Come on, Sandy. You had him for a year. You know what I mean. You said he came to school bright-eyed and eager to learn. But for me he acts like he doesn't care or he wants to be somewhere else. If I had the slightest clue what is going on, I'd bring it to his parent's attention."

"I think you'd be wasting your time, Deb. If there really is something wrong there's a good chance his parents are at the bottom of it. For my money neither one is worth a hoot in a high wind."

"Well somebody needs to do something about this."

"What? What are you are going to do? You just said you don't know what's wrong. Go ahead and tell Principal Sheffield and see how far you get."

Deborah sighed. "Somebody should do something."

"Stop trying to save the world, Deb. There are some people who don't want to be saved and some things you just can't fix."

*   *   *

Whether at school or at play Michael had always preferred to keep his own company, but this school year he was more of a loner than ever. Miss Johnson was right. He was angry, and he wanted to stay that way. He was convinced it made him stronger, and it was easier to stay angry if he was alone.

Michael didn't go to the cafeteria for lunch. When the bell rang, he got his jacket and went out onto the playground. He was sitting by himself in a protected corner when Charlie Marquardt found him. Charlie liked to make a nuisance of himself. He wasn't a bad boy, just a pest. When he saw Michael sitting alone he got an idea for a really good joke.

"Hey, Michael," Charlie called. "Where have you been?"

"What?" said Michael.

"Mrs. Franklin wants you."

"Mrs. Franklin?"

"Yes, she has playground duty this week. She told me to go find you. She has an urgent message for you."

"What kind of message?"

"How should I know? She just told me to find you."

Michael might have taken into account the source, but his mind was elsewhere. He got up and went to find Mrs. Franklin.

Mrs. Franklin, of course, had no message for Michael Long, so Michael started looking for Charlie. He found him playing marbles with three other boys on a sidewalk at the edge of the school grounds.

Charlie knew that Michael would be angry, that was part of what made it so funny, but he didn't expect to have to defend himself, not from puny Michael. He saw Michael coming toward him and said with a smirk, "Hey, did you get the message?"

"I sure did, Charlie. Now here's one for you."

Michael swung without setting his feet, but he was moving forward, so all of his weight, not to mention his anger, was behind the blow. His fist connected with Charlie's right eye and Charlie went down. He wasn't knocked out but he was hurt enough to guarantee that he wouldn't be fighting back.

Charlie groaned and rolled back and forth with both hands protecting his injured eye.

Michael stood over him with both fists up and ready. "You get *my* message?" said Michael.

"Jeez, it was a joke," Charlie moaned, "Can't you take a joke?"

"You leave me alone," Michael spoke with exaggerated clarity, his index finger pointing at the bridge of Charlie's nose. "That goes for all of you assholes," he snarled at the other boys in the group.

Michael returned to his corner and sat down again. He had his head down and his coat collar turned up, trying to keep warm. He didn't see the girl approaching.

Megan Sullivan, who sat directly behind Michael in Miss Johnson's sixth grade class, was interested in people, and she had the beginnings of a talent for understanding them. The skill had its foundation in a willingness to observe and evaluate the actions of those around her. The habit was neither defensive nor did it arise from a need to be liked. She was simply interested in what motivated people to do what they did. She never used the information to manipulate or curry favor. But she could see inside people, sometimes quite deeply. It was the kind of uncommon sensitivity that had a chance to mature into uncommon perceptiveness, and it was this talent that led her to decide she liked Michael.

She had known him since the first grade, and she evaluated everything she knew about him as being good—from his intelligence and eagerness to learn to the courage she had seen him display more than once.

She remembered the time Michael stood up for her in the fifth grade when she was being hounded by some other students. She could not help it that her parents could afford to buy her only two new dresses to wear to school each year. She was silent when kids called her "trailer trash" because she could think of no response that would make them go away, and that's all she wanted to happen.

She remembered that confrontation, Michael standing before them. Somehow he reminded her of a knight ready for battle, but his manner held no belligerence, no physical threat. He faced them calmly, chin high, eyes contemptuously observant. The others were all bigger than he was, some of them much bigger, but in Megan's eyes his words shrank them all to insignificance.

"Why don't you try observing the world you live in, for once." he said. "Can you really believe her parents' money determines what Megan is, or what she can become? Are you that ignorant?"

"Thank you," she said, when her tormentors went away.

"You should have known better." said Michael.

"What?"

"You should not have let them get to you. You're better than that."

They didn't speak often because Michael never said much to anybody, and she never seemed to find the right words to keep a conversation going.

She usually knew where Michael was on the playground and she happened to be watching when he hit Charlie Marquardt. She was shocked and puzzled by what he did. This was not like Michael. If he was acting like this, something must really be wrong. When Michael returned to his corner, Megan followed.

"Hi, Michael," she said.

Michael looked up, startled to realize that someone was nearby. "Hi."

"Is something wrong?"

"Nothing's wrong. Just leave me alone, will you?"

"Okay, you don't have to ask twice," Megan said without rancor.

She began to walk away. If he wanted to be alone, she would respect the desire even though she very much wanted to stay.

But Megan was right about one thing. Michael did not like hurting people, innocent people at least, and he did not want to hurt Megan. He did like her, and knew that if there was anyone who would understand what he was going through it would be her.

"Hey, Megan. I'm sorry," he said. "What do you want?"

"Nothing important, I guess. I didn't mean to bother you." She turned back to face him.

Michael stood up. "Listen," he said. "I'm not having a good day, so don't make me beg you to tell me what you want."

The beginnings of a smile played at the corners of her mouth. "I just wanted to know if you're all right."

"Why does everybody think that something is wrong with me?"

"I saw you hit Charlie Marquardt. There isn't a mean bone in your body. You never hit anyone. Something must be wrong, so I came over to see if I could help."

"Do I look like I need help?"

"I guess you don't look like it, but something is wrong," she said, "otherwise you wouldn't act so strangely. I came over because you helped me once, and I wanted to help you back."

In spite of himself, Michael began to be less angry. He remembered the incident last year that she was referring to. He would accept her company if it was offered as a repayment on a debt. Maybe he would even talk about what was wrong. He would have rejected her suggestion out of hand had she told him she was motivated solely by a desire to help him.

"Okay, Megan. You can't help but have a seat anyway." He gestured toward the empty spot beside him. "Do you really want to know what's wrong?"

"Yes I do," she said as she sat.

For a few moments there was silence and then he asked, "Do you ever have trouble with your parents?"

"Yes, sometimes," she answered.

"Well, I'm having trouble with my mother."

"What kind of trouble?"

"My mom is trying to force me to go to church and I won't do it."

"Why not? Everybody goes to church."

"I don't, not anymore. But that's a long story. Last summer Mom made our housekeeper stop washing my clothes, and last week she locked the pantry and cleaned out the refrigerator to stop me from getting my own food."

"Why?"

"Because I won't do what she wants me to."

"Like going to church?"

"Yes, among other things. It wasn't hard to learn how to wash clothes, but last week she hid the laundry detergent. I started washing my clothes in the bathroom sink with hand soap. It worked, but my skin itches all the time, and that's almost worse than being hungry."

"Can't you just buy something? I thought you were rich."

"My *dad* is rich, Megan. That doesn't mean I get any of it."

"Don't you get an allowance?"

"I used to, but Mom stopped that too."

"What about your dad? Won't he help?"

"He doesn't care."

"Are you sure about that? My dad can be real strict sometimes, but I know he cares."

"Take my word for it, my dad doesn't care."

"Why don't you just go to church? It can't be that bad. You don't have to believe it or anything, and it's better than going hungry."

"Megan, if you want to be my friend, don't ever say that again."

She fell silent. It wasn't the rebuff that stopped her, it was the suggestion that they could be friends. She decided she liked the idea.

Michael glanced at her. "Look, I know you don't understand why I won't go to church. You don't have the knowledge to understand it, and right now I don't feel like explaining. For now, just accept that I will not do it."

"Okay," she agreed. Maybe he would tell her later. "How long has it been since you've eaten?"

"Don't worry about it. I'm fine."

"Friends don't lie to each other, Michael. How long has it been?"

"A couple of days."

"I have some extra food you can have."

"I don't need your help, Megan."

"I'm not offering it to you because you need it. I just have more food than I want, and I want you to have it."

"I can take care of myself."

"Right, that's why you're sitting here dreaming of liver and onions and drooling all over yourself."

"I am not drooling, and I hate liver and onions."

"Well, ice cream and cake then."

"Shut up, Megan. Just shut up."

"I have half a sandwich in my lunchbox that I didn't want for lunch. Do you want it?"

"What kind of sandwich?"

"Liver and onions."

"You're kidding."

"Yes. Actually its strawberry jam."

"That's almost as bad."

"Do you want it or not?"

"Only if you are going to throw it away. You don't owe me anything, and I have nothing to give you in return."

"We're talking half of a stale jam sandwich, Michael. I'd have to pay somebody to take it off my hands."

"You have a point. I'll take it."

"Wait. I don't know if I can afford it. How much do I owe you?"

Michael gazed at her mildly. "What's half-a-jam sandwich between friends?" he said.

When noon recess was over and the students filed back into the room, Megan got the sandwich from her box in the cloak room and gave it to Michael.

"Thanks." Michael devoured it on the spot in two large bites.

"Boy, that must have tasted good," Megan teased.

When he finally managed to swallow Michael said, "I didn't have to taste it, just eat it. Thanks again."

"You're welcome. Any time."

In the front of the room Charlie Marquardt was holding his eye as he talked to Miss. Johnson.

"Uh-oh," Megan warned. "There's trouble."

"What?" Michael turned around to look. He hadn't seen Charlie enter the room.

Miss. Johnson noticed Michael looking at her and beckoned him toward her desk.

"You mean *that*?" Michael nodded his head toward the front of the room. "That isn't trouble, that's a walk in the park."

"Just keep it cool. I can't fix everything with a jam sandwich."

"Nothing is going to happen I can't handle."

Charlie glared at Michael as he made his way toward the front. Miss. Johnson didn't seem very happy either. Michael walked up to the desk and waited attentively for her to speak.

"Charlie tells me that you and he had a fight in the school yard. Is that true?"

"No, not really," said Michael. "Charlie played a joke on me, so I hit him. It wasn't a fight."

"Do you think he deserved to be struck just because he played a joke on you?"

"Well that depends on the joke. But no, I don't think he deserved to be hit. I thought so when I hit him but I don't anymore."

"You know I am going to have to contact your parents about this, and you will have to spend some time in detention."

"Yes, I know."

"All right. I think you need to apologize to Charlie for what you did."

Michael turned to Charlie. "I'm sorry I hit you Charlie," he said, "You're a complete pain in the ass, but most of the time you don't even realize it. So, no hard feelings?" He offered his hand.

Miss. Johnson was trying hard not to smile despite the gravity of the situation. Michael's description caught the essence of Charlie's personality, and his cooperative attitude surprised her. This was not the same boy she talked to before lunch.

Charlie looked at Michael's hand and then grudgingly shook it. "I didn't mean anything by it," he said, "It was just a joke."

"I know," said Michael. "Like I said, no hard feelings. How's the eye?"

"Miss. Johnson says it'll probably be black-and-blue tomorrow."

"Gee, I didn't know I could hit that hard."

"You hit pretty hard. It still hurts a lot."

Michael went back to his desk, and the rest of the afternoon passed uneventfully until just before the end of the day when he was called to the front again.

"You are wanted at the principal's office, Michael," said Miss Johnson. "Your father is here."

"My father?" said Michael.

"Yes, they tried to reach your mother at home, but there was no answer so they called your father's office. You know its school policy to inform a child's parents when there is trouble at school."

"All right. Do I go now?"

"Yes. You are to go immediately."

Dan Long and Principal Sheffield were talking in the lobby of the principal's office when Michael walked in.

Dan turned and gave Michael a look of extreme disapproval. "Do you think I have all day to be chasing around the countryside after you?" he said.

"Your office is six blocks from here, Dad. Did you get lost on the way?"

"Why is it always a smart-ass answer with you? This little incident has completely disrupted my day. The principal says you hit a boy on the school grounds. That kind of behavior is intolerable. He says school policy requires a day of detention for that. I have asked him to give you three, one for hitting that boy and two more for wasting my time."

"Sorry to be such a bother," said Michael. "They tried to call Mom but she must not be home. I'll do whatever you want."

"Huh?" Dan was used to Danny's behavior when he was caught. He expected to hear whining complaints and denials. Michael wasn't fulfilling his expectations.

"I said, whatever you want. I did it. I hit a boy on the playground today. Do you want me to start right now? I can serve the first day starting now."

His father paused. "No, I don't think so. They have to schedule these things." Dan looked at Principal Sheffield.

"Yes," said Sheffield. "We need to have a teacher present for any detention. That takes some planning."

"Ok. How about tomorrow? Can I start tomorrow?"

"You'll serve it when the principal says you'll serve it. Why are you so damned eager, boy? It isn't natural."

"Because I don't give a crap. I can do three days of detention standing on my head. You want to know how to really get my attention, Dad? You take a hardwood stick about two inches thick and you beat me with it until I can't stand up anymore. Then you tell me it's for my own good. And when I ask for help, you tell me to shut up and take it like a man."

"*What* are you talking about?"

"What's the matter, Dad? Don't you have a stick? Maybe Mom will let you borrow hers."

"Michael, I have no idea what you're saying."

"Right. Are you taking me home, or are you too busy for that?"

Principal Sheffield was shocked by Michael's lack of respect. He did not for a moment put any credence in what the boy was saying. Dan Long was one of the most respected citizens in town and the very idea that he would allow physical abuse of his son was ridiculous. The boy clearly had an overactive imagination. It was a good thing Miss Johnson brought this to his attention. These things had a way of getting out of hand if they weren't dealt with early in life.

"Well, I can see you two have a number of issues to discuss," said Sheffield as he beat a hasty withdrawal.

"Come on boy," Dan ordered. "Let's get you out of here before you get into real trouble."

"I've been in trouble before," Michael shot back. "It doesn't bother me."

Dan's eyes squinted in anger but he said no more.

6 - FLESH AND THE DEVIL

There were two tall windows in the room, but the one facing north was blocked almost completely by vines and shrubbery. The other window, mostly unobstructed, faced eastward and let in a beam of direct light for several hours each morning. On the floor beneath the east window a small rectangle of hardwood was lit by a patch of light so brilliant that, rather than providing illumination, it made the rest of the room appear gloomy by comparison. The air smelled heavily of cigarettes. A smoky haze hung thick in the shaft of light from the window, and stray currents moved the smoke particles about in a sluggish, random dance.

Dan sat at his massive oaken desk, his brow furrowed in thought, his arms framing a white sheet of writing paper with a single paragraph written upon it. He was chewing on the end of his expensive writing pen and tapping the fingers of his left hand on the desktop.

Danny's youthful frame lay sprawled on the large brown leather sofa that dominated the wall opposite his father's desk, one leg propped on the coffee table, the other stretched out beneath it. He wore a driving hat pushed back on his head and cocked to one side. A lock of thick blond hair hung down across his forehead, and his eyelids were half-closed with boredom. A cigarette hung carelessly from his lips, its smoke curling languidly upward until it was lost in the general murk.

When the Long family first moved into the house on the hill, the den had been one of Dan's favorite places. Furnished and decorated to his exacting specifications it contained everything he needed to do business from home or to enjoy a leisurely afternoon watching football on TV. But his desire to keep his distance from Edith meant he was rarely here, and the room had somehow lost whatever it was that made him like it. The den and its furnishings were all made of darkly stained wood and brown leather, a look that Dan had once though masculine and comfortable but now evoked a feeling of claustrophobia. The fireplace, a huge edifice built of native stone that hadn't seen a fire in ten years, was adorned by an equally massive moose-head, the relic of a hunting trip to Northern Minnesota made when Dan was still a teenager.

Danny didn't realize that he shared at least one emotion with his father: they both hated this room. He only came in here when his father summoned him as he had this morning. The old man needs to hire an interior decorator, he thought idly. This place is really depressing.

The ash was about to fall off Danny's cigarette when his eyes rolled downward. He observed the butt with mild surprise. How had the ash gotten that long? He must have dozed off.

"I'll have your hide if that falls on the floor," his father growled.

He never would have admitted it, but at the age of seventeen, Danny was still just a bit in awe of his father, especially here. This was his dad's innermost sanctum, where Danny usually did what his father demanded, even though he resented it. He displayed his resentment by moving with exaggerated slowness as he took the cigarette from his mouth and carefully flicked the ashes into the half-filled tray on the table. Then he took a last long drag and snuffed it out.

"Jeez, Dad," he drawled. "When are you going to finish with that? I'd like to hit the road sometime today."

"It will be finished when its right. I wouldn't be in too big a rush if I was you. You have a pretty big stake in how this turns out," said his father.

Dan was making his son wait for a reason. Lately Danny had been acting as though he could do anything and get away with it, and Dan didn't like it. It's a stage, he told himself. But he wasn't sure about that. Ever since his firstborn came to live with him Dan had indulged Danny's every wish, but he was beginning to suspect this may have been a mistake. Danny had become a narcissistic and careless young man, who acted as though nothing he did had any consequences. The boy had no judgment. If he felt like doing something, he did it. His mind seemed to hold no other consideration.

When he watched Danny tear down the driveway in the classic roadster Dan gave him for his seventeenth birthday, Dan worried. He worried even more when he paid his son's bail three days later. The complaint charged reckless driving and speeding, but that was only half the story. If Danny had not been the son of Dan Long, the police would have tacked on resisting arrest and assaulting a police officer. In fact the county attorney was still threatening additional charges.

This morning, Dan was writing a letter of explanation and apology to the chief of police, the arresting officers, and the county attorney in the hope that he could use his influence to head off the more serious charges. He was making Danny wait as a punishment for the actions that made the letter necessary, and because the two of them needed to get their stories straight. Danny wasn't cooperating. When asked what happened, he spun an unlikely yarn about a blue convertible trying to run him off the road and police brutality. Dan didn't believe a word of it. He was ready to lie for his son, but he hoped that Danny would come clean at least with him. If he knew what he was dealing with, he had a chance of beating it. He did not want his son to spend time in jail.

"Look, Dad. Why don't you just write down what you think will work and be done with it? There are things I want to do today."

Dan was getting angry. "Don't you get it, Danny? You're in big trouble. If you don't cooperate you're going to serve some jail time. Is this what you want?"

"*Jail* time?" Danny scoffed. "Come on, Dad. You have the best lawyers that money can buy. I'm not going to serve any jail time."

"You will if you don't straighten up and change your attitude. You were caught going fifty miles-an-hour in a school zone. That's not just dangerous, it's damn stupid. Then you ran when the police saw you and compounded your error by striking the arresting officer when he tried to handcuff you. Why were you driving that fast? What were you thinking?"

"I told you, a blue…"

"I don't want to hear it, Danny. Give me a little credit for recognizing a bald-faced lie when I hear one. If you won't tell me the truth, you might as well get out of here. I'll finish this, and you read it later so you know what I wrote."

"Sure thing, Pops. Well, I'll be on my way then."

"Not in your car, you won't. Remember, the police have your driver's license. Until this thing is settled I don't want you driving."

"Whatever you say, Dad." Danny threw the comment over his shoulder as he walked out the door.

Damn! That kid is going to be the death of me, Dan thought. This thing had him scared, and Danny's attitude wasn't helping. I was just like that at his age, he thought. But even as he thought it, he knew it was wrong. He wasn't like Danny at seventeen. At seventeen Dan had been sorry when he created a mess. Danny just didn't care.

The sound of a slamming car door barely touched Dan's consciousness. Then he heard the snarl of a high-performance engine and the squeal of tires on the driveway. He leaped to his feet and ran to the front door in time to see the streak of red that was Danny's deuce coupe hit the highway and turn west. The car was still accelerating when it disappeared behind a low rise.

Danny wore a contemptuous smile as he backed off the gas and lit another cigarette. *They* can't tell *me* what to do, he thought. And by "they" he meant everybody. His father couldn't tell him what to do. The police couldn't. *Nobody* could. He was a free agent, free to do whatever he pleased whenever it pleased him. He had wheels. He had a bank account. What else did he need? The fact that he had earned neither was irrelevant. He had old moneybags wrapped around his little finger.

The truth? The truth was he felt like going fast. The truth was he didn't feel like stopping went the police saw him. The truth was he didn't feel like being ordered around.

The speedometer needle quivered near seventy-five. He tossed the butt out the window, let out a wild yell and smashed the accelerator into the floorboards. In less than three minutes he was at the edge of the next town. It was an inconsequential little burg—a few bars, a grain elevator, some houses, a tiny grocery store—nothing but a bump in the road, certainly not enough to bother slowing down for. When Danny passed the twenty-five mph speed sign at the city limits he was doing ninety. He swerved into oncoming traffic to miss a little old lady negotiating a turn onto Main Street and popped back into his own lane just missing a pickup going in the opposite direction. He was already at the other side of town and accelerating when he heard the siren.

Danny laughed. Five-hundred roaring, turbocharged horses said the cop didn't have a chance, and it was going to be fun proving it.

* * *

Dan Long had learned to love his first son in the years since the boy came to live with him. In spite of the antics, he still did. He remembered fondly when Danny used to come running to him when Dan came home after work, and when they would go to movies and football games together. They were best buddies in those days. But it seemed those days were gone, and Dan didn't know how or why they disappeared. He thought about it frequently, but all he had were questions without answers.

Danny had a hard time adjusting when he first came to live with his father. Heartbroken over the loss of his mother, he had refused to accept Edith even as an authority figure. His stepmother, already predisposed to dislike the boy, was not about to take any sass from him, and the conflicts were many and sometimes threatened to become violent. Before their agreement over religion Dan had to step in often to keep the peace between his wife and son.

There was a rebellious streak in Danny, an attitude that denied any external constraint on his actions, and it became more pronounced as his son grew. Dan explained it to himself as the result of his son's early life without a father, but he never found the formula to change Danny's behavior.

When Danny was thirteen a country store owner caught him trying to steal candy bars when he and Dan stopped for gas during a hunting trip. When Dan asked him what he had been thinking, Danny shrugged and said, "Nobody ever caught me before."

Dan, more embarrassed than anything by the incident, gave the store owner twenty bucks to forget the whole thing.

As the two drove away Dan turned to his son and asked, "Why the hell did you do that?"

"To see if I could get away with it."

"For Christ sake, I could buy that place with pocket change and give it to you. You could have all the candy bars you wanted."

"What fun would that be?" Danny's smile was filled with devious cunning.

Dan remembered worrying over that smile.

When he was fourteen Danny stole a car and ran it into a ditch, destroying the vehicle and putting himself in the hospital. That incident cost Dan a lot more than twenty bucks to sweep under the rug, but it wouldn't do for his son to have a juvenile record. Danny was going to be a great athlete some day, and his character had to be above reproach.

Danny took over as the starting halfback of the Mansfield Tigers in the first game of his freshman year. At first he liked having Dan watch him play, and he enjoyed dissecting the games with him afterward, but there was something about football that held his interest more than anything else. It was the physical battle and the pain it allowed him to inflict upon his opponents without fear of retribution. In that pursuit, he was relentless, and utterly without scruple.

It didn't take long for Danny to gain a reputation as a malcontent and a punishing, often dirty, player. When the coaches were around, he followed team rules most of the time, and ignored them completely when they weren't. He tended to be disruptive during team meetings, and was in constant danger of losing eligibility because of his grades. But he was also very, very good—at football and a number of other useful pursuits. He could, for instance, turn an "F" into a "C" on his report card just by visiting the coach's office. It was a talent that served him more than once.

He was booted off the team when a marijuana cigarette fell out of his jacket while he was putting it on in the locker room after the sixth game of his sophomore year. A search of his locker produced several ounces of high-grade weed and some drug paraphernalia. He was selling it in school.

Any other student would have been expelled, but with his dad and a few other influential alumni leading the charge, his punishment turned into a relative slap on the wrist. Danny had to sit out the remainder of his sophomore year, but the next fall he was let back onto the team after he apologized to the coaching staff and his teammates, and agreed to serve a further three-game suspension to begin the season.

At the end of the three games the school administration, the coach, and Danny's teammates would decide if he would be allowed to play. There was never any doubt that his teammates wanted him back. They wanted to win. The coach would have given ten years of his life to have Danny's talent wrapped up in a more disciplined package, but the baggage that came with the talent almost made the coach wish he'd never heard of Danny. He had a hard time deciding which disaster was worse—a losing season, or having Danny Long on the team.

The principal was among Danny's defenders, but he knew this incident could not be ignored. The values of good citizenship and team discipline were at stake. So, Danny was required to practice and dress with the team, but he hadn't played a single down.

*　　　*　　　*

The Tigers had already lost the first two games of the season and were down 20-to-0 to the Drayton Spartans at halftime when Dan Long walked down the bleacher steps from his customary seat near the top. About half-way down he stopped and tapped Principal Sheffield on the shoulder.

"Look, Fred, don't you think this has gone on long enough?"

"What do you mean?"

"You know what I mean. The boys are getting killed out there and the solution is sitting on the bench. Don't you think Danny has been punished enough?"

"There is a standard of conduct involved here, Dan."

"There's a football season going down the toilet, and you have the power to stop it. They have no chance to make the playoffs if they lose again, and you and I both know they are going to lose if Danny doesn't play."

"What kind of message will this send your son?"

"Danny is heartbroken, Fred. Not being able to play has been really hard on him. He needs something to focus on, and you have taken football away from him. You have to get him back in there."

Principal Sheffield rose to his feet. "I don't know, Dan. I'll talk to the coach. He will need to approve."

Coach Eldon James was ambivalent about putting Danny in. "But he hasn't learned anything, Fred. He's still the troublemaker he always was."

"He's the best player you've had since his father played for you, and you know it. The decision is up to you Ellie, but unless you win this game the season's done, and your contract is up for renewal in the spring."

"That isn't fair."

"I know, but the decision to keep you on will not be mine. The school board will not stand for two losing seasons in a row."

Coach James' half-time speech was an eye-roller and Danny wasn't listening. Even when he expected to be playing, he never listened to his coaches' game-time speeches. As far as he was concerned they were vacuous little sermons filled with stupid little sports clichés, and when it came time to play he never needed to be provided with motivation or told what to do.

He was thinking about his girlfriend, Rachel, and what they had planned after the game. Normally he didn't think about girls during a game, but normally he didn't sit on the bench either. Danny's daydream was at the point where he was about to remove Rachel's panties when he heard his name being called. "Long, would you mind letting us all in on the joke?" It was Coach James.

Danny realized that he had a smirk on his face. "Uh, no joke coach. I was just getting fired up for another exciting half on the bench."

"Well get your mind on the game. You're starting the second half. You ready?"

For the moment at least, Rachel's doubtful innocence was saved. "Coach, you know I'm ready!"

The Spartans kicked off to begin the third quarter and the Mansfield return man let the ball land in front of him and bounce away. Then just as it was about to roll into the end zone for a touchback, he fell on the ball. Two big mistakes on one play. The Tiger offense took over at the one yard line.

Coach James knew what Danny could do in a game situation, so he wasted no time in putting him to the test. The first play was a halfback sweep to the right with the fullback faking up the middle. It was a dangerous play to run from the end zone but Coach James knew his guy had power and speed to burn. When Danny Long got going, he was almost impossible to bring down. The defense would be packed in, expecting the Tigers to take the safe option. If Danny got to the outside he was going to go a long, long way, and the team needed a lift. This was make-or-break time.

The quarterback handed off to Danny in the same instant a Drayton linebacker shot into the backfield through a gap that wasn't supposed to be there. The linebacker grabbed Danny's jersey, trying to pull him down. The crowd gasped as Danny staggered and almost dropped the ball, but he refused to be tackled. Somehow he regained his balance, tucked the ball away, and shed the linebacker with a brutal stiff-arm to the head. Now moving laterally in the end zone, he had no chance to beat the pursuit. The play was broken. If he was going to make yardage, he would have to do it on his own. He sensed a crack of daylight inside and cut sharply up-field into the teeth of the defense. He slipped one tackle and drove through another. A lightning cut to the right was accompanied by a roar from the crowd as Danny exploded into the open field.

Now there was nothing in front of him but eighty-five yards of empty real estate. The crowd was on its feet, cheering wildly. A Drayton safety was running across the field, trying to catch up to the play, but he wasn't going to make it and the crowd knew it. Danny knew it too. He slowed down and altered his course, switching the ball to his right arm. The safety wasn't catching up fast enough. Danny slowed even more. The safety overshot his target and turned back in an attempt to tackle his opponent. Suddenly Danny lowered his shoulder and drove hard into the player's chest just below the lacing on his shoulder pads. The Drayton player's feet went out from under him, and he fell on his back. Instead of avoiding the fallen player, Danny ran over him, his cleats coming down hard on the player's outstretched forearm as he went by. Danny heard the arm snap as he raised the ball high into the air and goose-stepped the last ten yards into the end zone.

The referee signaled a touchdown and Danny nonchalantly flipped the ball away and trotted back to the bench to a standing ovation. He glanced briefly at the medical team attending to the player whose arm he had just broken, then pushed through the crowd of teammates waiting to congratulate him. As he took off his helmet and turned around Coach James grabbed him by the arm. "What the hell were you doing, Long? You had him beat by a mile and you slowed down. I thought you pulled a muscle or something."

"There's nothing wrong with me, coach. I feel great!"

"Then you let him catch up on purpose? Listen, Danny, on this team you take care of business. Period. There will be no grandstanding stunts like that. Ever. You go sit your ass back down on the bench, and don't let me see you move it for the rest of the game."

"You've got it wrong, coach. It wasn't grandstanding. It was just my way of sending them a message." He gestured toward the group huddled across the field. "Pretty effective message, don't you think?"

"I send the messages around here. You go sit down."

Danny smiled. "I don't think you want to bench me, Coach. This crowd will have your head."

"You go sit down and shut up."

Coach James didn't like Danny's cocky attitude one bit. He never had. But he liked being a head coach very much. He wanted to tell the boy to go to the locker room and turn in his uniform but he knew he didn't have the courage to do it, and the knowledge irked him. For the good of the team he simply couldn't afford to bench this kind of talent. The touchdown play was amazing on so many levels. In nearly 30 years of coaching high school football, he'd seen nothing like it.

Drayton's offense started its next drive from the 35 yard line, but for some reason, it wasn't nearly as crisp as it was in the first half. The Spartans stalled at mid-field and had to punt. Mansfield took over on its own 23.

Danny got up from the bench and purposely brushed past the coach on his way onto the field with the rest of the offense. The coach opened his mouth to call him back but decided against it. Two plays later, Danny was in the end zone again.

The final score was Mansfield 43, Drayton 20. Danny gained 322 yards and scored five touchdowns on seventeen carries. He broke the Mansfield High School single game rushing record by fifteen yards while playing only the second half.

The previous record holder sat alone in the stands, his body leaning forward with his hands pressed against the bleacher bench on either side of him. Dan Long's eyes were focused on the empty field while his mind relived another game and another night more than twenty years ago, the night he set the record that had just been broken. He still counted that game as one of the great moments of his life, but this moment was greater. If he could have chosen anyone to break his record it would have been Danny, and the pride he felt was an emotion far more powerful than any he could remember feeling that night so long ago. He hoped Danny understood and appreciated the improbable nature of his feat. Achievements like this one and football players like Danny Long came along once-in-a-lifetime.

"Dad?"

Dan turned around. "Michael? What are you doing here?"

"I came to watch the game just like you did. I didn't know Danny was going to play tonight. I thought he was out until next week."

"Yes. Well, the coach changed his mind, I guess."

Michael sat down a few feet from his father. "Quite a game, wasn't it?"

"Yes, it certainly was."

"Danny's an incredible running back."

"That he is."

"Did you see how he broke that guy's arm? He had a clear path to the end zone and he just ran over him and broke his arm. He did it on purpose."

Dan gave Michael a hard look. The same thought had been percolating in the back of his own mind and he resented being forced to deal with it. "What are you talking about? It was an accident. The kid fell and Danny couldn't avoid him."

Michael looked at his father for a silent moment. "Oh yes. That must be it."

"What is this? You think you're gaining something by running your brother down?" Dan asked angrily. "Do you realize what Danny did tonight?"

"Perfectly."

"Football is a contact sport, Michael. The play was clean. The injury was completely unavoidable."

"I thought you'd say that, but I figured I'd check anyway. Well I guess I'll head for home. I have my bike here, so I don't need a ride. But thanks for asking."

77

"I haven't offered you a ride."

"Oh, my mistake. See you, Dad."

Before Dan could say anything more, Michael rose to his feet and ran easily down the bleacher benches, taking them two at a time. For a moment Dan paused to admire the physical skill and the speed of Michael's descent. The boy's feet seemed to barely touched the surface as he flew to field level. It reminded him of the kind of thing Danny could have done with equal ease. He hadn't known Michael had any athletic ability at all. He wondered for a moment why he'd never noticed before, but his mind quickly returned to Danny's game and the moment was forgotten. He wasn't going to let anything ruin this night for him.

But while he sat, his mind drifted back to the first play of the second half. Did Danny mean to hurt that kid? Of course not. Yes, he was wild, but he was a good kid at heart. Still…

Danny was not enjoying the moment as his father imagined he ought to be. In the Mansfield locker room the excitement was palpable, but Danny was not an active participant. He accepted the congratulations of his teammates with an air of distraction. As far as he was concerned the football fun was over until the next game, and besides, his mind was on other matters.

Rachel Pratt was waiting for him where she said she would be, under a security light near the locker room entrance. A vision of five-foot-five-inch perfection from her creamy skin and flowing auburn curls to her artfully sculptured lips and full breasts to her long, shapely legs, Rachel was a teenage boy's daydream—stunningly beautiful and, with Danny at least, amazingly willing.

She wore a navy-blue mini-skirt that exposed more than half the length of her thighs. Her blouse was white and semi-transparent, open to an inch below the beginning of her cleavage. Her cheeks were flushed and her nipples erect in the cool evening air, and since she was not wearing a bra he could see them standing proud against the translucent fabric of her top every time she breathed. She wore makeup, but not enough to look made-up. She looked healthy, wholesome, incredibly sexy and utterly flawless.

He didn't know where she got the clothes she wore, or how she got out of the house with them on, and he didn't care. The total effect was as electric as she hoped it would be. He wanted to tear her clothes off and take her right then and there on the pavement under the security light. If there had been a blanket available he might have done it.

She smiled happily when she saw him. "Hello, Danny," she said as she came slowly toward him. When she reached him, she pressed her body against his, put her arms around his neck and pulled his lips down to where she could reach them. She told him how much she wanted him with a smoldering, liquid kiss, and his response was immediate and hungry.

The kiss ended, but he did not let her go. He held her against him, looking deep into her bottomless brown eyes, savoring the smell and feel of her in his arms. Finally he said, "Gorgeous, you are just too spectacular for words, and I want you so bad I'm going to explode in a minute. Let's get the hell out of here."

She laughed with pleasure at the effect she was having on him. "Yes, let's! You have no idea how cold this outfit is. I need you to warm me up."

Rachel had her parents' car for the evening, she promised she would be home by eleven-thirty p.m. so there was no time to waste. It was already almost ten. Danny's coupe was too small for what they planned, but the back seat of the Pratt's Buick was big enough to host an orgy.

Danny and Rachel had met during the previous summer when she visited the Long house with her parents. Rachel, the daughter of Edith's pastor and his wife, Alice, attended a private church school in town. The Reverend Pratt liked to visit the homes of all of his parishioners at least once a year and usually he brought his wife along. This time he brought Rachel, too, at the special invitation of Edith.

Even though she wasn't supposed to meddle in Danny's life, Edith just couldn't help herself. The girl was about the same age as Danny and a very fetching child. Edith was horrified by the harlots Danny ran around with and thought this would be a good way to introduce him to a nice girl for once.

Rachel was indeed a very nice girl, but not precisely in the sense Edith used the term. While the Reverend, Alice, and Edith were in the house discussing the proper path to eternal life, Rachel took Danny to paradise of the earthly kind. In the garden, lying shamelessly naked in the grass under an apple tree, she gave Danny a breathtaking introduction to the many ways of the flesh.

Danny wasn't exactly a virgin, but Rachel gave him a perspective on sex he never imagined existed. By the time she left some two hours later Danny was utterly exhausted.

Rachel didn't think of herself as a "loose" girl, and she was discrete enough to keep her reputation essentially intact. But her virginity was long gone, and after it happened she came to believe she had nothing left to protect any longer, so she might as well enjoy the pleasure God gave her body the capacity to feel. Danny was so hot and cute and strong and cuddly. The moment she saw him, she had to have him, and after he got over his clumsiness he quickly became as good at making love as he was at everything else. Not only could he light her off like a firecracker any time he wanted, he made her feel desired in a way she had never known. Sex with Danny didn't make her feel empty and unfulfilled like most of her other experiences. It was just good, and very, very satisfying.

They drove to a spot they knew a couple of miles from town and made love in the back seat of the Buick. Afterward Danny kissed her closed eyelids and touched her cheek. She opened her eyes and sighed.

"I watched your face," he said.

"When?"

"When it happened. I wanted to see what you looked like when it happened."

"What did I look like?"

"Like…I was going to say like an angel, but angels can't possibly feel anything like that, and I pity them for the deficiency. You looked like the entire universe consisted of the pleasure I was giving you. Did it really feel that good?"

"Yes." she smiled and gently touched his hair, "Oh, yes. It felt like that and more, my beautiful boy."

"You need to be careful of me," said Danny.

"Careful? What a strange thing to say. Why?"

"Because I'm good enough to give you that. You might get to like it too much. You look beautiful when you come, Rachel. Very beautiful and very vulnerable."

"Oh, Danny, Danny! Is there anyone in the world as sweet as you? I am not nearly as beautiful as you think I am. There's a lot you don't know about me."

"I know everything I need to know, Baby. It was all in your face."

She remained silent until they were on their way back to town. "I watched you play tonight," she said. "Did you step on that player's arm on purpose? It looked to me almost like you did."

Danny frowned. He was silent for several seconds, and she glanced at him wondering if he was angry.

He wasn't angry, but he didn't know whether or not he should tell her the truth. Finally, he decided he would. "It was on purpose," he said. "I wanted to hurt him."

"But why? There was no need for that."

"I don't know why, really, it's just the way I am."

"Nobody is just the way they are, Danny. Maybe you don't know what it is because you haven't thought about it, but there's a reason you did it. I think you should find out what it is."

"Maybe." He never would have admitted it to anyone else. "Yes, maybe I need to know."

"I need to know too," she said. "It's very important to me that I know what kind of a person you really are because you are very important to me."

She left him in the school parking lot beside the coupe and drove off into the night. He watched her go until he could no longer see the Buick's taillights, and then he turned and got into his car. His head was filled with memories of the night: the football game, the touchdowns, the sound of that player's arm snapping, and Rachel, sweet, vulnerable, incredibly sexy Rachel Pratt. He really liked her a lot. It was a pity, really. He liked her and he knew he was going to hurt her. He just didn't know when.

7 - MOMENTS OF TRUTH

Megan Sullivan looked into the brown paper sack that carried her lunch and then back at her mother. "Mom, could I please have another sandwich today? Sometimes I get awful hungry before supper."

"Well, that's an unusual request," said Mrs. Sullivan as she took out the bread again. "Half the time you don't even finish one sandwich."

"And please make it peanut butter this time?"

Mrs. Sullivan stopped and looked at Megan curiously. "I thought you said you don't like peanut butter."

"Oh, yes I do. I used to hate it, but now I like it...some of the time anyway. It would be nice to have something different than jam once in awhile."

"Okay," said Mrs. Sullivan dubiously. It wasn't two weeks ago that Megan turned up her nose at peanut butter and refused to eat it when there was nothing else in the house for a sandwich. So even though the weekly budget was already stretched to the limit, Mrs. Sullivan had finally given her daughter twenty-five cents to buy a hot lunch at school. Now Megan was saying she *wanted* peanut butter. It didn't make any sense, but she reached for the peanut butter anyway, finished the sandwich, and placed it in the sack just as the school bus horn sounded at the corner.

Megan knew it wouldn't be easy to get Michael to take the peanut butter sandwich. He could be awfully stubborn about accepting help, but she was determined to try. He had to eat something.

When the bell rang at noon, Michael didn't go to the cafeteria. He went directly to the cloak room and then outside. Megan assumed it was because he had nothing to eat, so she decided that she would immediately take the sandwich to him in the schoolyard. She stuffed the peanut butter sandwich into one jacket pocket and the jam sandwich into the other. She found Michael in the same place as the day before.

When he looked up she simply took the sandwich out of her pocket and held it toward him.

"What's that?" Michael asked suspiciously.

"Mom made me an extra sandwich. Peanut butter. I told her I needed a bigger lunch, but it's for you. Here." She plopped the sandwich on his lap.

Michael inspected the neatly wrapped sandwich and then looked back at Megan with a curious twinkle in his eyes. "Thanks, but that wasn't necessary."

"I can't let you starve to death."

"If I eat that, what am I going to do with this?" he pulled a sandwich out of his own pocket.

"Where did that come from? I thought you said your mom was starving you to death."

"That's an interesting interpretation. I did tell you that she was *trying*, but that's old news. Last night I figured out how to get into the pantry."

"What did you do, beat the door down with a hammer?"

"No, I got pliers and pulled out the hinge pins."

"What are hinge pins?"

"The pins that keep the two halves of a door hinge together. The pantry door swings out, so the hinge pins are on the outside. I just pulled them out of the door, and it came out backwards, slick as can be. I raided the pantry, put the door back on, and hid the food in the carriage house. Mom will never figure it out."

"Brilliant! But what am I going to do with this sandwich? I *hate* peanut butter."

"Gosh, I guess you're stuck with it. Wait! I have an idea. Maybe you can pay me to take it off your hands."

"Very funny." Megan sat down beside Michael and took the sandwich back, stuffing it into her coat pocket.

They sat with their backs to the south side of the school building where it was sunny and protected from the wind.

"Why did you bring me that sandwich?" he asked.

"That's a stupid question. Because you needed food, and I had a way to get it."

"But you don't owe me anything."

"You said that yesterday. So what? I brought the sandwich because nobody should have to fight their parents just to stay alive. I will not stand by and let a friend struggle alone when I can help him."

"So we're friends now." He made it a statement, not a question.

"Sure."

"Is that why you want to help, because you think being my friend obligates you to help me?"

"I don't think of it that way. There's no obligation. I brought the sandwich because friends should not be wasted. I prefer them alive."

"Is that the only reason?"

"There are many reasons, actually, but why should they matter? You have your reasons, and I have mine. If we both get something good out of friendship, then we both win."

"But the key is knowing what 'good' means."

"Michael, what's the problem? What are you afraid of?"

"Not afraid. Cautious. I know a few people who ought to pay a little closer attention to the actual meaning of *good*. They claim to know what 'good' is and they know nothing of the kind. I don't want to make a mistake about people, that's all."

"I'm not sure I understand what you're talking about. I wasn't trying to force the sandwich on you. I just don't like the thought of your being hungry."

"You're not disappointed because I don't need your sandwich?"

"What a silly thing to say. Of course not. Why would I be disappointed?"

"I can't think of a single good reason."

"Michael, you can't always be sure of what motivates people. You just have to trust your heart a little bit."

"No, you don't."

She looked at him for a moment and then got out her jam sandwich. "Well, I'm hungry. I think I'll have my sandwich now."

Michael was thinking about all the times that Edith told him to trust his heart. What she meant was that he should ignore his brain and let himself be guided by emotions *she* decided he should have. His mother claimed to feel those emotions, but he knew she was lying. What Edith said she felt bore no conceivable connection to what she did. He was certain Megan didn't mean the same thing as his mother did when she spoke of trusting his heart. Megan just wasn't that kind of person. She might be mistaken, but she was nothing like his mother. Sitting beside Megan was good, the right kind of good. He stretched his legs out, leaned back against the building and exhaled a sigh of contentment.

"Thanks for bringing the sandwich," he said.

"You're welcome." She smiled at him around a mouthful of bread and jam.

*   *   *

In the 1960s, Mansfield public schools were all on the same block, separate buildings joined by short hallways. Students shared a common cafeteria and similar schedules, so there was daily contact between younger and older students at lunchtime and before and after school. Michael could have hitched a ride to school with Danny anytime but his half-brother always seemed to have things to do after school and couldn't usually take him home. So Michael took his bike when it was warm enough and rode the bus when it wasn't.

He was alone, pulling his bike from the rack near the elementary building, when Butch Lagred saw him.

Lagred was a twenty-year-old hoodlum who had finally reached the eleventh grade because every teacher who had him tried their best to get rid of him. His dad had once worked for Michael's father, but lost his job when he was caught stealing. Butch discovered who Michael was when he overheard someone mention his name in the cafeteria. He had it on good authority that the Longs were all stinking rich, so when he saw Michael getting his bike he decided to find out if the story was true.

Michael was just leaving the school grounds when Lagred jumped out from behind a hedge near the sidewalk and grabbed the bike by the handlebars. Michael got off his bike and backed away in surprise, but when Butch ordered him to empty his pockets, Michael refused. Butch was not the type given to careful observation, but he couldn't help noticing the strange look that appeared on Michael's face and vanished almost sooner than it registered on Butch's brain. It wasn't fear. Butch knew the look of fear. It was something he'd never seen and didn't have the capacity to understand. It looked strangely fierce and out of place on the face of an adolescent child. Butch expected cowering submission. His intended victim gave him defiance. Michael doubled his fists. "You want my money? Come and get it."

The flash of expression Butch saw and didn't recognize was the outward manifestation of a human mind identifying a fact. Michael did not know this plodding, slack-jawed punk, but he recognized in an instant that Butch and Edith were moral equivalents. The flash was the momentary desire to wade in and destroy the evil before him. What replaced it was the realization that he was in physical danger and the reasoned determination to face it and prevail. Michael was done serving as prey for meat-eating monsters in whatever guise they presented themselves. It didn't matter that he would probably get hurt. He knew what that felt like, and it didn't scare him anymore. It didn't matter that he had no money and nothing of value besides his text books. If this thug wanted to rob him, he was going to earn it.

Butch was deeply offended by Michael's resistance since it was a direct challenge to his status as the most-feared hooligan in the school. He advanced toward Michael, planning to give him a lesson in the finer points of suffering. Michael waited until Butch got close enough and then he calmly punched him in the crotch. Since Lagred was over a foot taller than Michael, the target was at just about the right height and Michael caught Butch dead-on with his best uppercut. Butch fell to the ground in agony.

His assailant unable to hurt him any longer, Michael retrieved his bike and rode home.

Although Michael noticed no on-lookers and told no one of the incident, somehow the story got out. By the next day it was all over the school. Butch Lagred, a thug whom even teachers feared, was left writhing on the ground by a little shrimp of a sixth-grader.

Danny heard about it from Butch himself, during the noon hour the day following the incident. Danny happened to walk by as Butch pinned a member of his own gang to the fence at the edge of the school grounds.

"It didn't happen and you better take it back or I'll rip your head off," Butch was saying. Little Kenny Schendel was going to have a hard time taking anything back unless Butch loosened his grip on Kenny's scrawny neck. But what Butch said next rendered immaterial any apology Kenny might have made had he been allowed to speak. It was as good as an open admission that the story was true. "I'm going to kill that little shit for sure," said Butch. "Nobody does that to me. That Long kid is going to die!" Butch made a point of emphasizing the word *die*. If his actual intent was not to kill Michael, he clearly meant to do some serious damage.

At the mention of his last name, Danny stopped. "Who's going to die?" he asked.

Butch turned at the sound of Danny's voice and immediately recognized who was talking. "I am going to kill that stinking little half-brother of yours," he said, dropping his grip on Kenny's neck and turning toward Danny. Butch was used to having his size do his talking for him. He was half-a-head taller than Danny and fifty pounds heavier, and he crowded Danny until the two stood chest-to-chest. "Your brother is going to die for spreading lies about me."

"I didn't know Michael knew you existed, Butch. When did you introduce yourself?"

Butch was confused by Danny's question and backed off a bit as he tried to think of a response that wouldn't incriminate himself. Butch was not blessed with an overabundance of mental acuity, but he did know he needed to be careful or he would admit too much. "Uhhh, what's it to you?" He said. It was the best line he could come up with under pressure.

"Well, I was just wondering, Butch. My brother is in sixth grade and you're a junior—uh, wait they *did* let you out of tenth grade last year didn't they Butch?" Butch nodded agreement. "Well then, you are a junior, and Michael is a sixth grader. How would he even know who you are unless you introduced yourself?"

"Uh, I don't know."

"I don't either, Butch. But let me tell you what I think might have happened. I know you are a thief and a fucking coward. I know you shake down little kids for lunch money because I've seen you do it. I think you tried to take money from my brother, and he got the better of you somehow. Is that what happened, Butch? Did wimpy little Michael Long make a fool out of you?"

Danny said it in a completely conversational tone as though verbalizing the obvious.

For a moment Butch wasn't sure he heard Danny correctly. Then it dawned on him that he had just been insulted. "Nobody makes a fool out of me!" he yelled, swinging a wild right at Danny's chin.

Danny was expecting this—he was counting on it. He was not acquainted with the phrase "plausible deniability" but he knew how to apply the principle. If you were going to have a fight in school, and Danny had been in several, then it was best to provoke your opponent into committing first. Butch's wild punch threw him off balance, and he stumbled forward. Danny simply stuck his foot out, and Butch tripped and went down hard. Before he could rise, Danny dropped on top of him, driving his knee viciously into Butch's back. His arms went around Butch's neck and locked in a choke hold. Butch, grunting in pain, could neither move nor speak. Butch's gang watched it happen without lifting a finger, too stunned to move. They had never seen Butch so much as challenged, yet Danny disposed of him with shocking ease.

"Now I want you to listen carefully, Butch. This is very important." Danny was speaking into Butch's ear, his voice barely above a whisper. "Are you listening, Butchie?" Danny's knee ground into Butch's back, and Butch rasped an inarticulate acknowledgement. "I'll take that as a 'yes,'" said Danny. "If I ever find out that you have bothered my brother, if he ever gets so much as a scuff on his shoe, I am going to hunt you down and make you bleed. Do you understand?" Another incoherent grunt. "You think you're a tough guy, Butch, but you're really just a stupid, clumsy coward. If there is to be a killing, you are the one who is going to die. Would you like to die, Butch?"

Butch was beginning to panic. He could barely breathe, and Danny's hold was getting tighter. Butch began to struggle, and Danny lifted his weight and drove his knee into Butch's back again. "Just be patient, Butchie-boy," Danny continued. "I'm going to let you up in a minute, so you'll have a chance if you have the guts to take it."

Butch stopped struggling, and Danny loosened his grip just slightly. Then he spoke quietly to Butch again. "You need to understand something Butch. I have nothing but contempt for wannabe hoods like you. You have no idea what it really means to be tough. Hell, my brother took you, and he's about as dangerous as a rabbit. When I let go of you, I think there's a good chance that you will run rather than fight because you're just that kind of guy, Butch, a gutless coward."

Danny released Butch and backed away, waiting for him to rise. Butch staggered to his feet rubbing his back and neck. He stood for a moment and then turned to his gang. "I don't want nobody buttin' in, you hear?" he said. "I'm gonna take care of this myself." He turned back to Danny. "Now I'm gonna teach you a lesson you'll never forget."

Danny was grinning from ear to ear. "Have at it, you worthless sack of shit."

Butch uttered a low growl and started to move in slowly, intending to back Danny into a corner and then beat him senseless. But Danny didn't wait to be boxed in. He attacked. Butch was used to creating fear in his opponents. Danny had no fear. There was only one thing on his mind: the incomparable joy of physically destroying Butch Lagred. Every blow Danny struck was designed to inflict the maximum amount of pain, and no part of Butch's body was off limits—a kick to the kneecap, a fist below the belt, a chopping blow to the throat, a finger in the eye—it could have been over in seconds, but Danny wouldn't let it end. Every time he knocked Butch down or Butch fell down, Danny stood back and waited for him to get up again, goading him to rise if he hesitated even for a moment. "Come on, Butch, drag your sorry ass out of the dust and give me that lesson you promised." As it began to take longer and longer for Butch to struggle to his feet, Danny's goading became louder and more impatient. "Remember your boys are watching this, Butch, and you can't afford to look like a panty-waist in front of them. Come on, boy. Show me how it's done. Show me how you beat up on sixth-graders. I want you to show me, Butch. Come on, don't stop now. I haven't learned my lesson yet."

Like many of the students on the playground at the time, Michael noticed the commotion near the street and went to investigate. A crowd had gathered around the fight completely obscuring the participants, and he couldn't see what was going on or who was involved. As he walked up to the edge of the commotion Charlie Marquardt pushed his way out of the crowd and saw Michael.

"It's your brother," said Charlie. "He's beating the shit out of Butch Lagred. You gotta see this!"

Michael knew immediately that the fight had something to do with him. It could not be a coincidence. He worked his way into the crowd until he could see Danny and Butch squared off against each other. Butch looked about finished, but Danny seemed to be completely untouched. Suddenly Butch attacked with a clumsy rush trying to grapple with his opponent. Danny simply sidestepped and let Butch stumble and fall to the ground again.

Danny turned to watch as Butch tried to rise and saw Michael standing at the edge of the circle. He grinned and called to his brother, "Hey, Michael. You want a piece of this? He's about your speed, but I guess you know that already, right?"

Michael shook his head. "No. It's over Danny. Just let him be."

"The hell you say! It ain't over until I say it is. Come on Butch. Don't go to sleep on me now."

Butch was up again and staggering. Danny waited until the bully had his feet under him and then he walked in again. A short, vicious punch split Butch's upper lip and he went down again. "Oh, come on!" Danny shouted. "At least *try* to stay on your feet!"

Butch could not lift his arms any longer, and Danny finished him with a roundhouse right. The blow struck Butch flush on the jaw, his eyeballs rolled up, and he fell like a sack of potatoes face forward into the dust. Danny stood for a moment over Butch's still figure, his fists clenched, waiting to see if Butch would rise again. He didn't move. Butch was done, but Danny wasn't ready for it to end, and he began to kick his downed opponent sadistically in the head and ribs. "I'm still waiting for my lesson, Butch. Come on, get up and fight you worthless jerk. I'm still waiting for the lesson you said I'd never forget. God damn you, Butch, wake up! We're not done yet." Butch didn't even twitch. Danny kicked him again and was about to land another blow when Mr. Sheffield broke through the crowd and pulled him away.

"Danny Long, what on earth are you doing?" he yelled, forcing his way between Danny and Butch's still form.

"I'm learning a lesson, Mr. Sheffield," Danny sneered. "Butch, here, is teaching me a lesson I won't ever forget. We were just getting to the important part when he lost interest."

"You head back to my office, mister, and wait for me there. Somebody call an ambulance!" Sheffield dropped to his knees to examine Butch, who was beginning to move again.

Danny headed toward Michael at the edge of the circle. As he passed his brother he leaned over and said, "Anybody asks, I did this for you. You got that?"

"That's a lie, Danny."

Danny looked around to see if anyone was watching them but all eyes seemed to be on Butch and Mr. Sheffield. He grabbed his brother by the shirt front and jerked him off his feet so the two were nose-to-nose. "Yeah, so what? You say it or you get what Butch got."

Michael smiled, gazing calmly at his brother. "Don't be scared, Danny," he said. "Your little secret is safe because nobody will ask me anything. Dad won't let it get that far."

It was the answer Danny wanted to hear, but it came in a form he could not allow. His fist tightened on Michael's shirt front as he lifted his brother farther off the ground. "You remember what I said, you little shit."

"Let go of my shirt, Danny. People might wonder why you are trying to intimidate the precious little brother you fought *so hard* to protect."

Danny looked around. Several people were now watching them. Danny let go of Michael's shirt and let him drop back to the ground. "Remember it, precious." he said, smoothing the wrinkles from Michael's shirt.

Danny sat in the Principal's office for more than an hour. Finally Sheffield returned and sat down at his desk. "Well, you're really lucky son. It looks as if Butch is going to be ok. He was conscious when I left him, and he was being taken to the hospital for observation. Your father is going to be here in a few minutes, and so are the police. That was a terrible, brutal thing you did out there. Why didn't you stop when Butch went down?"

"He started it. I just finished it. Go ask my brother what Butch tried to do to him."

"I know Butch started it, Danny, and I saw you finishing it. I talked to some students who saw the whole thing. The fact that Butch started it is the only reason you are talking to me now before the police arrive. I would like to think there is something salvageable in your character, and I want your side of the story. But there is no place in this school for the kind of brutality I saw from you out there. I want an explanation."

"Butch was threatening my brother. He said he was going to kill Michael. I had to do something."

"Why didn't you stop when he went down?"

"Hell, he was down most of the time," Danny said contemptuously. "It wasn't even a real fight. He didn't lay a hand on me. After awhile he stopped getting up, and you came along. I was defending my brother, and that's all. What the hell do you want from me? You know what Butch is like. Do you think I should have stood back and let that punk hurt my brother? If that's the kind of person you are, you can take your school and shove it."

"Relax, Danny. I said I was going to listen to your side of the story, didn't I?" Principal Sheffield wasn't shocked by Danny's behavior. He already knew the boy was a hothead, and the veiled threat to kick him out of school was nothing more than empty posturing. He had called the police because, under the circumstances, there was no other choice. But if there was a way to excuse Danny's behavior and keep him in school, Sheffield would find it. The football team needed this boy, not to mention the baseball and hockey teams.

There was a knock on the door. It was Danny's father accompanied by Phil Whitcomb, Dan's lawyer. Dan walked into the room, his eyes appraising his son. "They told me you were fighting on the school grounds again. You haven't got a mark on you. What happened?"

"It was nothing to speak of..." Danny began.

"It certainly *was* something to speak of," Sheffield interrupted.

"Did you see the fight? It doesn't look to me like my son has been fighting. Why did you call the police?"

"I called the police because Danny was in a fight with Butch Lagred. When I got there he had Butch unconscious on the ground and wouldn't stop kicking him. I had to pull him off. If this had been a typical schoolyard fight, we could have handled discipline internally, but Butch is in the hospital because of what your son did to him. It's a matter for the police now."

Dan turned to look at Danny. "Is that true, son?"

"I just got a little carried away, Dad. No big deal."

"It's no big deal that you put somebody in the hospital?"

"I mean… I mean I didn't mean to do it, and Lagred started it. He was the one who came at me."

Dan knew he wasn't getting the whole truth, but as always, he was determined not to let that stop him from doing what he could to minimize the damage. Danny was his son.

"Lagred…Lagred," said Dan. "That name sounds familiar. I used to have a Herb Lagred working for me. I fired him for stealing company equipment. I think he's still in jail."

"Herb Lagred is Butch's father," Sheffield admitted.

"Figures." Dan snorted. "Well I think we know what the problem is here, and it isn't my son."

"Regardless of who his father is, I think we ought to judge the son on his own merits," said a voice. Dan turned. There was a plainclothes policeman standing in the doorway, holding his hat in one hand and a badge in the other. He held the badge up for Dan's inspection.

"Detective Harvey Reed, Mr. Long. I was told that I would find your son here. I have a few questions for him."

"Do I know you, detective?"

"No, we haven't been formally introduced. I've seen you at a few VFW functions. I belong to the club across town, but I know who you are. And then there is the matter of Danny's other recent problem with the law."

"You heard about that, did you?"

"Everyone in the department heard about it. Your son seems to have a gift for trouble, and you seem to have a gift for getting him out of it."

Dan smiled ruefully. There was no way to deny it. This was the thing Danny didn't understand. You get a reputation with the police and it follows you everywhere.

Reed turned to Dan's lawyer. "Well, if it isn't Phil Whitcomb, defender of the truth and protector of the innocent."

"Hello Harv, nice to see you, too," said Whitcomb. "Dan has retained me to represent his son in this matter. Please direct any questions you have for him to me."

"I didn't expect that you were here for your health, Phil. If your client has nothing to hide why don't you let him answer a few questions?"

"I didn't say he wouldn't answer. I said you should direct your questions to me."

Reed flashed a thin smile. "And you will put words in his mouth and keep him from saying anything that will help us establish the facts. The result is essentially the same as refusing to answer, isn't it, councilor?"

Whitcomb smiled in return. "Nevertheless that's the way it's going to be. Take it or leave it."

"I assume your client will come willingly to the police station?"

"That depends. Is he under arrest?"

"Only if he wants to do it the hard way."

"In that case my client will be happy to meet with you at the station."

Reed looked at his watch. "Let's agree to meet there in, say, an hour. Will that work for you councilor?"

"That will be fine."

"Good. I'll hold you personally responsible for getting him there."

"My client will be at the station in an hour."

After detective Reed left, Danny related his encounter with Butch to Phil Whitcomb and his father. After hearing his story, Whitcomb agreed that Danny should be allowed to tell it directly to Reed. Danny left out of his account his role in provoking Butch and concentrated on the fact that Butch had threatened to kill Michael and had attacked Danny not once, but twice. Kicking Butch when he was down was not as easily justified, but Whitcomb told Danny to explain that as an emotional reaction to the moment. He was responding to a death threat to his brother, had just lost control, and was very sorry it happened.

Danny's story that Butch instigated the fight was confirmed by every witnesses who was interviewed except the members of Butch's gang, and word came from the hospital that Butch had a concussion and a couple of cracked ribs and would be kept overnight for observation but there were no permanent injuries. Butch already had two arrests for assault on his record, so the county attorney declined to press charges pending completion of the investigation, and Danny was allowed to go home with his father.

Before the pair left the police station, detective Reed spoke to Danny and his father. "Mr. Long, it isn't my place to tell you how to bring up your son, but you must realize this is wrong."

Phil Whitcomb bristled. "What are you insinuating?"

Dan put his hand on his lawyer's arm. "Relax councilor. Let's hear him out. What do you mean Detective?"

"I mean that if you help him escape the consequences of his actions he will learn nothing positive from this experience. I don't want to have to arrest him on more serious charges."

"Is that what you think happened here today? Do you think Danny got away with something?"

"Yes I do, and if you are an honest man, so do you."

"Thank you, Detective. Phil, we'll talk later. Danny, you come with me." Dan turned and walked out of the station with Danny trailing behind him.

Dan knew that Detective Reed was right, and he was incensed by Danny's poor judgment. The moment the two got into the car, Dan was all over his son. "What the hell were you thinking, boy?"

"That punk was threatening Michael," said Danny. "I had to do something to put some fear into him."

"Don't lie to me, Danny. I know you too well. Protecting your brother was the furthest thing from your mind. You just wanted a fight. Don't you get it, son? You've jeopardized your sports career and opened me up to a civil suit over nothing. This kind of thing has got to stop."

"What have you got against Michael? If Butch had gotten hold of him, he would have killed the kid. I was just trying to help my brother. Just ask Michael. He was there. He saw it."

"Damn it, forget that! Not another word about Michael! You leave your brother alone, and you stay out of his problems. He has his mother to protect him. He doesn't need you!"

8 - CHILDHOOD'S END

Megan Sullivan stumbled over a protruding root and almost fell. "Michael, slow down will you?"

Michael stopped and turned to wait for her. "Sure," he said, but his face held a look of mild impatience. In the woods he usually ran, but he couldn't do that with Megan along. They'd left the house nearly half-an-hour ago, and they were still far from their destination.

She caught up to him, and he turned and immediately began to walk again.

"Michael, stop. I need to rest." Not waiting for an answer, she found a fallen tree and sat down.

Michael turned around and walked back to where she was sitting.

"Sorry. This must be pretty tough going for you."

"Tough going? I can't even see a trail! If you come out here as much as you say, there should at least be a trail."

"I come a different way almost every time."

"Then you must have chosen the hardest way today."

"No. Actually this is one of the easiest. It's okay, Megan. You tell me when you need to rest and we'll stop. There's no rush."

They didn't see each other often on the weekends, and when they did they usually met in town in a park that was about half-way between their houses. But today Megan had shown up on Michael's doorstep without so much as a phone call. The look on her face told Michael that something was wrong.

"It looks to me like you need to say something," he said warily.

"My dad says I can't be your friend anymore."

Michael's face was unreadable. "Did he say why?"

"Mom and Dad had this big argument after I told Mom that you didn't go to church."

"You should have known better than to tell her that."

Megan was nearly in tears as she blurted out the story. "She asked why you didn't go, and I said it was because you didn't believe in God. Dad heard me and got all angry and said that I couldn't be around any damn atheists. I shouted at him that he couldn't make me stop being your friend, but he said he *could* stop me from seeing you. He told me I couldn't see you ever again. I got my bike and left before he knew I was gone. Michael, I'm so sorry."

"There's nothing to be sorry for. You trusted your parents. You made a mistake, that's all."

"What are we going to do?"

"Whatever we want to."

"It's not that easy for me."

"They can't watch us all the time, Megan. Forget about it. Come on, I want to show you something."

"You want to show me something at a time like this?"

"Why not? You said you wanted to see the lookout. It's about time I took you there."

It had been two years since Michael and Megan became friends, and little had changed for him. He still found his own food, washed his own clothes, and made do for himself in hundreds of other ways. Edith never caught on to the fact that Michael raided the pantry on a regular basis. The housekeeper noticed the disappearing food, but she did not tell Edith about it. Instead, she simply replaced the food whenever she purchased groceries for the family, and Edith was left none the wiser. The housekeeper would not have exposed Michael's frequent food raids under any circumstances. She liked the boy and detested his mother.

Edith knew that her attempt to starve Michael into submission was not working. She assumed Michael was begging meals from friends, perhaps from that cute little cherub she saw in Michael's company occasionally. But being forced to depend upon the charity of others was a valuable moral lesson, too. She smiled when she thought of it. The Lord certainly did work in mysterious ways, and sometimes she was privileged to catch a glimpse of His

Plan for her son's life. Let Michael beg, she thought. Maybe it will teach him some humility.

She never tried to beat Michael again after his first show of defiance, in part because the boy was growing so rapidly, nearly a foot in the past two years. He was now almost as tall as his mother. Any attempt to beat him now would entail a risk of retaliation more significant than a bite on the wrist.

Edith's relationship with her son had degenerated into little more than verbal abuse, all of it flowing from Edith toward Michael. Ironically, Michael felt a sort of bond with his father because of it. He was being treated exactly as Edith treated Dan. Nothing he did was good enough for his mother. She was on him constantly about everything, from the way he combed his hair, to the noise he made when he walked up the stairs to his room, to how often he took a bath, and how long it took him to do it. He endured the treatment with stoic indifference because he knew his mother could not stand that. She needed to get a reaction from him, some acknowledgement that her barbs were striking the mark. He knew his indifference could cause his mother's abusive behavior to intensify, but he refused to give her the slightest clue that her words mattered to him, and after a while, they didn't.

Megan was Michael's only confidant and sounding board, but they did not speak often of his family life. Their friendship was the only significant human relationship Michael cultivated, and he chose to keep it separate and uncontaminated by the life he had *not* chosen. There was never a discussion about it. Megan simply understood Michael's wish and saw no need to press him. She listened when he needed to vocalize his thoughts, and filled in the blanks with her uncanny talent for reading emotional cues. Her guesses were not always right, but she came to know Michael's battle and his determination to win it better than any person save Michael himself.

He wasn't sure why he wanted to show her the lookout. He'd never invited her or anyone else there before, but today it seemed like the right thing to do.

The treetops above their heads swayed back and forth in the brisk October wind, but the day was sunny and Indian-summer warm even here in the shade. Megan was hot and tired and more than a little frustrated by the pace Michael was setting, but she would not have missed this for anything. Even though she had never been here before, she felt like she knew these woods. Michael's descriptions were vivid, and full of detailed knowledge: Why moss grew mostly on the north side of trees and rocks, what left the trails, glistening with slime, on tree trunks in the morning, why the ground in a small clearing had been torn to shreds, what made the loud buzzing sounds she heard high in the trees. These were all questions she knew the answers to because Michael told her. But she knew much more than this. She knew that Michael loved the woods and the lookout on the hill, and she had a good start on knowing why.

The pair crossed the river valley and came to the sloping meadow at the base of the hill. They passed the abandoned plow and climbed the hill together. They sat for a long time on the hillside, saying little, just watching the traffic pass and the trains go by.

"I see why you like to come here," Megan said after awhile. "It's so lonely, and yet you're never alone. You think about where everybody's going—what's out there—and you want to go see it."

Michael looked at her with interest. "I'm going to find out before long."

"Isn't it too soon for that? You're not even fourteen yet."

"I can take care of myself."

"I know that, but it's safer here."

He laughed out loud. "You think so?"

She looked away from him, staring off into the distance. "Tell me before you leave?"

"I will. I promise."

The offices of Long Enterprises filled the top three floors of a downtown office building. Dan's large, corner office was nothing like his study at home. It was modern, efficient and well-lit. Floor to ceiling windows made the room relatively bright even on cloudy days.

At first he didn't hear the knock. He was reading a financial statement. When the second knock came, it was loud and impatient.

"Come in," Dan bellowed, angry at being interrupted.

The door opened and a large, muscular man in grease-stained coveralls stood in the doorway.

"There was nobody at the reception desk," the man said.

"Its lunch time. The receptionist is gone right now. What do you want?"

"I need to talk to you, Mr. Long, and I don't have time to

wait around. I'm due back at work in fifteen minutes."

"I don't even know who you are."

"I'm Jake Sullivan, and my daughter knows your son."

"Your daughter knows Danny?" God, now what? he thought.

"I don't know any Danny. I'm talking about your son Michael."

"What about Michael?"

"I want you to know that I told Megan she can't see Michael anymore."

Dan rose to his feet and walked around his desk to face Sullivan. "Mr. Sullivan, until this moment I had never heard of your daughter. I have no idea what her relationship is with Michael, or why you might forbid your daughter to see him. Why don't you fill me in?"

"I will not have my daughter consorting with atheists."

"What the hell are you talking about?"

"Don't you know what kind of Godless nonsense your son spouts?"

"My wife is responsible for Michael's education when it comes to nonsense. If you have a problem with what he says, take it up with her."

"Doesn't your wife go to the First Gospel Church on Fillmore Street?"

"I don't know where my wife's church is located."

"You don't know much about your family, do you?"

"I know my wife is no atheist, and I know I don't much care for your attitude. Get to the point."

"That is the point. I am told that your son refuses to go to church and talks like some goddamn communist, and I will not have him around my daughter. She is forbidden to see him, and I would appreciate it if you would make sure he stays away from her."

Jake Sullivan turned abruptly and walked out without another word. Dan returned to his desk to ponder the meaning of the visit. "Does it never end?" he muttered to himself. He should have known that Edith would bring the kid to this or something like it. You couldn't beat people into doing what you wanted them to do. Nothing good came from that.

Damn that bitch! She always found a way to make his life miserable. If it got around that his son was spouting this kind of talk, it could damage his business and would certainly embarrass him publicly. He could not allow people to think his son was an atheist. The term was too closely associated with the evil he fought in Korea. He knew not everyone who was an atheist was also a communist, but in this age of Cold War the assumption was automatic, and Dan was not prepared to depend upon the ability of his friends and neighbors to see the difference.

Dan spent the better part of the afternoon trying to work and failing. His mind kept coming back to Michael, and every time it did his anger grew. This simply could not be allowed. There was too much at stake in a small town like Mansfield. He needed to nip this in the bud, and do it now.

His car pulled up to the garage behind Danny's who was just getting home from football practice. Dan got out and called to his son. "Danny, where would Michael be at this hour?"

"Hell, I don't know. He could be anywhere."

"Go into the house and see if he's inside, will you? If he is, send him out to me. I want to talk to him without Edith around."

Danny looked at his father curiously. "What for?"

"I am going to put an end to this whole nonsense permanently. I should have done it years ago, and now it's way out of hand."

"What do you mean?"

"Did you know Michael is talking publicly about being an atheist?"

Danny threw his head back and laughed out loud. "Damn, that's a hoot! Wait till I tell Edith."

"You aren't going to tell her anything. Just go find your brother."

As Danny walked toward the house, Dan began to look for Michael outside. He called several times without getting a response. He was about to give up and go inside when Michael came around the corner of the garage.

"You were calling me?"

"There you are. Michael, you and I need to have a little talk," Dan said without preamble. "I know your mother has been giving you trouble for a long time, and I am going to do us both a favor and put a stop to it."

Michael looked at his father in shocked surprise. He almost

didn't believe his ears. Had he just heard Dan declaring his intention to put a stop to Edith's abuse? Despite his many previous disappointments, a spark of hope ignited in Michael's mind. Down deep—so deep he rarely acknowledged the feeling anymore—he still wanted his father's support and approval. He knew he deserved it, and had always wondered why he never got it. Was his father actually going to help him?

"Yes, Mom's been pretty hard on me," Michael said cautiously.

"Edith tells me that she's had to discipline you because you refuse to do what she tells you to, and I want you to stop it right now," said Dan.

"Me? Stop what?"

"Stop disobeying your mother. What did you think I meant? I can't afford to have this family's reputation dragged through the mud because you won't do what you're told, and I won't have you talking like some drug-taking hippy radical. People are beginning to take notice, and I can't have that."

"What are you talking about, Dad?"

"I got a visit today from some guy named Jake Sullivan. He says you know his daughter and you've been spouting some nonsense to her about being an atheist. I don't know where you've picked up this crap, but I want you to stop it right now. There will be no atheists in this family."

"You can't tell me what to think." The sentence was spoken not as a challenge but as a simple statement of fact. Michael looked at his father, his face solemn.

"Think what you want, but in this house I'll tell you what to do and what to say. From now on you'll do what your mother tells you with no arguments, and you'll keep the commie crap to yourself. If your mother wants you at Bible lessons, you be there. If she wants you to stop asking questions, you shut your goddamn mouth. If she wants you to shout God's praises to the heavens, then you'll damn well yell hosannas until you're horse. Do you understand?"

"I can't do that, Dad."

"What do you mean? Can't? There is no 'can't.' Just do what I tell you."

"Let me explain…"

"No!" Dan cut him off. "The foolishness ends now. This is a

simple question of doing what I tell you to do. I don't care what you think. Apparently you don't even have the brains to understand what's good for you. But, you will make up with your mother now. Tonight. From now on, you will do exactly what she tells you to do, and that will be the end of it!"

There was something in the way his father said it, with an air that dismissed Michael as utterly inconsequential. It wasn't the insult to his intelligence. That was the kind of thing his father said to him frequently, and he automatically dismissed it. But this time, the underlying motive behind the words suddenly became crystal clear.

In real time it took only a second, but Michael remembered that second afterward not as a single measured instant but as a long, slow-motion plunge toward certainty. There was a falling sensation while a dozen fragmented memories flashed through his consciousness like a series of movie clips so short they were almost subliminal, each a tiny sliver of evidence, each a little piece of innocence lost. It felt as though he struck bottom, and the terrible realization came suddenly into focus. In the eyes of his father he was not a son, not even a human being with a mind. He was a nuisance who was about to be disposed of.

In the first seconds that followed he felt a desperate longing to deny it. But the desire passed as suddenly as it came, and with it went the wish to deny anything. He should be thankful, he thought. His father had given him a gift even though he did not intend it as such. Nothing had really changed except Michael's understanding. That was Dan Long's gift to his son—the truth—the truth that Michael did not have a father in any sense other than the biological one. The reason this was so was not immediately significant, only the simple fact that it was true, and Michael had better get used to it.

The most important moments in a person's life often happen without the slightest fanfare, and at least on the surface, this moment was no exception. There was nothing obvious on Michael's face, only a grave look of honesty, as his most cherished childhood fantasy quietly died.

"Why?" he said after a moment. "Why am I the one who has to give in?" He already knew the answer but it was so enormously unjust that he couldn't let it pass without protest.

"Because you will and your mother won't."

"I'm sorry, Dad. I won't either."

"You won't what?"

"I won't give in."

"You'll do what I tell you, boy, or I will give you a whipping worse than your mother ever gave you!"

"I am not going to be whipped by you or anyone else. If you touch me, I'll leave this house and never come back."

"And go where? You think talking like a man makes you one? Who's going to protect you if you run away from home?"

"Who's going to protect me if I stay?"

"Don't be melodramatic. Just do as I say, and everything will be fine."

"I won't do as you say."

"Damn it, boy, I am trying to defend this family's good name!"

"By throwing me to the wolves, you goddamn bastard!"

Livid with rage over Michael's show of disrespect, Dan back-handed him across the mouth and knocked him to the ground. "You'll do what I tell you, boy, and there'll be no arguments!"

Michael's upper lip was cut where Dan struck him. A drop of blood formed at the corner of his mouth and began to trickle downward. He wiped the blood off with his sleeve and got to his feet. He looked directly at his father, eyes ablaze. The intensity of Michael's stare, and the realization that he had just committed an act of violence against his son, caused Dan to glance away for a moment. It took a conscious effort of will to turn his head back and meet Michael's eyes.

"I waited for you to stop her," said Michael. "I always wondered why you never did. Now I know. You can go to hell with her."

Nothing could have struck his father harder. The comparison with Edith was devastatingly apt, and Dan knew it even before Michael said it. He wanted to justify himself. "Michael, there are things you don't understand that make this necessary. I cannot explain it right now. You must have faith that I am doing the right thing."

They were the wrong words said at the wrong time. Michael blinked, and for a moment he seemed to be on the verge of responding. Then he turned abruptly and walked toward the house.

"Where do you think you're going?" said Dan.

"None of your goddamn business." Michael said it without turning around.

Despite Michael's promise to leave if his father touched him, Dan was certain that Michael did not really mean it. His experience with Danny told him that children often made threats in the heat of the moment that they had no intention of carrying out. Call the bluff and wait them out. That was the best thing to do. What his father did not realize was that there was no "child" left in Michael. The last of what remained had just been destroyed.

Although Michael currently relied on his family for a roof over his head, that's where his dependence ended. He was otherwise isolated from whatever resources a normal family might provide. He could survive without them, and if he didn't? Well, from Michael's point of view there were worse things than dying, and what his father demanded was one of them. In essence, Dan had given him the same untenable option his mother had given: deny his mind or be beaten into submission. He saw no reason to tolerate either alternative.

When Danny found him, Michael was in his room packing a few things in a small bag. "Did Dad talk to you?" Danny asked.

"Yes."

"What did he say? He told me he was going to put a stop to your Mom's abuse."

Michael smiled ironically. "Yes, that's what he told me, too. Did he tell you *how* he was going to accomplish this miracle?"

"No."

"You should ask him sometime. Well, I'm out of here, Danny."

"What are you talking about?"

"I'm leaving. I can't live here anymore."

"What the hell did Dad say to you?"

"Ask the son-of-a-bitch yourself."

"This is stupid, Michael. You aren't old enough to survive on your own."

Michael ignored his brother's comment, picked up his bag and walked down the stairs.

"All right, you dim-witted little shit," Danny yelled after him, "I hope you get what you deserve. I hope you fucking die out there!" The kid was such a goddamned *fool!* All he had to do was pretend to give in, act a little contrite, pay a little lip-service, and everything

106

would be fine. Instead he always did it the hard way. To hell with him, Danny thought.

Edith was in the sun room, immersed in a volume of reflections on the glorious raptures awaiting her in Paradise. She didn't notice when Michael walked by on his way out the door.

Dan came into the house and went to his study to have a smoke. When he heard the front door close, he leaned back in his chair and smiled faintly. For the moment he had talked himself into believing that Michael was running a bluff. His main concern was what he would say when Michael came slinking back to the house.

Michael's bike was leaning against the garage where he left it when he came home from school. He got on and pedaled into the night. Thirty minutes later he gave a quiet knock on Megan Sullivan's bedroom window.

"I have to leave, Megan," he whispered when she opened the window.

"Leave?"

"I'm leaving home."

"When?"

"Tonight. Right now."

"Why?"

"My dad says I will have to obey my mother, or he will beat me up. I am not going to be beaten again, and I will not obey my mother."

"This is all my fault!"

"Don't be an idiot. This was going to happen sooner or later anyway."

"Wait, I'll go with you."

"You can't go where I'm going."

"But who's going to look out for you?"

"The same person who always has."

"Michael there has to be a better way."

"There isn't. I just stopped by to say thanks. You've been a good friend, and I promised I would say goodbye. So…goodbye."

"Be careful, Michael."

She saw the dim flicker that was the back of his tan jacket and for a moment she heard the muffled crunch of bicycle tires on gravel, and then he was gone. After several seconds she closed the window and lay down on her bed. She didn't know what to do.

Michael returned to his house and quietly stood the bike next to the garage. Then he walked down the brick drive to the highway. Dropping his bag at the edge of the road he sat down on top of it and made himself comfortable. Every time a car passed he stuck out his thumb. About ten minutes later a car stopped. It was headed west, but the direction didn't matter one way or another. He got in.

*   *   *

As soon as Michael walked out the door Danny went find his father. "What did you say to Michael?" he asked.

"I told him to stop getting into trouble with his mother."

"That's how you were going to stop it? Well, that worked out well. He just walked out the door with a bag in his hand. He's going to run away, you know."

"Yes, I know. He pretty much told me he was going to do that."

"And you're going to let him go?"

"No, I'm going to let him go while I finish this cigar. Don't worry about Michael. If he isn't sneaking back to the house right now, he will be shortly. He isn't going to run away. He just wants me to think he is."

"I'm not worried about him, Dad, and I don't care if he comes back or not. He has himself to blame for this. The stupid little shit deserves whatever he gets."

"I thought you felt sorry for him."

"Maybe a long time ago. Not anymore."

Dan did not really believe that Michael would be sneaking back into the house any time soon. He had seen the look in Michael's eyes and he was afraid he knew what that look meant. But he could not allow himself to act upon the knowledge. To act would mean admitting he was wrong about many things, and had been for a very long time. He was not ready to do that.

Evening came and went, and Michael still hadn't appeared with his tail between his legs. Edith knew Michael was gone. When she asked if anyone knew where he was, Dan told her what had happened.

So, Michael claimed to be an atheist, did he? Edith mused to herself. Well, let's see what a thirteen-year-old atheist believes after spending the night out in the cold. It will serve him right if something happens. He should have known better than to run off like this. He should have had more consideration for his mother's feelings for one thing. Her best efforts were being repaid with ingratitude and abandonment. A night without a roof over his head would put the fear of God back into him, and besides, the Lord would decide Michael's proper fate with or without her approval. There was no use worrying over events that were pre-ordained.

By the time he walked into the den after dinner, Dan emotions had deteriorated from uneasiness into fear. If he was going to cave in and come back, Michael should have done it by now. He couldn't help wondering where the boy was and whether he was hungry. He regretted the way he handled the conversation with his son, and he wished he could take it back. "You can go to hell with her," Michael had said. Dan knew exactly what that meant. He had handled the confrontation in the same manner his wife would have, and he despised his wife. He kept seeing Michael's angry, accusing eyes staring at him, the smear of blood on his chin. Why had he done it? Why had he hit the boy? Was it because he believed what Edith told him, that Michael hated him? Thinking back on it there had been no hatred in Michael's eyes, not until Dan put it there with a single careless swipe of his hand. First there was hope, and then hurt and betrayal, but until his hand struck there was no hate.

For much of the night Dan lay staring at the ceiling. Every time the house made a noise or he heard something outside he was wide awake. Finally around five a.m. he fell asleep. His alarm went off at six, and he rose immediately to check Michael's room one more time. It was still empty. The bed had not been slept in.

At seven a.m. Danny left for school. Five minutes later Dan was walking toward his car to go to work when a young girl on a bicycle rode into the yard.

She got off her bike and threw it to the ground in obvious anger. He had an idea that this was Megan Sullivan, and he was not going to like what he was about to hear.

"Mr. Long, my name is Megan Sullivan, and Michael came to see me last night. He told me he had to leave home."

"Where is he?"

"Gone, thanks to you."

"He did not have to leave. He had a choice." said Dan.

"What choice, you bastard? What kind of choice did he have?"

"I beg your pardon?"

"You heard what I said. What kind of choice did you give him?"

"He was given every chance to obey."

"His mother abuses him, and you treat him like he doesn't exist until he gets in your way and you call that a choice? What is he to you, a piece of garbage you can throw out with the rest of the trash?"

"How would you know how I treat him?"

"I know for a fact that his mother has abused him for years. He doesn't say much about it, but I know what she did and I know what she does. You have to know, too, unless you're a complete idiot, and you just let it happen! She used to beat him so hard... how could you not notice? He has scars all over his back."

"How do you know that?"

"Not because Michael wanted me to know, I can tell you that. He tries to hide it, but I saw the scars through his tee shirt when we went swimming."

"I think you are exaggerating, young lady. I'm sure you speak from a concern for Michael and I will not fault you for that, but this is none of your business."

"Don't you dare patronize me!" Megan was shouting now. "I want to know why you're such a complete jerk. I want to know what you are going to do to find Michael and make this right! I want to know if you are going to be a father for once instead of a worthless piece of crap!"

"Now just a minute, young lady, Michael has been nothing but a problem for years. He has been treated exactly as he has deserved to be treated."

"God, are you blind? Do you know what his mother did to him? Do you even care?"

"She's a little hard on him, that's all."

"For God's sake, ask him to take his shirt off and take a look at his back, then tell me she's been a little hard on him."

"Michael doesn't want my help."

"How do you know that?"

"He told me."

"Oh, and I can imagine how that conversation went. Be his father for once. He needs a father!"

Dan stared silently at the little spitfire who had just peddled into his life. He knew she was right, and it didn't matter that she was exaggerating. He'd known it from the moment Michael walked out the door. It didn't matter what he thought of the boy or what the boy thought of him. He was Michael's father. That was the bottom line. He had to face his responsibilities.

"Megan, I am going to walk inside and call the police right now," he said. "Would you like to come in while I do that? I would like for you to stay and talk to the police with me. Maybe you have some ideas about where he's gone. Do we need to let your parents know where you are?"

At three p.m. Edith finished the devotional she had started the day before. She closed it and reverently placed it on the stand beside her chair. Then she leaned back in her rocker to contemplate the unfathomable mysteries of God's Infinite Love. Her book ended by repeating that blessed promise from the Book of John. "For God so loved the world, that he gave his only begotten Son, that whosoever believeth in him should not perish, but have everlasting life."

Edith's heart swelled with the infinite magnitude of the Master's loving sacrifice. She wondered how unbelievers managed to survive, bereft of divine protection, always waiting for the next catastrophe to befall them, helpless prey to Satan's every random wickedness. Surely the unbeliever lived in constant fear. She shuddered at the thought of the fear Michael must be experiencing right now. If he truly did not believe, then he must be cowering somewhere in terror.

If God saw fit to punish her son for holding blasphemous ideas, it was for Michael's own good and the good of those around him. Edith was not afraid. Her faith in God was unshakable. Her mind was at rest. She had done the best she could. If it was God's Will that the boy be returned to her care, she hoped the Lord would teach him the wisdom of minding his elders in the meantime. If her son was taken from her she would suffer of course, but the Lord knew best and she was ready to accept His Will as her own meager sacrifice to His Plan. She was not the first Christian to suffer a loss in service to God's Will. She would not be the last.

*   *   *

Near noon on the seventh day after Michael's disappearance the phone rang at the desk of Detective Harvey Reed of the Mansfield Police. "Harv, the chief wants to see you."

Reed walked up the flight of steps that led to the chief's office and stuck his head in the door. "You wanted to see me, boss?"

"Come in, Harv, and close the door will you? I've got a tough one for you."

Reed closed the door and sat down.

"You know Dan Long, don't you Harv?"

Reed knew immediately what his job was going to be.

"They've found the boy," he whispered.

9 - THE WAGES OF SIN

The storm began as a heavy downpour that became a mix of freezing rain and sleet. Now the moisture fell in angry frozen pellets driven hard before a relentless northwest wind. The pellets were so small they could barely be seen close up, but they looked dark grey in the distance, slanting down from clouds that hung low and tattered over the sodden landscape.

Dan placed one hand on the side of the large dining room window and leaned forward to study the weather. The temperature was falling rapidly, and a ring of ice was beginning to form around the edge of a large puddle of standing water near the driveway. The ice particles, flying almost horizontal in the wind, peppered the windows furiously and tore foliage from the trees in bunches. Just a few hours ago the trees in the front yard had been lush with fall color. Now they were almost bare, and the wind howled through the naked branches twisting the few remaining leaves violently with each new gust.

The window glass vibrated in another icy blast and Dan pushed back a step. The storm windows were still in storage, and he could feel the ferocity of the wind in the frigid draft that emanated from the window well. The cold passed through his heavy sweater and settled in his bones. For the first time in his life he felt old—old and tired. If Michael was out in this weather he was in serious trouble. Seven days since the boy walked out the door and disappeared. Seven days of waiting and wondering and hoping for news that never came.

A random drop of moisture condensed on the inside of the glass high on the window pane. It hung for a moment, gathering weight, and then slowly found its way to the bottom, cutting a meandering path downward through the film of moisture created by Dan's breath on the chilled surface of the glass. He watched it slide down the pane until it joined the layer of ice forming at the bottom of the window. The drop followed a path like the emotional course of the past seven days, his hopes drawn relentlessly toward the frozen depths at the bottom of his soul. He was afraid he would never see Michael again. And if he didn't, he knew he had no one to blame but himself.

Dan looked up as an unmarked police car drove into the yard. He recognized Detective Reed as he got out. There could be only one reason why the police would visit. Dan walked quickly from the dining room to the front door, opened it and stepped onto the covered porch. He didn't bother to put on a coat.

Edith also saw the car arrive and guessed immediately that the man walking toward the house was bringing news of her missing son, but she did not go out to meet him. If the man brought news of Michael, Dan would tell her. God's will be done.

Dan stood waiting, his feet braced against the storm, while detective Reed fought the wind and sleet from the driveway to the front door. He waited until Reed climbed the steps, then he said, "Detective Reed. You have news of my son?"

"Yes, Mr. Long. Michael has been found. He's alive."

"Thank God." The sense of relief was overwhelming. "What happened? Where is he?"

"He's in a hospital in Minot, North Dakota. Do you want your wife to hear this too?"

"No, tell me now."

"All right. I'm afraid the news isn't good. Michael was beaten and stabbed. He's badly hurt. A railroad worker found him unconscious under a coal car in the Minot rail yard early this morning."

Detective Reed tried to make himself say the rest but he couldn't. It was too much. The doctors would have to tell Dan the whole story. He just didn't know how to say the words. There were some forms of evil done to children so hideous that respectable people could not contemplate them for long.

"How bad is it?" asked Dan.

"I'm sorry, Dan, I can't answer that. You're going to have to talk to his doctors in Minot. Here is a phone number you can call." He handed Dan a small piece of paper. "I do know that Michael had emergency surgery this morning. I know he survived it. That's all I have."

"How did he get all the way to Minot?"

"I have no information on that. I'm sorry."

"All right, thank you."

Dan pocketed the paper and began to turn back toward the door when Reed put his hand on Dan's shoulder. "I'm sorry, Dan," said Reed. "I'm really sorry. I wish the news could have been better."

They knew each other but they weren't friends. It was a gesture Harvey Reed should not have allowed himself, but he liked Dan Long. He was thinking of the news he couldn't bring himself to deliver.

"Thanks Harv," Dan responded, "but they've found him and he's alive. That will have to be enough for now."

Dan turned and walked purposefully back into the house. He was already planning the fastest way to get to his son's side. Only as he began to climb the stairs to his bedroom did he remember Michael's mother. "Edith, would you come here please?" he called. "I'm going to my room to pack."

Edith found him throwing clothes into a suitcase. "What is it?" she asked. "Michael has been hurt hasn't he."

"He's been found alive. He is in a hospital in North Dakota. I'm going to hire a plane to take me there. If you want to come along, I'm leaving in fifteen minutes."

"You know I don't like to fly."

"Well, I am going now. If you don't come with me, you'll have to find your own way."

"Is there a reason you have to fly?

"To get there as soon as possible."

"Feeling a little guilty, are we?"

"Edith, maybe you should ask what happened to your son before you start in on me."

"The Lord has watched over him as I knew he would. That's all I need to know."

"For God's sake, woman, what are you saying? Put the hymnal away and think about your son for once! Michael is in the hospital fighting for his life. He has been beaten and stabbed."

"I knew it would be bad. He has been very disobedient, and you are a terrible father. You are *both* being punished. Whatever happened was the Will of God. I'm sorry that Michael has to suffer, but both of you are responsible for it."

Dan looked at his wife with incredulous contempt. "Are you coming or not?"

"No. You go to him, Daniel. Fly to your son's side. You are the one with the guilty conscience. I will follow on the train tomorrow."

"Very well. Please tell Danny where I've gone and why. I will be gone for as long as necessary."

"Oh, I'll tell him. I wonder what he'll think when he discovers that he has competition for his father's attention."

Edith's mindset was so engrained that even the news that her son was in the hospital did not stop her from using the circumstance to gain advantage. Every emotion was a potential weapon in the Lord's service, and Edith would not pass up the chance to exploit the available ordinance. If the situation offered an opportunity to push a wedge between Danny and his father, then Edith would use it. Who could tell? Everything that happened was a part of God's Plan. The ways of the Lord were far beyond her meager understanding, and it was really Dan's fault that Michael ran away. He had hardened his heart against God, forcing Edith to bring Michael up in the ways of righteousness alone. Now, God was punishing him for it. It was Dan's lack of support that had forced Edith to resort to violence and intimidation from the beginning. If God saw fit to allow Michael to be badly injured, then perhaps this was one of His reasons—to show Dan the wages of sin and prompt him to accept Jesus as his Savior. Perhaps then her fondest dream would be realized, and the family would at last be together in the loving arms of Christ.

Of course Edith would never willingly wish harm on her son, but she couldn't help thinking that the more catastrophic Michael's injuries were, the more likely they would move Dan to find his proper place at the Master's feet. Everything happened for a reason.

The moment Edith declined to go with him, Dan forgot she was in the room. He focused his attention on finding enough socks and underwear. When she left he didn't notice.

Edith is right about one thing, Dan thought. Michael had paid a terrible price for his father's mistakes. It wasn't love for his son that motivated Dan's desire to go to Michael as quickly as possible. He was honest enough to admit that. He did not suddenly love him because the boy was hurt. In the years since his marriage he had at least learned that love and guilt were not interchangeable concepts. But he was acutely aware that he was responsible for an enormous injustice. Whatever his feelings toward Michael, the boy did not deserve this. No child did. He had to try and make it right before it was too late.

Dan did not give Edith a chance to change her mind about going. When he was done packing, he walked down the stairs and out the door, pausing only to select a warm jacket from the hall closet and an umbrella from the stand by the door. The sleet stopped falling and the wind seemed to be dying down as Dan drove rapidly to the airport, but the clouds still threatened. He had rented aircraft many times before in the course of doing business so he knew that the charter service would be reluctant to fly in this kind of weather. He intended to make it worth their while.

"Hello, Frank," said Dan as he walked into the airport office. Frank Cushman had been his pilot on many flights over the years, and the two knew each other well. "I need a plane and a pilot to take me to Minot, North Dakota."

"Now? Dan, this is pretty dicey weather. You sure this can't wait?"

"Very sure. I need the fastest plane you've got."

"The twin's available. But I still advise against flying in this kind of weather."

"Look Frank, I'm in a hurry and don't have time to argue. I'll give you a thousand dollars over and above your regular fee if we are in the air in twenty minutes."

Cushman paused for a moment to consider the proposal. The offer was more than fair, a full five percent of his annual salary. "Let me check with the weather service first," he said. "The money means nothing if I don't live to spend it, but they've been predicting a break for several hours now. Maybe it's close."

"All right," said Dan. "In the meantime maybe you can have somebody roll out the plane and gas it up. I have to make a couple of phone calls before we leave."

Cushman smiled to himself. Dan never would take "No" for an answer.

The plane broke into the clear less than a half-an-hour after take-off, and Cushman began to breathe a little easier. Flying in this kind of freezing soup was always dangerous. He was happy the weather service got it right, and he was going to be able to spend the extra thousand bucks. He relaxed into his seat, removed his headphones and flipped on the auto-pilot.

As the plane flew northwest over the farmland of Minnesota and Eastern North Dakota, Dan wondered anew what motivated people like his wife. It wasn't love, though she spoke of love incessantly. It was something else, something... sinister and... dishonest. What kind of person could contemplate the vision of her son lying beaten and stabbed under a coal car as an outcome he deserved? What kind of person was capable of worshiping a being she believed had Willed that this obscenity occur? If there was any meaning to the word "evil" this was the purest form of it he had ever encountered. I must have it wrong, he thought. Was inflicting pain Edith's only motivation? Did she *want* her son to suffer? He could not bring himself to believe that, even of Edith.

But there was another kind of evil, the evil of omission, and *that* he knew was his own guilt. He was not required to love this son or even like him, but he did have an obligation to protect him until he was old enough to take care of himself. This is *my* evil, Dan thought. I am Michael's father. I could have prevented all of this. Instead I turned Edith loose on him. When the boy asked for help, I wouldn't listen. When he needed comfort and understanding, I was nowhere to be found. And in a final act of betrayal, I gave my son, my own flesh and blood, no alternative but to submit to his mother's bullying or leave the only home he knew.

Suddenly, Dan remembered seeing something more than hatred in Michael's eyes in the seconds after he struck the boy. He saw it when Michael got to his feet and looked straight at him. He didn't recognize the look then. He'd seen it before but did not recall where. Now, it came to him. He saw it first in a landing craft on the way to the beach at Inchon. He saw it many times in the long, hard days at Chosin Reservoir. It was the look of fear accepted and discounted as a primary motivation, the look of men who knew what they faced and were prepared to do what needed to be done despite the knowledge that they might not survive it. It seemed incredible, but Michael's face held a quality that was almost the equal of what he remembered on the faces of grown men going into battle. *His son* knew exactly what he was doing. He was afraid, but determined to go ahead in the face of it.

I have known that fear myself, Dan thought. I have known it, and learned from more experienced combat veterans how to live with it. But where had Michael's bravery come from? How had it grown with no one to show him the way? How on earth had Dan failed to recognize that his son was capable of this kind of courage? How did he allow himself to become its enemy? He did not think Michael would ever forgive him. He knew he would never forgive himself.

When the plane landed, a car was waiting to take Dan to the hospital. He barely waited for the aircraft to stop rolling. Without a word of farewell he jumped out and walked rapidly to the car. "Trinity Hospital," he said to the driver. "Get me there as fast as you can."

*   *   *

When he first saw the boy, Doctor Samuel Graham did not expect him to live. In fact, during those first frantic minutes in the emergency room he would have bet his reputation that there was no hope for the kid. His injuries were so massive that he should have died before he was found. That he was still alive was due partly to the fact that he had been naked, his body cooled to less than 80 degrees by the frigid November air.

And then he did die. Twice in the emergency room his heart stopped beating, and both times Dr. Graham and his team brought him back to life. Now, after a two-hour fight to stabilize him and a five-hour operation to repair his injuries, his young patient lay nearly motionless in the ICU, still breathing, his heart pumping slowly.

Dr. Graham hated the term "miracle." In his experience it was an over-used and entirely inappropriate metaphor, a term that was carelessly slung about out of medical ignorance. He was prepared to admit that the reason one patient died and another lived was not always physical, nor was it always due exclusively to the attending physician's training and skill. He believed there was such a thing as the will to live, and it was stronger in some patients than in others. The source of the will to live, he believed, lay in the human mind, and the human mind was not a miracle, it was a fact.

So it was that Dr. Graham gazed upon his young patient with an admiration bordering on the incredulous. He did not trivialize the child's struggle by calling it a miracle. He knew what was keeping this boy alive. It was his will to live. And it must be a powerful force, indeed, to keep him going despite injuries as massive as these.

And there was something else. The lad was a victim of more than just the wounds he suffered in the rail yard. Sometime in the relatively recent past there had been other incidents of physical trauma. There were many scars, mostly on his back and shoulders. X-rays showed evidence of healed fractures to three ribs, and his nose had been broken at least twice. Wherever he came from, whatever had happened to him, this child was a survivor, and contemplating his bruised and broken body, Dr. Graham resolved that if he had anything to say about it, the boy was going to survive this battle too.

The doctor re-hung the child's chart at the foot of his bed and opened the door into the common area. There was a man leaning against the glass wall of the room and Dr. Graham stopped to observe him. The man's right palm and his forehead were pressed against the glass as though he needed the wall's support to remain upright. His shoulders were slumped forward in a posture that looked like utter despair. His face was twisted with anguish, his eyes fixed upon the bandaged child lying on the bed.

"Who are you? Do you know this boy?" Graham demanded.

The words were aggressive, motivated by a desire to protect the lad from every possible danger, but the man seemed not to notice the doctor's tone. He slowly pushed back from the wall and nodded briefly in affirmation, his eyes never leaving the still figure on the bed. "Dan Long," the man choked out the response. "I am his father. Are you his doctor?"

"Yes. I'm Dr. Graham."

"Will you please tell me what has happened to my son?"

"Let's find a place where we can talk in private." Graham led Dan to a small sitting room just outside the intensive care unit.

Before the doctor had seated himself, Dan spoke. "I want you to give me his prognosis first. Will Michael get through this?"

"Michael." said Graham. "I didn't know his name, but it fits him, a strong name for a very strong child." Graham sat down and paused for a moment. "He has a chance, Mr. Long. My experience tells me not a good one, but there is a chance. Your son has survived the kind of injuries I would have expected to kill a grown man in perfect health. Yet he is alive, and when a patient is alive there is always a chance he will stay that way."

"What happened to him?"

"You haven't spoken to the police?"

"Only at home in Minnesota and only briefly. When I called the hospital, they didn't give me much either. I have almost no information."

"Nobody knows for sure exactly what happened," said Graham. "He's been unconscious since he was brought here. He has suffered a severe concussion. His left arm and both legs are broken. He was stabbed several times causing lacerations to his liver and other abdominal organs and damage to his diaphragm. His spleen had to be removed..." Graham paused again. "I want you to prepare yourself for what I am about to tell you. It will be difficult to handle."

What could be worse than what he'd already heard? Dan nodded in grim agreement and steeled himself.

"The boy's attacker sexually assaulted him," said Dr. Graham.

"What do you mean?" The doctor's words were spoken clearly, but Dan did not comprehend their meaning.

"Your son was raped, Mr. Long."

For a moment Dan was stunned to silence. When he spoke his voice was ragged with emotion, "*Oh, Michael! Michael, what have I done to you?*"

Dan's hands shook as he ran them through his hair in agitation, his face blanched to the color of ashes. "Who did this?" he demanded. "What kind of monster...?" He knew *he* was responsible, but he wanted to crush the life out of whoever actually did this with his bare hands, and then he wanted desperately for his own life to end.

"I can't answer that, Mr. Long except to say that we both know such people exist. But it doesn't matter who did it. Your son is alive, and our job is to keep him alive."

Dr. Graham's eyes missed nothing as he observed the man before him. Michael's father did not look or act like a child beater, but you never knew.

"Do you know how he got where he was?" Graham asked.

"I know why he ran away from home but not how he got here. It was my fault he left. I should have protected him, and I didn't."

"Protected him from what?"

"From everything a child should be protected from."

"What do you know about his previous injuries?" said Graham.

"For God's sake, what previous injuries?"

"The broken bones and the scaring on the boy's back. Your son appears to have suffered systematic physical abuse over a long period."

"Broken bones? She hit him that hard?"

"Who, Mr. Long? Who hit him?"

"His mother. She took care of him. I wasn't around much."

"And you knew nothing of this?"

"I did not realize—no that isn't exactly true—I guess I always suspected, but I didn't want to know how bad it was because I didn't want to deal with it. I told myself his mother wouldn't really hurt him. She never did it when I was around. Michael's brother told me what was happening but I thought he was exaggerating, so I did nothing. How bad was it?"

"You would have to beat a person awfully hard to break bones and inflict scars like that. I think it qualifies as very bad."

"Oh, God," said Dan. He wasn't listening anymore. No wonder his son hated him. What had Edith done to him and for how long?

"Mr. Long? Mr. Long, are you all right?"

"Yes? Yes, I'm…fine. Anything you need doctor, anything at all."

Dr. Graham was satisfied that the boy's father was not directly responsible for his abuse. "Just be here when Michael regains consciousness," he said. "I will do my best to make sure it happens."

Dan nodded. "I'd like to be with my son now."

"Yes of course."

"And doctor…"

"Yes?"

"I'll need to make a phone call later. Is there a pay phone nearby?"

"By the elevators. You can't miss it."

"Thanks."

*   *   *

The phone rang just after supper, and Jake Sullivan got up from watching TV to answer it.

"Mr. Sullivan, this is Dan Long."

"Yes, Mr. Long?" Sullivan's response was cool. He hadn't decided yet whether Dan Long was just a fool or an actively evil man, but he had no time for either type. A man who didn't take care of his family wasn't much of a man.

"I'm sorry to bother you, but Michael has been found and I think your daughter has a right to know."

Megan ran down the hallway from her room. She had heard her father say "Mr. Long" and she was certain there was finally news of Michael. "Is that Michael's father? Have they found Michael?"

Mrs. Sullivan heard the name, too, and rushed into the room from the kitchen. "Megan, be quiet," she said. "Your father can't hear what he's saying."

Sullivan looked thanks at his wife and said into the phone, "Go ahead, Mr. Long."

"I'm at Trinity Hospital in Minot, North Dakota. Michael is here. They found him in the rail yard this morning. He is unconscious and in critical condition."

"Minot?"

"Nobody knows for sure what happened or how he got here, but that's where he is."

"What can I tell my daughter?"

"You can tell her this: Tell her Michael has been badly injured and is fighting for his life, but his doctor's are the best available and his dad has finally figured out what his job is, thanks in part to her. Tell her I will not leave here until Michael does. Tell her I will be happy to pay for her to come and visit him if that's what she wants to do."

"No," said Jake Sullivan.

"I understand your attitude perfectly, Mr. Sullivan. It is for my son's sake that I make the offer. I already know enough about your daughter to realize how highly she regards Michael, and judging from the fierceness of her loyalty I suspect he feels the same way about her. He'd be a fool if he didn't, and I've had recent occasion to learn that my son is no fool. Her presence will be good for him, and he will need every advantage to get through what he is facing."

"I'll think about it."

"Thank you. That is all I have to say now. With your permission I will keep you informed of any changes in Michael's condition."

"All right. Megan will appreciate it. Thank you for calling."

Jake Sullivan hung up the phone and turned to Megan.

"Sit down, child," he said.

"What did he say? Tell me what he said. How is Michael?"

"He's alive. Now, sit down and I will tell you the rest." He waited for Megan to take a seat on the sofa.

"As you've figured out that was Mr. Long," he began. "Michael was found unconscious in the rail yard in Minot, North Dakota this morning. He's in the Minot hospital, and he's in critical condition."

"I want to go to him!"

"Not right now. If he regains consciousness, we'll see."

"What do you mean, 'if'? Is it that bad?"

"Mr. Long didn't say exactly how bad but I suspect it could be very bad. Megan, Michael might never wake up. You need to prepare yourself for that."

"I want to help him!"

"You can't. Let his doctors do their jobs, and if he wakes up we'll talk about going to see him. In the meantime Mr. Long will let us know if there's any change."

*   *   *

Edith found Dan at Michael's side when she arrived a day later.

"What are you feeling right now, Daniel?" Edith asked after Dan finished reviewing Michael's injuries with her.

"Nothing I want to discuss with you."

"Look at your son. Look at this poor, pathetic child. He has suffered dreadfully for your sins. The guilt must be gnawing at you. What are you going to do about it?"

"What would you have me do?"

"You must take Christ as your Savior! He is calling you to do the right thing. Open your heart and let Him in."

"What the hell good would that do?"

"God will heal him if you repent from your sins."

"Like you did?"

"Yes, like I did! Together we can redeem our son's soul, and his suffering will not have been in vain."

"Does that mean you won't needlessly beat him anymore?"

"I *punished* him, and it was not needless. He had to be taught to obey God's Will."

"God's will or yours, Edith?"

"I have no will beyond what God wants."

"And you think God wanted him beaten?"

"I did not beat him! I am his mother, and I did what I know is right. 'For the wages of sin is death; but the gift of God is eternal life through Jesus Christ our Lord.' No one escapes the Truth, Daniel, not Michael, not you."

"It isn't the truth I want to escape, Edith."

Dan looked at his wife for a long moment and then made a decision he realized he had been considering since Megan Sullivan called him a bastard. "I am relieving you of all responsibility where Michael is concerned, Edith. Our deal is off. I will take care of Michael from now on."

Edith's mouth dropped open. "What?"

"You're done, Edith. Go home."

"But you can't do that! You have no right! I am his mother! We have a deal!"

"It's over. It should have been over years ago. I have enough concrete information about how you have treated Michael to deny you the right to ever see him again if you make a fuss. Now get out of here and go home."

"I won't go."

Dan walked over to his wife, put his hands on her shoulders and looked directly into her eyes. "I have never raised my hand to you," he said gently, "even when you deserved it as richly as you do right now. But if you do not accept this, I will beat you to a bloody pulp and have you removed from my house permanently. You will take nothing with you that is not your own. You have been no wife to me and no mother to your child. It's time we put an end to this."

"What about you, Daniel? You made him run away! It's your fault Michael is dying."

"God, you worthless bitch!" Dan yelled at her. "Michael is not dying! He is fighting for his life, and I am not going to give up on him, not ever again. Now get out!"

"But you can't take him away from me. He is a child of God. He belongs to the Lord!"

"It's already done. Go home, woman!"

Her hand lifted to slap him. He caught her wrist in a crushing grip. "Go home, Edith." His face was an inch from hers. "Leave before you really get hurt."

Edith's face was white as she winced in pain. "Let me go, Daniel." She forced the words out through clenched teeth.

"With pleasure." He dropped her wrist. "Now get out of here."

Without another word Edith turned and stomped from the room. God was testing her again, but she would wait to act until the Spirit moved in her.

Refusing all offers to find him a place to lie down and rest, Dan kept vigil at his son's side day and night. The hospital staff accommodated his needs as much as possible. He was allowed to use a shower. He purchased his meals from the hospital cafeteria and slept in the chair by Michael's bed. Dan was determined to be there if and when his son awakened.

The police came to the hospital to check on Michael and to ask Dan some background questions. He stepped outside to meet with them so as not to be in the way of the hospital staff. Otherwise he spent all of his time in Michael's room.

Dan asked the police about what they knew of Michael's movements and contacts. They had very little. They were waiting for Michael to wake up in the hope that he could tell them something.

"A couple of people saw the boy at a local soup kitchen the night before he was found, but he didn't seem to be with anybody," one of them said. "This is a railroad town. Itinerants move through here all the time. My guess is it was one of them, but we may never know. Maybe the boy can tell us something when he wakes up."

Michael's heart stopped again and was restarted by the vigilant staff of the ICU. Another operation was required to relieve pressure on his swollen brain and to repair a small bleeding artery that was missed during the first operation. A third operation took care of further intestinal bleeding. Through it all, Dan Long stayed by his son's side, leaving the room only when Michael was wheeled to the operating theater, but Michael was to remember none of this.

The boy's condition slowly improved, and on his fifteenth day in the hospital he began to show signs that he might be waking up.

On the seventeenth day, Michael recognized his father.

10 - THAT SHALL HE ALSO REAP

He did not come easily to the light. The qualities that made him human and unique, his thoughts, his sense of self and purpose, slept unaware, while the physical substance of his brain and the rest of his body strove toward recovery. For many days he drifted between a state of total oblivion and the twilight of semi-consciousness. Most of his automatic functions were working, sometimes he even responded to his environment, but he neither consciously controlled nor remembered what he had done.

Finally, answering to a cause or causes not yet fully understood by the science of medicine, he opened his eyes and kept them open long enough to take note his surroundings. The room slowly resolved into objects, and he began to recall that the objects had names. He heard somebody moving near him and turned his head to see who it was. His father rose from his chair at the side of the bed and looked down at him. Michael thought he should know this man but he could remember neither his name nor where he had last seen him.

"Where am I?" The words were mumbled rather than spoken, but his father, leaning over him, understood.

"You are in a hospital. You've been here for a long time."

"What happened?"

"You've been hurt, Michael."

Yes, that was his name, he realized. He nodded his head once in acknowledgement, closed his eyes and slept again.

When he awakened for the second time about an hour later he remembered where he was. Somebody told him he was in a hospital and that he was hurt. Funny… He didn't feel hurt. He lay quietly for a long time, feeling comfortably weak and lazy, not really thinking anything in particular, just being alive. He stared up at the ceiling for awhile, then his eyelids became heavy again and he began to drift off. It felt so good to be alive…

His eyes snapped open. He *was* alive, yet he suddenly remembered dying. He remembered the fear and the awful pain, the knife slicing into his body again and again, his vision fading out, the certainty that his life was over. But it wasn't true. He wasn't dead. He was lying in a hospital bed. Now he remembered that, too. His father told him he was hurt, his father sitting in a chair beside him. His father. His betrayer.

Dan was leafing through an old magazine. Michael heard the noise and knew immediately that his father was still beside him.

"What are you doing here?" The words came slowly, but more distinctly than before.

His father looked up, startled to hear his son speak. He closed the magazine and rose from the chair so he could look at Michael directly. "Waiting for you to wake up, son," he responded smiling. "How are you feeling?"

"Go away."

"I have nothing better to do until you can leave this hospital. I'll wait."

"Get out."

Dan's face lost its smile. He gazed at Michael calmly. "I see," he said. He knew why he was being told to leave. "I'll step outside for awhile."

"Go home."

"I won't do that. I will not leave here until you have safely recovered and are able to leave the hospital. I will stay away from your room if that's what you want, but I will not leave until you do."

"Leave me alone." Michael turned his head toward the wall.

Dan felt a confused jumble of emotions. He knew he deserved this. He needed to pay for what he did. He wanted to pay for it more than he had ever wanted anything in his life. He wanted to serve his sentence and be done with it. He wanted his terrible guilt to go away. He wanted desperately to take Michael in his arms and comfort him. He wanted to apologize. He wanted to wipe out everything and start over. He wanted to make his son well and whole and happy. He knew none of this was possible, so he gave Michael the only thing his son wanted from him. He turned and left the room.

Dr. Graham walked into the ICU just as Dan entered the common area from Michael's room. The look on his face caught the doctor's attention. "Is something the matter?"

"Michael's awake."

"That's wonderful news!"

"Oh yes, and I hope the fact that he remembers what I did to him means he's suffered no permanent brain damage." Dan paused for a moment, and then said, "He wants me to leave, doctor. He wants nothing to do with me."

"Are you surprised by that?" There had been more than one conversation between the two regarding Michael's circumstances.

Dan shook his head. "Of course not," he said. "He is absolutely right that this is my fault...in ways that even he probably doesn't understand. I do not deserve his respect, and I certainly haven't earned his trust. But I won't abandon him. I'll stay here until he is well enough to leave, and then I'll try to convince him to come home with me. If he refuses to go, I will not force him. If I have lost him for good, I will make sure that he has a nurturing environment to grow up in until he is old enough to take care of himself, even if I must do it without his knowledge. I must make whatever amends are still within my power to make regardless of what Michael thinks of me."

"So, what do you want to do now?" asked Dr. Graham.

"I will stay away from his room for the time being. I'll get a hotel room, but I will be here every day. I want Michael to know that I have not left him, but I will not force my presence on him. If he asks for me for any reason, I want to be informed immediately and I want to be kept abreast of his treatment and progress. Do you think you can do that for me, doctor?"

"Yes, that can be arranged."

Dr. Graham entered Michael's room and lifted his chart from the hook at the end of the bed. "Hello, Michael," he said. "Your father told me you're finally awake." Michael watched the doctor with interest but said nothing as Dr. Graham quickly scanned the entries for the past several hours and then looked up again. "My name is Dr. Graham. I've been your doctor since you were brought into the ER. You gave us quite a scare."

"I want to get out of here."

Graham chuckled. "You have some injuries that will take a long time to heal. Even if you had the strength to do it, it would take you a very long time just to remove all the fixtures and attachments. You couldn't get out of that bed if you tried right now. You were hurt very badly, Michael."

"How long?"

"How long have you been here?"

"How long before I can leave."

"I can't say right now. It depends on how fast you heal. We'll know more when we get you back on solid food and get all of your organs functioning properly again. You've been through a terrible ordeal, both physical and emotional. It will take time, there is no doubt of that, and I think you should concentrate on getting well rather than when you can leave."

"Sure, Doc. Whatever you say."

Michael wasn't interested in anyone's advice and his level of trust in others was at an all-time low. He wanted to be out of the hospital and away from his father. Dan's presence didn't mean a damn thing. It was guilt, pure and simple. He was through waiting and hoping and trusting and paying the price for his father's behavior. The chord was cut and it was going to stay cut. There was nobody to trust except himself and that's how he wanted it.

Two days later, Dr. Graham brought up the topic of Michael's injuries.

"Michael, how much do you remember of how you got hurt?"

Michael looked at the doctor. "Everything," he said. "I remember everything. Not that it's any of your damn business."

"Do you want to talk about it?"

"Does it sound like I do?"

"We have people on our staff that specialize in helping people get through things like this. They can help you if you let them."

"What makes you think I need help?"

"People who have suffered the kind of mental and physical injury you have need professionals to help them heal."

Michael laughed weakly. "Is that what you call it around here? Mental and physical injury?"

"You're going to need help, Michael."

"Go away."

"We can help, but only if you let us."

"Leave me alone."

"Well, let me know if you need anything, son. I'll do my best to get it for you."

"You can get me out of here."

"That will happen in good time, but the more you try to rush it, the longer it will take."

"I've got news for you, Doc. I'll leave when *I'm* ready."

"You need to trust my judgment, Michael. Otherwise I'm going to have a hard time helping you."

"Then don't help me! I can't pay you anyway."

"Your father is taking care of that."

"Is that information supposed to make me feel better? Do you think I should be grateful? Do you know why this happened?"

"Your father told me some of your story, Michael. He also said he was very sorry for what happened to you, both before and after you ran away. He feels responsible for it."

"I'm touched. Let me shed a tear in honor of my father's regret."

Michael closed his eyes. He knew he was in no condition to walk out of the hospital. He would have tried to leave if he thought he could make it, but even his brief conversations with Dr. Graham wore him out. He just wasn't up to it and wouldn't be for some time. Since he couldn't leave, he went back to sleep.

When he awakened again, there were two policemen waiting outside and his father was in the room. "What are you doing here?" Michael demanded.

"Michael, I know you'd rather I wasn't here, but these officers would like to ask you a few questions and they asked me to be present when they did. They want to ask about what happened the night you were attacked."

"There isn't much to tell, but if they want to ask questions I'll answer them."

"Would you rather I wait outside while they talk to you?"

"No point in that. They'll just tell you what I say anyway."

Dan motioned for the officers to enter the room. One of them introduced himself as a Officer Simonson. The other's name was Gordon.

"Michael, do you have any idea who did this to you?" Officer Simonson asked.

"No."

"Okay. How did you get here? We're interested in particular in anyone you were with or may have met along the way."

"I wasn't with anybody. Most of the time I stayed away from people. It took me two days to get to Fargo. I thumbed rides twice and rode on a freight train for the last eighty miles or so. I hung around Fargo for awhile and then hopped a freight. When the train stopped, I got out and went looking for something to eat. I smelled food and followed the smell."

"We had a report that someone fitting your description was seen at the Mercy Mission near the rail yard. Were you there?"

"I never knew what it was called. If you mean that soup kitchen on the north side of the yard then yes, I was there."

"What happened the night you were attacked?" The question came from Officer Gordon.

"I left the mission and somebody followed me."

"Did you notice anyone looking at you or acting suspicious when you were there?"

"Everybody looked suspicious."

"Anyone in particular?"

"Not that I remember. But the place felt dangerous."

"What do you mean?"

"Just the look of the people there, shabby, dirty. I needed to find a place to stay for the night, and I didn't want to stay there. I got out as soon as I finished eating."

"How did you end up in the rail yard?"

"That's where they dragged me."

"They? There was more than one?"

"Two."

"Can you tell us what happened?"

"I heard footsteps behind me. I looked for a place to get away but there was a fence topped with barbed wire on both sides of the street. I could see the shadow of this guy behind me. He had a bat in his hand that he kept swinging against his palm. I didn't know it was a bat at the time. I found out later."

Dan sought the support of one of the chairs in the room, dreading what was coming.

Michael continued his story. "He was getting closer to me, so I started running, but I was looking back when I should have been looking where I was going. Somebody tackled me. I didn't even see it coming. There was no way I was going to get away after that. I must have hit my head when I fell. I couldn't move for a while."

Dan's hands gripped the chair back. He wanted desperately to escape, but his sense of justice would not let him leave. This was Michael's story, but *his father's* confession. It was proper that he learn the full magnitude of his guilt directly from his son.

"That's where they assaulted you, under the railroad car?" asked Simonson.

"Yes."

"Did you manage to put a mark on either one of them? Scratch them maybe?"

"Damn right I did! I got one of the bastards good. I found a stick on the ground and shoved it in his face, gouged his fucking eye out. He screamed and got off me. That's when they started in with the knife and the bat."

Dan gripped the chair back harder, his knuckles dead white.

"That's it." Michael finished the story. "I don't remember anything after that."

"Do you remember how they looked or what they were wearing?"

"I never got a real good look at their faces. Too dark. I do remember they both had heavy jackets. I don't think they were from around here. They talked different."

"Different? How?"

"With an accent, like they came from the South or something."

"All right. Thank you."

Simonson turned to Dan. "Here's my card. Call if he remembers anything else you think might be important." He turned back to Michael. "You're a very brave young man, son. Your father should be proud of you."

The comment did not have the desired effect. Michael looked at Officer Simonson scornfully. "How the hell would you know that?"

Simonson glanced at Michael in surprise. "I'm sorry if I offended you, son."

"I am not your son, and my father is not proud of me. He's just feeling a little guilty. But he'll get over it, right Dad?" Michael looked at his father. "In order to be proud of me the asshole would have to know who I am, and he doesn't. But feeling guilty isn't nearly as much work."

Dan ushered the policemen out of the room.

"I know Michael meant no disrespect in what he said to you Officer Simonson. He's angry with *me*, and with good reason."

"He's survived an incredible ordeal, Mr. Long."

"Is there a chance of finding the men who did this?"

"To be honest, not much. If they were itinerants from the South, they were probably headed that way when they stopped in Minot. All these guys head south for the winter. They're probably long gone. We'll do the best we can with the available information but you shouldn't be too optimistic."

"All, right," Dan frowned. "Thanks for your help." He turned back to Michael's room.

Michael had been watching his father talk to the police outside his door, but when Dan opened the door again he pointedly turned his face away.

Dan understood the signal but he spoke anyway. "Michael, do you mind if we talk for a moment?"

"Get out."

"This will take just a minute, and then I'll leave. I am so sorry this happened. You have suffered incredibly because of what I did to you. I don't know what to do to make amends."

"Don't waste your time trying. It's too late."

"Maybe, but I must try. There is no reason you should forgive me for what I did to you, for forcing you to leave and everything that came before it. I'm not asking for that. I always felt contempt for Edith because she was such a terrible person. But the fact is that I'm as bad as she is for letting her do what she did to you. I want you to know that I understand this. I also want you to know that I understand that trust is earned, and I haven't earned yours."

"There's a news flash."

"Let me try to earn it now, Michael. You are not ready to leave home. This experience should tell you that." Michael opened his mouth to speak, but Dan raised his hand to stop him. "No, don't answer now, please. Just think about it. Think about it for awhile, and I'll ask again when the time comes."

"Dad, does it really make that much difference to you where I get raped?"

"I...I don't understand." Just the word "rape" from the mouth of his adolescent son was enough to shock him. Michael said it so easily, like it was a concept he had long been familiar with. "What do you mean?" Dan stammered.

"If I went home with you, would it be the same as always? Were you still planning to force me to submit to Mother, or have you changed your mind about that? I will not attend another Bible lesson. I will not be what other people want me to be. I will not pretend for anyone's benefit, and I will not be a sacrifice for anyone under any circumstances. Now *you* think about it, you fucking piece of shit...or go to hell, I don't care which."

"You may not believe this, Michael, but your mother and I will never hurt you again."

"You're sure-as-hell right about that one, Dad!"

Dan looked down at the floor and then back at his son. "Michael, I am so sorry." He turned and walked out, the door closing slowly behind him.

11 - A SOUL WITHOUT PITY

Jake Sullivan looked down at his daughter and chuckled. The chuckle was at the memory of telling Megan that she was forbidden to see Michael Long ever again and the sound of the conductor's voice announcing that the train's next stop was Minot, North Dakota. Megan smiled in answer. He didn't have to explain. She knew why her father found the announcement amusing. She thought it was funny too.

Sullivan had no regrets. When Dan Long called to tell them that Michael was awake and out of danger, Megan made it her mission in life to go see him. The fact that Jake hated disappointing either of the women in his life made it almost impossible for him to say no. When Darla added her vote to Megan's, he was lost. Never mind about the boy's subversive opinions. Although she was only thirteen, Jake Sullivan was beginning to trust his daughter's judgment when it came to people. She was almost as reliable as her mother that way. If Megan said that Michael Long was a good boy, it didn't take a lot to convince him it was true. It was obvious that Michael meant a great deal to her and, after due consideration, Jake came to believe that his daughter could not possibly be that wrong about somebody.

Sullivan refused Dan Long's offer to pay for the trip. If there was a good reason to do something he would pay his own way. He took a long weekend, withdrew a portion of the family's savings to buy the train tickets, and he and Megan were off to North Dakota. Mrs. Sullivan stayed at home to save money.

When they reached the hospital Jake let his daughter go into Michael's room alone. He knew they both would be more comfortable without him there.

Michael was delighted when Megan walked into the room. And now, twenty minutes after she opened the door, it felt almost as though nothing had happened. It was good to have a friend nearby. Michael felt more at ease with Megan than with anybody else. She sat in a chair at the edge of his bed and talked, while Michael mostly listened. For the first time since he left home he actually began to feel good. She always had this effect on him. Megan didn't ask about his injuries, and Michael didn't volunteer. She did not yet know the whole story, but it would not have changed the conversation if she had. She knew that Michael would talk about the attack if and when he was ready. There was no need for her ever to know exactly what happened. It was enough that he survived it.

"How did you get here?" Michael asked.

"Dad brought me on the train."

"I thought he didn't want you to see me."

"He changed his mind."

"How did that happen?"

"I changed it for him."

Michael laughed. "I don't need to ask how you did that."

"What? I just convinced him it was the right thing to do."

"You wore him down until he crumbled."

"That, too. Has anybody else been here to see you?"

"Yes, Dad's here somewhere. I can't get rid of him. Mom was here before I woke up but nobody else."

"I went to see your dad the morning after you left home."

"What for?"

"I hated him for making you leave, and I wanted him to know it. I called him a bastard."

"And you got away with it? He knocked me down when I called him that."

"He regrets doing that. He wants you to come home again."

"Yeah, he's already talking about it. It's not going to happen."

"You should have seen him talking to the police, Michael. He told the truth. He told them he hit you, and it was his fault you left. He said he would do anything to take back what he did."

"It's too late for that."

"Your dad thinks so, too."

"He's right."

"Okay." Megan, dropped the subject. "I like the room."

"I don't."

Michael was out of the intensive care unit and in a private room. Doctor Graham told him the reason he had his own room was because of his injuries, but he knew that was a lie. He was here courtesy of his father's money. He'd asked to be moved to a regular room, but Doctor Graham said there were none available. That was a lie, too, but if they wouldn't move him, there was nothing he could do about it. For now, he was stuck in whichever bed they put him in.

"Why don't you like it?" Megan asked. "I bet this is the only room in the place that's private. Somebody must think you're special."

"You mean somebody thinks my dad's money is special. I wouldn't be here if he wasn't paying for this."

"Is that so bad?"

"I don't want that son-of-a-bitch paying my bills."

"Why not? It's about time he started acting like a father."

"He's just trying to make himself look better. It's just like always. All he's worried about is his image."

"Or he wants to make up for what he did."

"Come on, Megan, that's ridiculous! Anyway, that can't be done and you know it."

"Maybe. Only you can be the judge of that."

"He's as guilty as hell, and I want him to pay for it."

"But you can't make him pay unless he knows he's guilty. I don't think he's trying to make himself look better, and I don't think you really do either. I think he's really sorry, and I think you know it."

"Tough. He still has to pay."

"I think he is."

"Good."

"Michael, you don't owe your dad anything. I would never suggest you forgive him, or even that you stop making him pay. I can guess, but I don't know how much he's hurt you. Only you know that. But refuse him with your eyes open. I think he realizes what he did was wrong and he really wants to be your father and make up for it. If it's too late for that, it's too late. But think about it before you reject him."

"I can't trust him, Megan. He betrayed me."

"I know he did. I won't mention it again."

*   *   *

Jake Sullivan was sitting in the lounge at the end of the hallway when Dan Long came in and began to rummage through the pile of old magazines on a corner table. Dan didn't notice that anyone else was in the room until Sullivan got up.

"Mr. Long, maybe you remember me. I'm Jake Sullivan."

"Oh, sorry. I didn't recognize you." Dan reflexively offered his hand. "Frankly, I'm a little surprised to see you here."

"Frankly, I'm a little surprised to be here, but Megan is convinced your son's the greatest. She's hard to resist."

Dan offered a faint smile, "I wish she'd talked to me sooner. I think I owe you an apology."

"What for?"

"I wasn't very civil at our first meeting. I'm sorry."

"I wasn't either. Forget it. How is Michael doing?"

"Fine. He seems to be healing just fine. The doctors say he'll be able to leave the hospital in a few weeks."

"Well, I hope everything turns out all right for both of you."

"So do I."

"Has anyone been able to tell you what happened? Does Michael remember?"

"Yes."

"Well, I'm glad you were able to find out."

"Yes."

Sullivan didn't pursue the issue. The boy's father clearly didn't want to talk about it.

After several minutes Jake broke the silence again.

"There's one thing that really puzzles me," he said.

"What's that?"

"From what my daughter has told me, you didn't care much for your son. Our first meeting gave me that impression too. But you told me on the phone you realized you needed to step up and do the right thing. I have to tell you that I am still not sure if you fit either description."

"What don't I fit?"

"Why have you stayed here since Michael was found and why did you call to tell us what happened to him?"

"People sometimes learn from their mistakes. If they're lucky, it happens soon enough."

"I would think a father who almost lost his son and really cared for him would want to spend every possible minute with him. If you've learned from your mistakes why are you here instead of with Michael?"

"I didn't learn soon enough."

Jake stuck his head into Michael's room. "Everything all right in here?" he asked.

"It's all good," said Megan. "Come in and meet Michael Long, Dad."

Sullivan opened the door and walked over to Michael's bed.

Jake stuck his hand out. "No need to get up," he smiled at his own joke.

Michael took the offered hand and shook it. "Good thing. They have me stapled down."

"I've heard a lot about you."

"I've heard you don't approve of what you've heard."

"I wouldn't worry about that. I'm a stubborn old Irishman who's suspicious by nature."

"I'm not worried. What you think is your problem. Thanks for bringing Megan to see me."

"You're welcome."

"How long can she stay?"

"Just until the early train leaves tomorrow morning. We have to look for a place to sleep for the night, so I think it's time we left Michael alone, don't you Megan? Even you must be talked out by now, and it's time we got something to eat. Say goodbye and meet me in the hallway."

"Take care of yourself and come home soon," Megan said after her father walked out the door.

"I don't know that I'll ever come home again. Don't expect me to."

"Then write to me."

"Okay. I promise to do that at least."

"Goodbye, Michael. I'll miss you." Megan leaned over and gave him a brief hug and then left the room to join her father.

*   *   *

Michael gasped for breath. His heart was pounding so hard his throat hurt. He had to get away! The man was a shadow, holding a knife in one hand and a baseball bat in the other, and Michael had to get away.

His eyes snapped open. He started to rise from the bed and felt a tug on his arm. He didn't know what it was, but he knew he had to get rid of it to get away. He violently threw the covers back and saw a tube running up the side of the bed and into his arm. He ripped it free, and threw it on the floor. The heart monitor lead followed, but when he started to get up his catheter stopped him. His mind reoriented with a jolt and he realized where he was. His head fell back on the pillow. He was still in a panic but now that he understood where he was, he could do something about it.

"It's okay." He whispered the words aloud to himself. "You aren't there anymore. It's okay. It was a dream. You're in the hospital. You're safe." He deliberately slowed and deepened his breathing and focused his mind on observing his chest as it rose and fell. His panic gradually receded, and after a few minutes he pushed the call button.

"Can I help you?" said a voice through the speaker above his bed.

"Yes," said Michael, "I pulled out my IV."

"I'll be right in."

Nurse Jane Simmons rapidly walked the few steps from the nurses' station to Michael's room. She took only a second to appraise the situation. "Goodness, young man, what have you done to yourself?" Nurse Simmons was the motherly type, full of warmth and genuine concern. She insisted on calling Michael 'young man' because she thought it would make him feel more grown up. Michael didn't mind. Being mothered was a new and pleasant experience for him, and he knew she meant well. He gave her lots of points for that. He didn't have to search for a hidden agenda or threats in her words. When she asked him if he was feeling well, it was because she wanted to know. When she expressed empathy for his pain, it was real.

Nurse Simmons began the task of reinserting the IV. "It must have been terribly painful for you when this came out," she commented. "What happened?"

"I had a dream."

"It must have been quite a dream. Look, you've completely destroyed this vein. I'll have to find somewhere else to put this."

Michael admitted that it hurt a little because Nurse Simmons seemed to think it should, but he didn't really remember. He was busy going off the deep end at the time. Michael lay back on his pillow and waited for her to finish.

When the job was done she patted Michael's arm. "Feeling better now?"

"I'm fine, thanks."

"Was it another nightmare?"

"Yes."

"I wish we could give you something to help you stay asleep."

"I'll be fine."

"Well, you know how to get hold of me if you need anything. Make sure you call. How's your water? Can I get you some fresh water?"

Michael smiled. "The water's fine, thank you. I'll call if I need anything."

"Make sure you do, young man." She patted his arm again and left the room.

Jane spoke up about Michael at the morning shift exchange meeting. "He had another nightmare at around four o'clock this morning. It was a bad one, and he tore out his IV before he realized where he was. Isn't there something we can do to help him?"

Head nurse Brenda Jackson sighed. "Let me have a talk with doctor again. Dr. Graham doesn't want to give him sleeping pills while he's recovering from a concussion. There are other things you can use, but you have to be very careful with those. For right now he's been given as much medication as the doctor allows."

Brenda knew exactly where the nightmares came from. She knew well before he came under her care. The story of the boy in the ICU spread through the hospital in a matter of hours after he was admitted. She knew that Michael was unwilling to discuss his dreams with anyone. Beyond his brief statement to the police he refused all attempts to get him to talk about the attack or any other aspect of his life.

Seven a.m. came, and Dr. Graham stepped from the elevator onto the floor. Nurse Jackson told him of Michael's nightmare.

"Absolutely no sleep medications."

"Have you had any luck getting him to see a therapist?"

"None whatsoever."

Dr. Graham walked into Michael's room. "How are you this morning, Michael? Feeling any better?"

"A little."

"Nurse Jackson tells me you had another dream last night."

"Nurse Jackson is a blabber-mouth." Michael smiled slightly when he said it.

"Yes, I know." Graham chuckled. "I count on her a great deal for that, and she is very good at her job. What are we going to do about that, Michael? Don't you want to make the dreams go away?"

"Sure, go ahead and cut, Doc. Just make sure you get them all."

"You know that isn't what I meant."

"Yes, I know what you meant, and you can forget it."

"Michael, I really think it would be to your advantage to see a therapist."

"*Doc, will you please just let it go?* I have dreams. So what? They aren't real, and they can't hurt me. People think I need to talk about it. What I really need is for everyone to shut up about it."

"How are you going to deal with it if you don't talk about it?"

"I *am* dealing with it. I deal with it twenty four hours a day. I deal with it every time I try to move. I deal with it every time I wake up in the middle of the night."

"All right," Graham let the matter drop. "Is there anything you need before I leave?"

"Actually, there is. I know my dad is around somewhere. Would you tell the bastard to come in here, please?"

"Of course. I will tell him right away. Would you like him to come see you now?"

"Any time would be fine."

Dr. Graham could not suppress a smile as he walked out the door. At least the boy wanted to talk to *somebody*. It was a start. Michael needed a parent, a real one, more than he needed anything else.

As usual, Dan was waiting by the nurse's desk when Dr. Graham walked out of Michael's room.

"How is my son doing today?"

"Why don't you ask him yourself? He wants to see you."

"Are you sure about that? He said he wants to talk to *me*?"

"I wouldn't tell you that if it wasn't true, Dan. You can go talk to him right now if you like. But understand that Michael has his own reasons for asking for this, and you may not like what he has to say. Don't walk in there assuming all is forgiven. He is still a very angry young man."

"Of course." Dan looked at the door to Michael's room and back at the doctor. "Okay," he said with a nervous laugh. "I'll go talk to him."

He rubbed his palms on his pants and walked toward Michael's room. He knew that he had to take it slow. He had to follow, not lead this conversation. He had no right to do anything other than accept what Michael gave him.

His hand touched the half-open door, and he entered the room. Michael was sitting up in bed, reading a magazine. He looked up when Dan entered.

"Good morning, Father."

"Hello, Michael."

"I asked to see you because I want to ask you a few questions."

"Anytime you want to talk to me, day or night, I'll be here for you."

"We'll see if you still feel that way after we talk."

"What would you like to talk about?"

"Well, I thought maybe you could tell me why I had to nearly get killed for you to discover I was your son."

Dan paused. "You aren't going to make this easy are you."

"Is there a reason I should?"

"I can't think of one."

"Well at least you have the honesty not to try and justify what you did."

"It can't be justified."

"Can you explain it?"

"I can try, but I'm not sure I understand it myself."

"That's not very encouraging."

"Michael let me just start by telling you how I feel right now. I know I have wronged you terribly. Even if you were to forgive me, I couldn't forgive myself. This will be with me for the rest of my life, no matter what happens between you and me. I want to make amends for what I've done, but I know there are no amends great enough to compensate for it."

"Why are you saying this? Do you expect pity from me?"

"God, no! I'm just trying to explain that I know how enormously unjust I've been."

"Got a pencil? I want to give you a point for recognizing the obvious."

"I know you don't trust me, and there's no reason you should. Be angry. Question everything. Make me pay. If you don't make me earn it, your trust will mean nothing."

Michael looked inquiringly at his father. "Why now, Dad? Is it just guilt?"

"At first that's what it was. I won't deny that. It was guilt when I heard what happened to you. It was guilt when I saw you lying unconscious in the ICU. But it's more than that now. What you did took the kind of courage I know I would not have had at your age. There is strength in you, Michael. What you went through would have destroyed me. I have no idea how you did it, but you seem to have turned yourself into the kind of young man that any father would be proud to call his son. To my everlasting shame and regret I had nothing to do with it. The accomplishment is yours alone."

"Do you expect me to believe that? Do you expect me to believe any of it?"

"I have no right to expect anything. All I can do now is be as honest as I can and hope you will give me a chance to prove it."

"Damn it, Dad, what took you so long?"

"I don't know."

"What made Danny your son and not me?"

"That's a long story."

"Well we don't have anything else to do, do we? I want to hear it."

"Okay." Dan paused for a moment and then continued. "When you were five years old, Edith demanded that she be allowed to raise you without my interference. I let her do it as long as she left Danny and me alone. We'd been fighting for a long time, and when she got religion it just got worse. She preached all the time, and I needed some peace."

"But she never stopped preaching."

"She did for awhile."

"Why me? Why did you give me to her?"

"You were really her child from the beginning, Michael."

"You didn't want me?"

Dan hesitated. How could he say this without hurting his son's feelings? But before he had a chance to say anything, Michael spoke again.

"No, that's not the right question," said Michael. "I know you didn't want me. What I want to know is why."

"Son, you have to understand that Edith and I fought all the time. Our marriage wasn't fit for a child. I think I was already angry at your mother when we got married. When you were born I transferred some of the anger to you."

"But what did I have to do with it?"

"Nothing. Like I said, I can't justify it. When you were a baby, Danny came to live with us, and it didn't take long for me to realize that your mother hated him. I owed Danny. I abandoned him once before, and I had to protect him."

"So you abandoned me."

"That's not what I intended, but that's how it turned out."

"Dad, that's monstrous."

"Yes, I know."

Michael turned away from his father and stared at the wall. After a moment he said, "Leave me alone now. I want to think about this."

"All right. If you want to talk again, just ask one of the nurses to let me know."

Michael did not respond, and after a moment Dan got up and left the room.

*   *   *

Dan had spoken over the telephone several times with Edith in the days after she returned to Mansfield. He did not really care what Edith did or how much she knew, but each time he phoned to talk to Danny, Edith took the opportunity to ask about Michael. Dan answered her questions but he volunteered no information, and Edith said nothing about returning to the hospital.

But when Dan was leaving the hospital to get some lunch after his conversation with Michael, he noticed a taxi pull up to the main entrance. The door opened, and Edith stepped out. Dan altered his path immediately to confront his wife.

"What are you doing here?" he demanded.

"What kind of a greeting is that? Obviously I am here to see my son."

"I told you to stay away."

"I must see Michael. I have prayed long and hard about this, and The Lord has called me to protect my son."

"From what? He's in the hospital. He has everything he needs."

"Evil is everywhere, Daniel. It is my duty to protect him from evil."

"What if Michael doesn't want your protection?"

"It will be as the Lord has ordained. He's my son. I know he still loves me. Of course he wants my protection. If there is anyone he doesn't want around, it's you."

"What makes you think he isn't angry with you, too?"

"We've discussed this before. You have no right to question my child-rearing methods. You have never been a father to him. Unlike you, I care about what happens to him."

"Is that why you abused him?"

"And you didn't? I don't have to explain my actions to you, Daniel. Clearly, you would never understand them anyway."

"But I am beginning to understand, Edith, and that is why I have denied you access to him. Better late than never. But now that you're here, why don't we just ask Michael what *he* wants."

"But he's just a child. He doesn't know what he wants. *I* am the guardian of his soul!"

"Edith, has anyone mentioned how delusional you are?"

"Michael is my son! I must protect him!"

"Only if *he* wants it. If he doesn't want you here, you will leave. Is that clear?"

"You can't make me do anything, and Michael will not want me to leave. He's a smart child. He knows what's good for him."

"We shall see." Dan took Edith by the arm and escorted her to Michael's room.

Michael was sitting up in bed reading a worn paperback from the hospital library when his parents walked in. He frowned angrily when he saw his mother. "What the hell are you doing here?" he said.

Edith started to speak, but Dan held up his hand. "Just a minute, Edith. Michael, I'm sorry for the interruption, but your mother has demanded to see you. I've told her that the choice will be yours. If you want her to leave, I'll make sure that she does."

Michael looked at his mother. "What do you want?"

"Does a mother need a reason to see her son?"

"*What* do you want?"

"I'm just a mother who misses her beloved son."

"If you want to say anything at all to me, start with the truth."

"Michael, what a thing to say! I'm here because you need me now more than ever. The Lord has spoken and called me to his service. He has great things in mind for you. God withdrew his Grace because you turned away from Him. I am here to help you understand that. You have always wanted to understand, Michael. This is your chance to learn the most important lesson of your life."

"What lesson would that be, Mother? That God is an evil pervert? Is that the reason you worship God, out of terror that you might be his next victim?"

"I worship God because He made me and redeemed my soul, Michael. I worship Him out of gratitude and love."

"If you were God's special little project, why would he need to redeem your soul? Did he screw it up the first time?"

"I can't answer that, my son. The ways of the Lord are beyond man's understanding."

"Yes, I've heard you say that so many times I'm sick of it, but if it's true I wonder how you can claim to know *anything* about what God is, or wants, or does. I know you feel something, and I know you claim that it's God stuffing those feelings into your brain, but your claims mean nothing to me. And there's one question I keep coming back to every time I think about God, Mother. If there is a loving God who cares about what happens to me and he sent you to protect and teach me, I keep wondering what the hell he was thinking."

"Oh Michael, what a terrible thing to say! Why must you hurt me like this?"

Michael turned to his father. "You said the choice would be mine. Please remove this…*thing* from my room."

"Michael, you may not speak to me in that tone of voice! I am your mother!"

"I wasn't speaking to you. I was speaking to my father."

"I want an apology this instant!"

"Somehow I think you are not going to get an apology today, Edith," said Dan. "It's time for you to leave."

"No! I want an apology now!"

"Come with me."

"Stay out of this, Daniel. I'm warning you. This is none of your affair."

Dan took hold of Edith's arm above the elbow and squeezed. "Edith, come with me, please."

"Ouch, you're hurting me!"

"Come with me and I'll stop hurting you." He steered Edith into the hallway and the door to Michael's room closed.

"You can't make me leave," Edith was indignant. "I am Michael's mother, and I have a right to be here any time I want to be. I'll get a lawyer! I'll file an injunction!"

"Not with my money, you won't."

"There are other ways of getting a lawyer."

Dan laughed. "Yes, there are. They won't be good lawyers, but I admit you can find one without paying for it in cash. What form of compensation did you have in mind?"

"What are you insinuating?"

"Your body is the only thing you actually own, Edith, and it doesn't appear to be worth much anymore."

"Don't be offensive."

Dan's smile was ironic. "Have you thought about what will happen if we bring the lawyers into this? Go ahead and give it a try. If there is a hearing, Michael will testify. My lawyers will see to it that everything is revealed. After that, no judge on earth will allow you within a thousand yards of Michael. Now I want you to leave. Do not return to this hospital again without being asked to return. Do not attempt to see or call Michael without prior permission. If you do, I will throw you out of the house for good. Do we understand each other?"

"I want to say goodbye to my son."

"No. You will leave now."

"You will live to regret getting between us, Daniel."

"I regret not having done it long ago."

Only after she disappeared onto the elevator did Dan turn back to the door to Michael's room. He opened it and stepped into the room only far enough to let the door close behind him.

"Michael, I am very sorry we bothered you but your mother insisted, and she had to hear it from you. If you want to talk to your mother at any time, of course, you have the right to do so. And if you let me know that's what you want, I'll make sure it happens. She will not bother you again unless you ask for her." Dan turned to go.

"Dad," said Michael as Dan opened the door.

Dan looked back. "What is it, son?"

"The only reason I let you throw her out was because I'm chained to this bed. Don't think for a minute I owe you anything for this."

"The thought never crossed my mind."

12 - AN INSTRUMENT OF DEATH

The phone rang several times at the Long house before it was answered.

"Hello?" a girl's voice said with a giggle.

"Hello," said Dan. "Who is this?"

"You first," the girl responded.

"I'm the person who owns the house you're standing in and the phone you're speaking into. Please put Danny on the line."

"Danny, it's your dad!" The girl yelled at the top of her lungs. After a moment she spoke into the phone again. "He's coming," then she began to laugh hysterically as though she had just delivered the world's funniest punch line.

A minute later Danny came on the line. "Hi, Dad. What's cookin'?"

"Maybe you should answer that question first."

"You mean Rachel?"

"The girl who answered the phone."

"That's Rachel. She's just a chick I know."

"I see. Can't you do any better than that?"

"Come on, Dad. No need to talk like that. Rachel's all right. She likes to have a good time, and so do I."

"Yes, I know how you like to have a good time. If I find out you have drugs in the house again, I'll have your hide. You understand?"

"Ease up, will you? I don't have any drugs. I haven't had any since that time you caught me."

"You'd better not. Where is your mother?

"Some church deal. She'll be home late. Do you want to talk to her?"

"No. Just do me a favor and make sure that Rachel is gone by the time she gets there, will you?"

"Mom knows her, Dad. She introduced us."

Dan laughed out loud. "She introduced you? How thoughtful of her. Well, at least make sure she has her clothes on when your mother gets home. I have no interest in dealing with Edith's complaints over this. Don't give her a reason to call me."

"Sure thing, Dad."

"How are things going with you, Danny?"

"Fine. Why do you ask?"

"Well, I've been away for a long time. I just wondered how you are doing."

"I'm fine Dad. Everything's fine."

"Michael is coming home soon. He could be released sometime this week. I would like to spend some time with you when we get home."

"Don't be weird Dad. I'm not Michael, you know. I have my own life. Don't mess it up."

"All right, Danny, if that's the way you want it."

"That's the way I want it. Listen, Dad, I gotta run. Can we talk later?"

"Sure, Danny. Talk to you later."

Danny hung up and stared at the phone for a second. He hoped this didn't mean that his dad was going to take a regular interest in his life again. That was the last thing he needed. He was in a spot of trouble right now, and the less his dad knew the better.

Danny picked up the joint smoldering in the ashtray beside the phone, took a long hit and held it in. He exhaled and smiled to himself in blissful contentment. This had to be the best shit he'd ever smoked.

He turned away from the phone and yelled up the stairs. "Hey Rachel, where the hell are you?"

"In bed, lover boy," her voice called back. "Come to mama."

"Rock-'n-roll!" Danny said it to himself as walled up the steps.

Everything was going to be fine. Everything was always fine. Sure he had some things to take care of, but there was always a way out. He always found a way out. The Baker boys could wait until tomorrow. He wasn't going to waste time worrying about them now, not with Rachel waiting for him upstairs, bare-ass naked and ready for anything. Damn, that babe was hot!

*   *   *

The snow fell heavily for most of the day, and by early evening the sidewalks on Riverside Avenue were six inches deep in slush. Huge, fluffy white flakes temporarily covered the grime and decay, and made the West Bank look almost clean for once. The drug dealers and unemployed leftist radicals who called the neighborhood home were gone from the streets, driven inside by the weather, and in the last moments of twilight before the streetlights came on and destroyed the illusion, the storefronts looked almost presentable.

Danny eased the coupe up to the curb in front of a dive called "Ace in the Hole" just as the bottom half of a garish neon sign announcing "…on tap" buzzed and flickered on for the night. If you looked closely, you could see that the top half of the sign said "Budweiser," but the top half wasn't working. He killed the ignition and patted his jacket pocket to reassure himself that the package was still there. Then he reached over and pulled a .38 revolver from the glove box. It was easy to buy a gun on the street if you knew where to look. Danny bought it for protection after being mugged by a dude with a knife when he was trying to score some reefer. For perhaps the tenth time that evening, he checked to make sure it was loaded, shoved it into the back of his waistband, and covered it with his coat. Taking a deep breath, he got out and walked into the bar.

The bartender looked up as Danny entered and frowned. "We don't sell root beer in here, Junior" he said.

"Relax Grandpa. You've got nothing I want. I'm looking for Billy Ray."

The bartender jerked his head in the general direction of the back of the joint and turned away. Danny squinted. In the gloom he could barely see the shadow of a very large man sitting alone at a corner table. "Billy Ray?" he asked, walking toward the back.

"Who wants to know?" said the shadow.

"None of your business."

154

The shadow chuckled, "Well, Mr. None-of-your-business, what do you want Billy Ray for?"

"I was told he was buying what I'm selling."

"You're nothing but a kid. I doubt you have anything that Billy Ray would be interested in."

"Well, why don't you trot him out here, and we'll find out."

The shadow snorted. "Don't be such a punk, Boy. Maybe I'll just take what you got."

On the surface he appeared to be fearless, but Danny's insides were churning as he widened his stance and leered scornfully. "Give it your best shot and see what happens, fat man."

Billy Ray dismissed both the threat and the insult with a contemptuous grunt. "Well," he said, "since you took the time to find me, I guess I could have a look. Step into my office."

Billy Ray got to his feet and motioned for Danny to follow him. In the dim light Danny hadn't realize just how big the man was, but standing, he looked like a mountain. He was at least six-and-a-half feet tall and well over three hundred pounds. Danny looked like a child beside him, and he didn't care much for the image. The .38 felt comfortably hard in the small of his back. "Let's do it," he said.

He followed Billy Ray to a small doorway hidden behind a large plastic plant in a back corner of the room. When Billy Ray stepped aside and held the door for him, Danny walked past him into the room and immediately found himself pinned, face to the wall, with his right arm twisted behind his back.

"Relax kid, I'm not gonna hurt you. Just gotta see what you're packin'."

Billy Ray found a crumpled paper bag folded several times around its contents in an inside jacket pocket and flipped it onto the packing crate that served as a desk. The .38 followed it a second later. "You'll get that back when you leave. I'm not gonna do business with a punk when he's carrying. There's too much chance for a misunderstanding."

"How did you know I had it?" said Danny.

"My business." Billy Ray replied shortly.

The office was a converted broom closet containing just enough room for the packing crate and two folding chairs. He sat down and motioned for Danny to do the same. "All right, let's have a look," he said as he opened the bag and dumped its contents onto the packing crate.

Billy Ray whistled through his teeth. The bag contained several exquisite pieces of jewelry. There was a gold ring with a complex setting that featured a diamond of at least three carats, an emerald broach also set in gold, a pearl necklace, a platinum bracelet incrusted with precious stones, and miscellaneous other expensive baubles.

Billy Ray's eyes narrowed. "Where the hell did you get this stuff?" he asked suspiciously.

"Never mind where I got it. The police aren't looking for it, and neither is anyone else. How much will you give me for all of it?"

"If the police aren't looking for it, why did you come to me?"

"Look," Danny said, "I didn't come here to answer stupid questions. If you're interested, tell me what you'll pay. If not, I'll be on my way."

"Okay, relax." Billy Ray dropped the subject and reached first for the ring. He produced a jeweler's loop and examined each piece in turn.

"I'll give you sixty-five hundred for everything," he said. "That's the best I can do."

Danny began to gather up the merchandise. "I can get more than that at a pawn shop," he said with disgust. "This stuff must be worth at least ten times that much."

"Not to me it isn't. I need to cover my overhead, and no pawn shop I ever heard of would buy this off you. They'd think it's hot, too. Tell you what. Let's make it an even seven-grand."

"I want twenty-grand," Danny bluffed. "It's twenty or I walk." Danny already knew no pawn shop would buy it because he'd tried several.

Billy Ray could have turned a hefty profit even if he paid the kid twenty, but his policy was to squeeze the last drop out of every deal. "Ten is my final offer," he said. "Take it or leave it."

Danny thought for a long moment. It wasn't enough, but what choice did he have? "I'll take it," he said finally.

He was in no position to force the issue. Fences didn't exactly advertise their profession, and if Billy Ray didn't buy the merchandise Danny had no other options. Ten-thousand dollars was better than nothing, but it was only half of what he needed.

Dan had given Edith most of the jewelry before they were married, but Edith's religious convictions prohibited the wearing of personal adornments. Danny found the jewelry box hidden in a bottom drawer several years ago when he was searching for money to steal. At the time he was too young to realize the value of what he had found. But in this moment of need he remembered the box and went looking for it. It was still where he remembered finding it the first time, buried and forgotten beneath a pile of clothes his stepmother hadn't worn in ages.

Danny needed the money to cover a gambling debt, and he didn't want his dad asking unnecessary questions, like "how the hell did you manage to lose that much money?" He could just hear his dad saying it. The old man always asked way too many questions. He hated having to justify himself to his father because Dan was never satisfied with his answers. In fact, Danny didn't know how he managed to lose the money. It just happened somehow. Danny liked to play poker. It was *his* game and he was pretty good at it—well, he thought he was good at it anyway.

He hung around with Al and Joe Baker because they knew where to get drugs when Danny wanted them. When they let it slip that they played a high-stakes poker game every Wednesday night Danny just had to get in. Joe warned Danny that the game was for heavy-hitters only, but that just made him want it all the more. The boys knew what they were doing. They never talked about the game unless they were baiting the hook. They knew Danny thought he was good and they knew he had money to burn. The boys fleeced him of every cent he had on him in three hours flat. When he compounded his bad judgment by signing an IOU and trying to win back what he lost, they took him for the entire contents of his bank account and left him twenty-thousand dollars in the hole.

The boys told Danny he had five days to come up with the money, or he'd wish he was dead. It was no idle threat. He knew the Bakers played for keeps, but Danny never worried about anything until it was time to do something about it. Usually his dad bailed him out. This time his father didn't know.

All Danny owned that was worth any real money was his coupe and he had no intention of parting with that. Then he thought of the jewelry. It was the perfect answer. It wasn't his jewelry, but that was one of the reasons it was perfect. He wouldn't have to give up a thing. He needed the money. The jewelry was easily taken, so he took it. It was a great plan except that he was still ten-grand short and time was running out.

Danny was already thinking hard as he walked out of the Ace in the Hole. There had to be a way to get what he needed. Well, ten-thousand dollars was a start. Maybe he could come up with a story good enough to pry another ten large out of his mother's penny-pinching hands. She'd ask questions, but he could come up with a story good enough to fool her. With his dad it was another matter.

Maybe the money he had would buy him a little more time to raise the rest. Maybe Al and Joe would call it even and let him go. He'd go talk to them.

He knew the boys were running a game somewhere, but that didn't help much. They rarely used the same place twice. It took him several hours to track them down in the back room of a seedy strip-joint near the river.

The place was imaginatively called "Gentleman Jack's." He'd been there many times before. It was known to every under-age delinquent in Mansfield and a hundred other small towns around the city as a place where you could get a drink, see the sights and cop a feel without being asked embarrassing questions. As he neared the door to the back room the Bakers' body guard appeared as if by magic.

"Where do you think you're going?" The menacing voice came from behind him.

"Come on, Ax." Danny stopped but did not turn around. "Let me talk to Al and Joe."

Danny knew enough to be careful with "The Ax Man." He wasn't called "The Ax" because he looked like one. He was five-and-a-half feet tall standing or laying down, a cube of solid muscle. His name was Axel Fjordbak; hence, "The Ax Man." His reputation and his physical appearance were such that he rarely had to hurt anyone. The threat was usually enough. But sometimes he hurt people just for fun, and when he went into action he held nothing back.

Once Danny had seen The Ax attack and physically destroy a man who had objected to being fleeced and hadn't had the good sense to back off. At the end the guy was disabled and begging for mercy, but Ax didn't stop until his victim was an unrecognizable bloody pulp. The man was permanently disfigured and paralyzed from the waist down. At the time Danny thought the whole incident was funny. The guy should have been able to figure out he was in trouble before it went too far, and he deserved what he got for being so stupid. But when Danny's ass was on the line, the situation wasn't so humorous.

"You need to be invited," said The Ax. "Were you invited?"

Danny turned around. "No, I wasn't invited, but this is important and I'm sure the boys would want to talk to me if they knew why I was here."

"No invitation, no entrance," said Ax. "That's the rule."

"I know the rule, Ax, and you know I would never ask you to break it if it wasn't important. I really need to see the boys tonight."

Danny reached into his pocket and pulled out a twenty-dollar-bill. He'd stolen fifty from his mother when he took the jewelry. "How about this? You just tell them that Danny Long is here with the money."

Ax made the twenty disappear. "Your funeral." He walked over and rapped on the door.

The knock caused an audible commotion in the room beyond. Ax knocked again. "Open up boys. Somebody to see you." After a delay of several seconds, Al Baker opened the door just a crack.

"Ax," said Al, annoyed at the interruption, "What the hell are you doing? When a game is going, the door stays closed."

"I know it, boss, but this might be an exception. Danny Long is here, and he says he has the money. I thought you might like to know."

Al stuck his head back into the room and called to his brother. "Joe, put your cards down and come out here for a minute, will you? Ax, you watch these guys."

He opened the door and stepped outside, motioning for Danny to take a seat in an empty corner booth. Joe joined them a moment later.

"This had better be good, Danny," Al warned. "If you have the money, fine, we'll take it. Otherwise, this is going to cost you more than you know."

"I have half of it," Danny said, "but I might need some extra time to come up with the rest. How about giving me a few extra days?"

Al looked at his brother and chuckled. "Jeez, what do you think, Joe? Should we give this weasel a break?"

"Danny, Danny my boy," Joe shook his head in mock sorrow. "I don't think we can do that. A deadline is a deadline. We'll take what you have now so you don't misplace it, but you need to have the rest tomorrow."

"That's just the way it is, Danny," Al chimed in, "and, of course, we'll need something for wasting our time tonight, say an extra five-grand."

"Look, guys, let me explain. You've got to cut me some slack here. I came here tonight because I wanted to get ahead of this thing. I was going to borrow the money from my dad, but he's out of town right now."

"A real sob story." Joe was smiling. "My heart goes out to you. But you gotta understand our position. It's nothing personal. We just can't afford to be sentimental. You need to do whatever it takes to come up with the cash. The money needs to be in our hands by two o'clock tomorrow afternoon."

"So that's it?" said Danny. "The ten-grand isn't even going to buy a few more days?"

"Let's see the money," Al demanded.

Danny reached into his jacket and pulled out a roll of bills.

Al didn't bother to count it. He just tossed it to Joe who stuck the money in his pocket.

"We'll consider it an installment payment on a note that comes due tomorrow. The only thing it buys you is a free walk out the front door. You still owe us fifteen-thousand tomorrow."

"But I gave you ten already, damn it. Count it."

"Oh, we trust you. Don't we, Al." Joe looked at his brother, the smirk on his face saying far more than his words. "But half of it went to cover the surcharge for listening to you whine. That leaves fifteen that you still owe. Besides," he said, "we were both thinking that you wouldn't meet the deadline. Right, Al?"

"Right," Al agreed. "That's kind of what we had in mind."

"We were looking forward to the pleasure of watching Ax beat the crap out of your worthless, rich-boy hide. In fact we're gonna to be real disappointed if you manage to come up with the rest of the money in time. Right, Al?"

"Right," Al agreed again.

"This isn't fair guys. I need more time."

Al laughed out loud. "Not fair? Joe, he says it isn't fair. Danny boy you kill me! Listen kid, if you waste any more of our time, we might decide to turn the Ax loose on you tonight."

The pair stood. "We'll see you tomorrow, Danny," Joe said. "Don't be late, now. We won't like it if you're late."

The boys returned to their poker game, and Danny was left alone.

He walked over to the bar and ordered a whiskey.

The bartender poured the drink but held it back. "You got the money to pay for this, kid?" he asked.

"The name's Danny Long, genius. I have a tab. Just keep the liquor coming and shut up."

The bartender didn't like the Baker boys, but he liked Danny's answer even less. He decided to tell Danny about the game.

"I saw you talking to the Bakers a minute ago," he said. "I bet you owe them money, right?"

"That's none of your business."

"Hey, kid, it's nothing to me one way or another, but you should know the cards were marked."

"What do you mean?"

"I mean they played you like a fish, and you were too damn stupid to notice. Makes you feel real good doesn't it? …Genius."

The bartender turned away.

Danny was a lot less street-wise than he thought, but he was smart enough to realize that the bartender was probably right. He'd been running with the Bakers off and on for months. He knew they cheated other people, but he was their good buddy, part of the gang, a member of the inner circle. Apparently it didn't make a damn bit of difference. Or maybe they'd been playing him all along.

If he went to them claiming he didn't owe the money because the game was rigged, he would only look more foolish. Danny didn't like looking foolish, but he didn't like being played either. He was more determined than ever not to go to his father now, looking like a complete idiot.

When Gentleman Jack's closed for the night, Danny went to another bar he knew that served illegally after hours and drank some more. The sun was up when he drove into the yard. He was getting a hang-over and wished he had another drink to calm his nerves. His head throbbed in time with his heartbeat, his eyes felt like a gravel pit, and he was no closer to covering his debt. Less than six hours until two o'clock, and he was still short by ten grand, fifteen if you counted the damn penalty charge. He knew if he talked to his stepmother the news would get back to his dad eventually, but he was becoming desperate. He had to do something and he couldn't afford to wait until she got up. Danny climbed the steps to Edith's room and woke her up.

"Danny," Edith looked at her stepson in amazement, "What do you need that much for? Who is this 'guy' and why do you owe him so much money?"

"That isn't important," Danny returned. "I just need the money. Dad was going to give it to me, but he isn't here."

"But Danny, I can't come up with that kind of money, at least not today. Your father keeps me practically penniless. I have a weekly allowance, and I have my car. There is a fund for the upkeep of the house and grounds and the purchase of groceries, but that's a very limited account. There's never more than five hundred dollars in it. I guess you could use my jewelry, but I don't even know where it is anymore."

"Forget the jewelry, Edith. You probably won't find it and it won't bring enough to cover the debt anyway."

"Probably not. I don't even know if it's real. Your father said it was, but I never believed him. Most of it looks pretty trashy. But the most important thing is that I will not give you anything if you don't tell me why you need it. I have a moral obligation to know where the money is going."

Danny swore explosively and Edith started to reprimand him for his language, but he interrupted her . "Look Mom, I need that money right now. Are you going to give it to me or not?"

Edith was unmoved. Danny only called her "Mom" when he wanted something from her. "No, I will always give you what you need, but what you really need is to make peace with God. The money is unimportant."

"You have no idea what you are talking about." Danny's frustration was beginning to boil over. "If I don't have that money in the hands of the people I owe by two o'clock this afternoon, I'll be killed."

"Oh come now Danny. Surely you are exaggerating. And even if what you say is true, the most important thing is to make peace with God. Then no matter what happens, you will have the assurance that God will receive your soul into Heaven."

"Is that what you want? Do you want me to get killed?"

"All right, Danny, I will try to help you on one condition."

"What's that?"

"That you at least listen to the voice of God in your heart."

"What are you talking about?"

"You must get down on your knees with me right now and beg God's forgiveness. Then you must come with me to meet with Reverend Pratt."

"We don't have time for that."

"There is always time for God in the hearts of those who sincerely seek Him. God will forgive your debt."

Now Danny understood what his mother meant by help, and his fear exploded into rage. "Do you really think that's going to help, you stupid bitch? Are you that fucking ignorant?"

"Do not mock the Lord in my presence, Danny."

"Far be it from me to mock the Lord, but you must be a stark-raving lunatic. Hell, you belong in an insane asylum. I need cash! Cash, do you hear me? Cash, money! Now are you going to help me or not?"

"God is calling you, Danny," said Edith serenely. "Do the right thing and you will have nothing to fear."

Danny knew he had plenty to fear, and for the first time he was beginning to realize how much. He should have known better than to ask Edith for help. He should have known that this was the kind of bullshit answer she would give him. He had to have the money, and he had to have it now!

"What's Dad's phone number in Minot?" he demanded.

"I don't have it. He never gave it to me. He said you had it."

"What's the name of the hospital?"

"I don't remember."

Danny pushed away from Edith with a grunt of disgust and marched back down the stairs and out the front door.

Danny remembered vaguely that his father had given him a phone number, but he hadn't bothered to write it down. At the time the last thing he wanted to do was call his father. Besides, he shouldn't have to call him. Dan should have been *here* when he was needed and not off in some forgotten hole in North Dakota. Damn it! If Michael hadn't run off, and if Dan hadn't run after him, none of this would have happened.

Assholes! The mental exclamation was not specific, but rather an indictment of the universe in general. This was beginning to really piss him off. He had only a few hours left, and the later it got, the angrier he became. If there was anything he hated it was being forced to do something he didn't want to do. It was already too late to get help from his father, so fuck him. Danny was going to take care of this himself.

He was back in the coupe now, cruising down the highway just under the speed limit. For the first time in his life he was thinking about the future rather than feeling the moment. It wasn't far in the future, but if he could get through today with his skin intact, that was all that concerned him.

Danny decided immediately not to go to the Bakers without the money. He knew what The Ax could do to people, and he had no intention of letting it happen to him. Besides, the more he thought about it the better he understood that his real problem wasn't money, it was Axel Fjordbak and the Baker boys, and there was more than one way to make that problem disappear.

He was supposed to meet the boys at a West Bank bar at two o' clock. He knew the Bakers lived in a broken down house only five blocks from the meeting place, but they never walked anywhere. Even if the trip was only a few hundred yards, Ax always drove them in a big Lincoln. No matter where they went they always kept the Ax and the Lincoln within easy reach. But if he picked the time and place right he might be able to catch them by surprise, and surprise was essential to the daring plan growing in his mind.

Danny knew there were few people up and about at two p.m. in the neighborhood where the Baker boys lived, and any possible witnesses in that part of town would have their own reasons for not running to the police. He stood a good chance of getting away with what he planned, at least a much better chance than if he waited for the boys to find him.

When the Lincoln pulled up at ten minutes to two, he was hidden behind a dumpster, loaded .38 in hand.

The narrow street was actually an alley behind a row of buildings that fronted a larger avenue. The dumpster was across the alley and a few feet down from the Bakers' house. It was pushed up against a large bush that grew out of the widening crack between the alley paving and the brick foundation of the building directly behind it. Danny approached his planned position by cutting through a chain-link security fence and climbing through a refuse-strewn walking space between the buildings. The walking space came out almost directly behind the dumpster and the bush. He now stood sandwiched between bush and dumpster with an unobstructed view of the Bakers' house and the street in front of it. Branches hung over his position partially obscuring it, yet he could get out quickly by stepping around the corner of the dumpster and into the alley or by going back the way he came.

The Ax walked to the front door and knocked. The Bakers came out a minute later and began to walk toward the car with Ax in front. Danny had little experience with a pistol. He hadn't actually shot the weapon he held in his hands, but he knew how to shoot a rifle, and he'd seen his dad shoot a pistol many times. The principle was basically the same with any firearm: relax, sight along the barrel at the target, and squeeze the trigger. He gripped the gun with both hands and steadied it on top of the dumpster, aiming at the middle of The Ax's wide chest no more than seventy five feet away.

The first the Bakers knew anyone was around was when they saw The Ax turn and fall. The sound of a pistol shot echoed in the narrow street as the bullet hit Ax high and wide, breaking his right shoulder. Not a killing shot, but it took his gun hand out of action and knocked him down.

Al and Joe both ducked and looked frantically around, trying to find the shooter, but before the echo died Danny was out from behind the dumpster. He ran across the street toward the Bakers with the gun raised in front of him. "Don't move," he commanded. Danny held the gun steady in his hands and the fact that the Ax was down was proof enough he knew how to use it. The Bakers did what they were told. They seemed shocked by the turn of events, and it took them a few moments to comprehend that their adversary was Danny.

Al recovered first. "Danny Long?" he said unbelievingly. "What the hell? I didn't think you had it in you!"

165

"You made a mistake," Danny snarled. "Where's my money?"

"What money?"

"The money I gave you last night. The money you cheated me out of."

"Now wait a minute Danny." Al held his hand up as if to ward off the reality of Danny's statement. "We won that money fair and square. It's ours now, and I don't like being called a cheater."

Joe was looking down at Ax, who was struggling to get his gun out but was obviously in great pain. "That was a really stupid thing to do, Danny," he said, "Now you're a dead man. The Ax is going to kill you for sure."

With his gun trained on the Bakers, Danny reached down and removed Ax's weapon from its shoulder holster and tossed it aside. He smiled at Joe. "You think so? You think I'm too stupid to figure this out?"

"I think you're a punk who's in way over his head."

"I guess we're going to find out who's in over his head boys. Where's my ten-grand?"

"We haven't got it," Al replied.

Danny glanced down at Ax. Then he looked back at the Baker boys. "Are you sure about that?" He pointed the gun at The Ax's head.

The Ax stared up at Danny with a malevolent glare. "Danny I am really going to enjoy killing you." His voice was tight with pain.

Danny looked down at The Ax and grinned. "If you were in any condition to do that you would have tried already."

"Don't do anything stupid, Danny." It was Al talking. "I said we didn't have the money and we don't."

"That's your last word?"

"It's the only word."

Danny glanced down at Ax again. "Sorry Ax," he said. "The boys just don't think I'm serious."

The pistol went off with a roar, and a hole appeared in Ax's forehead. The Ax stopped breathing.

Al was staring at Danny as if he had never seen him before. "Jesus! That was cold. Joe, give him the money."

Joe handed over the roll of bills, but his eyes were wide with hatred. "Where do you think you are going to hide after this? We'll hunt you down."

"Joe, shut up," said Al. "Danny, Joe doesn't know what he's talking about. We're willing to let this whole thing blow over. We're in a position to cut you in on some serious action. So what is it going to take for you to forget about this? I'm sure that we can come to some kind of a financial agreement."

"I thought about that, Al, I really did. But I can't afford to be sentimental. It's nothing personal."

The gun barked twice. Then a few moments later there were two more shots, slower and more deliberate than the first pair, as though the shooter was making absolutely certain he hit what he was aiming at. Somewhere a dog yelped and then there was silence.

The Baker boys were out of business.

13 - THE PATH TO RIGHTEOUSNESS

There was a drunk sleeping in the stairwell again. He was snoring loud enough to wake the dead, and Joey could hear him before he opened the door. Joey Lonneman had a running battle going with a couple of neighborhood drunks, who thought the walkup to his second floor flop was a great place to sleep off a bender. You couldn't reason with these guys. They were never lucid enough to carry on a conversation, let alone remember what was said. So Joey began using a different approach. He figured if he hurt them enough they might get the message and never come back. So far the plan wasn't working, but he kept trying. If it didn't work at least he felt better.

The smell of urine and cheap wine enveloped him in a caustic fog the moment he opened the door. Joey gagged and swore under his breath. It was Bags again. He could tell from the smell. The bum was the most putrid human being Joey had ever encountered. In this enclosed space his body odor had the impact of a biological weapon. Joey held his breath and prepared to run the gauntlet.

Bags was sleeping on the second floor landing, and as Joey climbed past him he planted a vicious kick in the bum's mid-section. Bags didn't even wake up. He just coughed once and threw up on Joey's shoes.

Joey swore again, wiped his shoes on the drunk's clothes, and kicked him in the head. This time there was no effect of any kind.

Joey Lonneman was a petty thief and pickpocket by trade, a good one if success is measured in avoiding jail time. Since deciding to make a career out of it, he had stolen just enough to stay alive.

Joey was no risk-taker, preferring starvation to incarceration, and thus spent a lot of time hungry. He had been arrested several times and charged twice, but so far nothing stuck. Joey's singular talent lay in anonymity, his ability to fade into almost any background. He was of medium height, medium build, and neutral complexion. He was neither handsome nor ugly and had cultivated an absolutely unremarkable demeanor. He dressed in non-descript clothing. He was of above average intelligence but scrupulously suppressed all outward signs of it. As a result he could blend into almost any random crowd consisting of more than two other people. It was a talent he often used to avoid being caught.

The flop consisted of one small room on the second-floor-rear of Crazy Eddie's Hookah Heaven, a head shop just off Twentieth Avenue. Kitchen, living area, bedroom and bathroom were all crammed together. The stool and shower didn't work but there was another bathroom downstairs he could use. A later era would call this an "efficiency apartment." Joey called it a pit, and that term was certainly more descriptive. The rats and cockroaches owned the place, but Joey paid the rent to Crazy Eddie once a week—if he had it. At the moment he was about three months behind. Crazy Eddie was always threatening to kick him out, but Joey knew he wouldn't do that. Eddie wasn't likely to find anyone else willing to put up with this dump, let alone pay rent for the privilege of staying there.

It was early afternoon, and Joey wanted to take a nap before going out to ply his trade. He lay down on his bed and had been sleeping for about a half-hour when a loud noise awakened him. It sounded like a gunshot? He thought about getting up to look out the window but dozed off again. There was another loud noise, and this time he came fully awake. It was definitely a gunshot! He got up and carefully drew the shade aside just enough to see out. Across the alley below him there were three men standing close together and another lying on the ground. Joey whistled. He recognized the one on the ground. It was The Ax Man. Somebody finally got to that bastard, Joey thought. He knew two of the other three as well. Al and Joe Baker were facing the gunman, and Al was talking. Joey had the feeling the gunman wasn't buying the line. A few seconds later the feeling was confirmed. The gunman suddenly raised the gun and pumped a shot into Al's chest then turned on Joe. They both went down. The gunman deliberately shot each man in the head then stuffed the gun behind his belt and covered it with his jacket. As he turned back to cross the alley Joey got a good look at him. Why it was just a kid! Then with a jolt of recognition Joey realized he knew the boy. He'd seen him with the Bakers several times. Danny Lund? Donny Land? Something like that. Anyway the punk couldn't be more than eighteen at most. What a story! The Baker boys done in by a shave-tail kid. Too bad nobody would ever hear about it. Joey had no intention of talking. His mind didn't work that way. Better to keep his mouth shut and live.

The bodies lay in plain sight for more than six hours before a patrol car cruising the alley behind Twentieth discovered the Baker boys and their bodyguard Axle Fjordbak lying dead within a few feet of each other. Within an hour Minneapolis Detective Sergeant George Anderson was on the scene.

"What have we got, Ed?" Anderson asked patrolman Ed Boyd.

"Three dead, detective. You're gonna love this. It's the Baker boys."

"No kidding!" said Anderson.

Patrolman Boyd was pleased by the effect of his news. "Yup. And The Ax is lying right beside 'em."

"It figures," Anderson said. "Whoever did it would have to take care of the Ax first." He walked over to the bodies to have a look.

The crime scene technician was Howie Morgan, an old-timer like Anderson. Morgan was standing next to the bodies, speaking into a hand-held recorder. Anderson waited until he was finished and asked, "Find the murder weapon?"

"Nope."

"Time of death?"

"From the temperature and condition of the bodies I'd guess about six to eight hours ago."

"More than six hours in plain sight and nobody called it in," said Anderson. "Welcome to the friendly West Bank."

"They each got two bullets," Morgan continued, "one to the body, one to the head. Call me stupid, detective, but this was no crime of passion. It looks almost like a hit, except the shooter was probably not a professional."

170

"What makes you say that?"

"His choice of weapons for one thing. Looks like he used a .38. I found a slug over there." Morgan pointed to a small object marked with a red flag near the car. "It must have gone through one of the vics and made that dent in the fender. Never heard of a pro using a .38."

"The first shot came from over there, behind that dumpster," the technician pointed across the alley. "Cigarette butts, scuff marks, broken branches, and gunpowder residue. They all point to the shooter waiting behind the dumpster and the first shot coming from that location. That's another thing: the shooter's location. He had to be one hell of a shot, or the luckiest guy in the world to hit anything at that distance with a pistol. A pro would never have taken a chance like that."

"Prints?" Anderson asked.

"None so far."

"Who got it first?"

"The Ax, probably. The shooter was across the street when the Ax went down. It was the only bullet fired from a distance. The rest all left powder burns. It got him in the shoulder and it looks like it shattered the joint. It would have knocked him down, and he may not have been able to move much after being hit. The other shots are all from close range. The shooter must have been waiting for them and hit The Ax first, and then ran across the street to finish them off. Each victim was shot twice. In each case there is a non-lethal wound to the body and a second shot that blew the victim's brains out. The shooter must have been making sure the job was done right. Cold-blooded, calculated murder."

"Ok, Howie. Let me know what else you find."

Anderson walked back to patrolman Boyd. "I want you and your partner to take two other patrolmen with you and canvas every business bordering the alley and every apartment with a window facing the scene."

"Sure thing, but we aren't going to find anybody who'll talk. Not around here."

"Just do it, Ed. You never know. There might be a solid citizen where you least expect it, just waiting to leap out and bite you in the ass."

"Thanks for the warning, detective."

*　　*　　*

Michael dropped the small bag that contained his few belongings on the floor just inside the door and took a deep breath as he looked at his surroundings. The bag was new and so were his clothes, but the house looked exactly the same. The broad oak stairs that led to the second level and his bedroom, the dark frame of the sun room door just down the hall, the kitchen at the far end that led to the back entrance and the carriage house behind the garage, everything appeared just as it had the day he left, but it didn't feel the same and he wasn't sure why.

His decision to come home was not final, but he let his father convince him to give it a try. He was here mostly because of Megan. He didn't want to lose contact with her. She had been able to visit him only once more after the first time she came to the hospital and Michael missed having her nearby. They wrote to each other, but that was not the same as being able to talk face-to-face.

Michael picked up his bag again and began to climb the steps to his room. There was something important he wanted to take care of right away.

The house was silent and wintry cold. Dan called Edith's name as he walked down the hallway to check on the heat, but there was no answer. The thermostat was set to fifty degrees. Dan turned it up. The house felt empty, smelling of dust and old food. A pile of mail so deep it overflowed onto the floor buried the phone stand in the foyer. Annoyed, Dan picked up the mail and carried it toward his study, calling Edith's name again. She didn't seem to be in the house.

Before they started home, he'd called to tell her that he and Michael would be home today. She answered the phone and acknowledged the message, but now she seemed to be gone. He glanced quickly into the sun room as he walked by the door with the mail. He took another two steps then stopped and backed up. The reading lamp wasn't on, but Dan could see Edith sitting in her chair, gently rocking back and forth. She was wearing a wool cap and a heavy winter coat, and her arms were wrapped tightly around her Bible.

"Edith, what are you doing?" Dan asked. "It's like a deep freeze in here."

172

"I'm trying not to spend your precious money," she snapped.

Dan gave a tired chuckle. When he pointed out to her that she had no resources beyond her husband, he knew she would try to throw it back in his face somehow. This was vintage Edith.

"You have my permission to keep the house comfortable until I tell you otherwise. If you want to say hello to your son, he's upstairs."

"I'm sure he doesn't want to see me."

"Suit yourself."

Just then there was a pounding noise from upstairs followed by a crash and the sound of glass breaking.

"Michael?" Dan called. He listened for a moment, but there was no answer. "Michael, are you all right?" Still no answer. Suddenly there was another crash, much louder than the first, and entire house seemed to shake. Only something very heavy could have made that much noise. The mail scattered as Dan ran for the stairs. Edith rose from her chair to follow.

Dan's only thought was that something had happened to Michael. Edith had the same thought, although not for the same reason.

Dan took the steps two at a time. He reached the top and shouted, *"Michael where are you?"*

"I'm in here, Dad." The voice seemed to come from Michael's room.

Dan raced down the hallway, put out his hand to brake himself on the door frame of Michael's room and skidded to a stop. Edith took longer to reach the top of the stairs and was several yards behind.

A quick glance told Dan that his son was fine. Michael stood near the dormer window in his reading niche. The bookcase filled with his religious books was face-down on the floor next to him with its contents lying in a pile underneath.

Michael saw his father at the door and said, "Dad, can you give me a hand with this stuff?"

"Michael, what are you doing?"

"Taking out the trash."

"What?"

"I don't want these books in my room anymore, so I'm getting rid of them."

"By tearing the house down?"

"I climbed up on the bookcase to get to the books on the top shelf, and it sort of tipped over. Sorry."

"Michael, you could have been badly injured or even killed. That thing could have crushed you!"

"You're telling me. I can hardly move it."

"And what about that?" Dan pointed at the dormer window. Its lower pane was almost completely broken out.

"I couldn't get the window open. It seems to be frozen shut. It broke when I tried to pound it open with a book. Dad, are you going to help me or not?"

"I'm not sure I understand what you want to do."

"I'm going to throw these books out the window, pile them in the back yard and burn them."

Edith, who had just arrived at the doorway moaned as though suddenly stricken with a terrible pain.

"Hello, Mom." Michael looked at his mother. "Is there something you wanted to say?"

"Michael, I gave you those books. Why are you doing this to me?"

"I'm not doing anything to you. I'm just rearranging my room. These books have to go to make room for some others I want to put here."

"But the books are meant to guide you on the path to righteousness."

"I'm not following your path to righteousness."

"Don't you understand how much it hurts me to hear you say that?"

"Do you think I owe you any concern for your feelings?"

"All right, I don't understand your attitude, but I will accept that you are angry with me for some reason. The Lord will give me the strength to bear this. I'm certain I have made some mistakes with you. I'm not perfect. But I have only done what I thought was best for you and the rest of the family. If you don't want the books, give them back to me. I'm sure there is someone somewhere who will appreciate their value."

"No, I will not give them back. They are my books, and I intend to dispose of them."

"But why? Those books are filled with goodness. You cannot deny it."

"I'm not going to deny it, Mother. I'm going to burn them."

"Michael, you must not do this. For the sake of your immortal soul you must not! 'For by thy words thou shalt be justified, and by thy words thou shalt be condemned.'"

"What does that mean, mother? Is God going to punish me for burning my own books?"

"Do not tempt Him, my son. Surely you, more than anyone, must realize the folly in that."

"Shut up, mother." Michael turned back to the bookcase and said, "Dad, help me lift this thing, will you?"

Dan helped Michael stand the now empty bookcase upright and situate it against the wall.

"Michael, make sure the whole place doesn't go up with the books," he said. "Please put them in the refuse barrel before you burn them."

"Okay, Dad."

Edith's hands were on her hips, her lips compressed into a line of determination. She turned to her husband. "So you are going to let him get away with this?"

"Yes, Edith, I think I will."

"I might have known. You two had this planned, didn't you? He wants to hurt me for some reason, and you are helping him do it out of spite."

"What makes you say that, Edith? Feeling guilty?"

"Nonsense. I have nothing to feel guilty for."

"Then why do you think Michael wants to hurt you?"

"Because you have poisoned his mind against me."

"Michael and I talked quite a bit while he was in the hospital, and I recall a few times when your name came up, but we had no discussions about how to hurt you. I had no idea this would be the first thing he did when he got home, but if he wants to rearrange his room, I think we should let him do it."

"I won't let this go, Daniel. It isn't right. God is not mocked."

"Right, Edith, whatever you say. But for now let's leave Michael alone, shall we?"

Dan steered Edith from the room, as Michael stooped to his task behind them. One by one he picked the books up and threw them out the broken window.

When the books were all lying on the ground, he put on his coat, grabbed a box of wooden matches from the kitchen, and went outside. He gathered the books, and using a wheelbarrow he found in the storage shed behind the garage, he moved them to the refuse barrel. The books made an impressive pile, and he had to make several trips. He couldn't even begin to get them all in the barrel. He would have to burn them a few at a time.

He piled the first batch in the barrel, tore off a few pages and lit a match. The wind blew the fire out. He tried several times, but the books wouldn't stay lit. The barrel was too full and the wind kept blowing out the flames.

Suddenly he had an idea. The big gas can used to fuel the mowers and snow blower was stored in the shed. He had seen it when he got the wheelbarrow. He could use that to get the fire going. The can contained almost four gallons of gas, and in his enthusiasm Michael poured on a little too much. He set the can down several feet away, walked back to the barrel, struck a match and threw it onto the pile. The books exploded with an angry whoosh, and flames leaped high into the air. Michael stumbled backward and fell down. His hair and eyebrows were singed, and his face stung. He stared wide-eyed at the roaring flames remembering his mother's words: "by thy words thou shalt be condemned." He burst out laughing.

Did God reach down invisibly from on high to punish Michael on an inexplicable schedule by means of unexplainable magic, or did Edith randomly assign supernatural causes as her faith found it convenient? If Michael had been hurt, his mother would claim that it was God's punishment. Since he was not injured, she would claim it was God's warning, but neither explanation explained anything. The only actual cause in evidence was that a mixture of fire and volatile materials produced combustion.

For the first time in his life he understood the central failure of his mother's method of thinking. You could justify virtually any nutty conclusion if you were willing to arbitrarily pick your starting point out of thin air. Calling his mother's starting point 'arbitrary' was an understatement of monumental proportions. That's why she got so angry when he questioned her beliefs. That's why she beat him.

When he refused to take her baseless assertions as truth, it was the only real answer she had to offer.

There was a reason being home felt different. It was *he* who was different. She could not bully him anymore. She could not even make him feel uncomfortable. Her only weapons were physical coercion and guilt. She was not strong enough to threaten him physically any longer, and he knew beyond all doubt that he was guilty of nothing.

His task finished, Michael found his father reading in the study.

"I'm done, Dad."

"Okay. There's a man coming from the hardware store to replace the window."

"Thanks."

"Just a minute," his father said as Michael turned to leave.

"Yes?"

"I'm curious, son. What was that all about? Those books are just words in a row, and they've been in your room for years."

"They're a lot more than words in a row, Dad. Words have meaning and the books were there for a reason. You told me in the hospital that things were going to be different from now on. I had to find out how much different, and there was no use wasting time."

"You were testing me?"

"That was part of it. If you had tried to stop me or let Mother try, I would have left and never looked back. I had to find out where things stood."

"But why burn them? It seems so barbaric. Words can't hurt you."

"You're wrong, Dad. If you believe them, the wrong words can destroy you. I could not allow them to fall into the hands of someone less equipped to handle them than I am."

"I think you're overstating things. I can understand that you are angry, but they were just books."

"Were they? Books deliberately designed to cripple my ability to think? Exactly how do I survive without my mind?"

"Well, I've never read the books but they can't be that bad. Lots of people teach their kids religion. They turn out all right."

"Compared to what?"

"Well if the books are evil, you managed to overcome them."

"Yes I did, and if I owe Mother anything its thanks for being as pure as she is."

"What do you mean?"

"It's easy to recognize an evil presented in such an undiluted form. The difference between her religion and yours is that she actually attempts to practice what the Bible teaches. It's all right there, Dad. You can read it for yourself any time you care to."

"Where does it say that parents should beat their children?"

"You haven't read the Bible, have you?"

"Well, no, but I know it preaches love and brotherhood."

"Oh yes, God loves you, and you must love him and worship him and obey him or he will make you suffer in agony for all eternity. A message of love delivered with a threat isn't a message of love. It's just a threat."

"There are good things in the Bible. What about loving your neighbor as yourself? Civilization would fall apart without that."

"Lots of Christians don't even like their neighbors, Dad, let alone love them."

"That isn't what that means. You have to get along with each other to have a society. It's a basic principle."

"You have it wrong, Dad. What the Bible *implies* in this instance, and says explicitly in many other places, is that love ought to be completely independent of any logical thought process. You must not judge with your mind. I can't think of a concept more evil than that."

"Michael, I think you have let your hatred for Mother cloud *your* judgment. You speak as though all Christians are evil."

"Not at all. Most people who call themselves Christians are definitely *not* evil. But almost none actually do consistently what the Bible says they ought to. What a horror the world would be if they did."

Dan laughed. "I know a lot of Christians who would be deeply offended by that remark," he said, "especially if they knew Edith."

"Maybe they should read the Bible and find out exactly what it says."

14 - THE PRODIGAL SON

In the predawn hours of an early spring morning in 1965 an automobile traveled a solitary course down a narrow back-country road. The road meandered snake-like through the shadowed hills and valleys, passing by turns between dark stands of timber and broad fields, fallow and muddy with melting snow. A waning three-quarter moon hung low in the west, and in its dim light, what remained of the shrinking snowdrifts could just barely be seen under the trees as smudges of dirt-peppered gray on black. On high ground the air was crisp and clear, but in the low spots a heavy mist covered the earth with a ghostly white blanket that rose several feet into the air. The car faded in and out of the fog, at times even the headlights disappearing as it made its slow traverse through the silent countryside.

The driver had no destination in mind. He rode slouched in the seat, guiding the car with an indifferent disregard for the attention the job demanded. His right wrist rested idly on top of the steering wheel. His left arm hung limp out the open car window. The driver's eyes were wide open, but his mind barely registered the twists and turns of the road. His focus was not on where he was going, but on what lay behind.

Danny Long remembered every detail. For the past several hours the events in the alley had been replaying in his mind over and over again: the gun bucking in his hand each time he pulled the trigger, the splattering blood and flesh, the groans of agony, the muted thud of bodies hitting the ground. But most of all he remembered the eyes, first staring up at him, filled with fear and pain and helpless hatred, and then staring at nothing.

He recalled the aftermath, getting into his car and leaving the city, roaring down the highway as though trying to outrun the devil that made him do it. He had been shocked at first by his own gristly handiwork, shocked by the knowledge that he was capable of doing it, but the shock was fading.

He suddenly realized the cigarette butt hanging from his mouth was dead, long ago burned down to the filter. He flipped the butt out the window in disgust. "Jesus Christ, get a grip man! They deserved it," he said aloud as he straightened in the seat. It was true, he thought, they *did* deserve it. If there were three human beings who deserved to die, they were Al, Joe and Axel, and he was a pathetic piece of crap for not seeing that from the beginning. So he killed them. So what? They needed killing. It wasn't murder, it was a public service. People ought to thank him. People ought to send him flowers and name their kids after him. People ought to build monuments to him.

He considered the thought for a moment and then smirked in self-contempt. God how he hated pretense. Heroes were for fools and children. He killed the Baker boys because the bastards asked for it and he wanted them dead. He didn't have to justify himself. He was nobody's hero and liked it. He was a man who took care of business, a strong man, strong enough to kill when the occasion demanded it.

The road looked familiar, and it dawned on Danny that he knew where he was. If he doubled back and turned east at the last intersection, he'd be in Mansfield in less than an hour. He downshifted and slowed to turn the coupe around. There was a moment's hesitation as the thought crossed his mind that maybe he should just keep going. No, that was stupid! Nobody knew what he did. If he kept his cool, everything would turn out fine. He completed the turn and headed home.

It was just after dawn when the coupe rumbled up the drive and into the yard. Danny noticed with surprise that his father's car was parked in front of the garage. He felt a flash of anger. Damn it! A day late and ten grand short. If his dad had been here for him he wouldn't have had to kill anybody.

The anger evaporated. But then he wouldn't know how much he liked the solid feel of the gun in his hand, the intense awareness of power that came with the liberating knowledge that he had the courage to use it. If his dad had been here, Danny might never have known any of that.

He twisted the ignition key and the engine died.

There was a light on in the kitchen. Michael was up and making his breakfast.

"Well, well. Look whose home."

Michael turned to face his brother. "Hello, Danny. How have you been?"

"What did they feed you in North Dakota. You look like you're about a foot taller."

"I've grown some."

"Don't be modest, Junior. You've grown a lot. What's for breakfast?"

"Whatever you want to make, Danny." Michael gestured with his spatula toward the cupboard.

"What the hell do you mean by that?" Danny asked angrily.

Slightly bewildered by his brother's aggressiveness, Michael gave Danny a questioning look. "What did you think I meant? What's the matter, did you forget how to cook?"

"There's nothing the matter. Not one damn thing." It was *true*. Danny felt fantastic, powerful, dangerous. He felt like nothing could stand in his way.

"You need to learn something, boy, and it might as well be right now." He walked toward Michael, pointing his finger. "I used to let you get away with a lot, but that's all over now." He poked Michael's chest with his finger for emphasis.

"Stop that. It hurts when you do that."

"Oh, it hurts? I'm soooo sorry." Danny deliberately poked harder.

"Damn it, Danny, stop it!" Michael pushed Danny's hand away.

"Or what?"

"Or I'll stop you."

"You threatening me, boy? I used to let you mouth off to me because you were little and stupid. But you're not so little anymore, and just being stupid isn't going to protect you." The finger was again poking Michael's chest.

Michael slapped Danny's hand aside and intentionally stepped closer. "I don't need protection, and you're in no position to question

181

my intelligence. It's true that you're stronger than I am. But that gives you an advantage only if I don't know you're coming. I always know when you're coming, Danny."

"What the hell is that supposed to mean?"

"Think about it. Think real hard. You might get lucky and figure it out."

"Why you…" Danny grabbed for Michael's neck but Michael ducked under his brother's grasp, and using the handle of his spatula like a spear, drove it hard into Danny's solar plexus.

The blow didn't finish Danny, but it made the fight even.

From his bedroom on the second floor Dan heard the commotion and rushed downstairs to find his sons battling on the kitchen floor. "Hey, what is going on here?" he shouted. He waded into the fray and pulled Danny off by grabbing his hair and pulling until he had no choice but to let go of Michael or lose his hair. Dan dragged his son to his feet while still gripping his hair, and then shoved him backward over a chair.

Dan turned back to Michael. "Are you all right, son?"

"I'm fine, Dad."

"You're sure?"

"Yes, I'm fine." Michael snapped. "I was doing just fine a minute ago, and I'm fine now."

Dan glared at Danny. "What the hell got into you? Michael just came home from the hospital, and now he has to fight you?"

"The little shit wouldn't get into trouble if he learned some respect."

"That'll be enough!" Dan said furiously.

"So you're taking *his* side now?"

"Yes, if Michael needs me on his side that's where I'll be. I've let you get away with murder far too long, Danny. It has to stop."

"A little late for that."

"What?"

"Never mind, I don't need you telling me what to do. In fact I don't need you at all."

"Okay," Dan agreed. "When do you plan to move out?"

"What?"

"If you don't need me then I assume you have a job and you're ready to move out of the house and begin to make a living on your own."

"Oh, I get it. One son at a time, huh? Michael's home, and now it's time for me to get the boot."

"Not at all, Danny. There's is plenty of room in this house for both of you. It's a big house. But you just said you didn't need me, so I naturally assumed you were going out on your own. Of course you're welcome to stay, as long as you keep in mind who pays your bills and act accordingly."

"What's that supposed to mean?"

"The first thing it means is that you are going to treat your brother with respect."

"What about him? I'm the one who isn't getting respect!"

"You should have known better than to attack someone who is recovering from serious injuries."

"How do you know I started it?"

"I don't think you've ever been in a fight you didn't start, boy. Now, I think you owe your brother an apology."

"You go to hell!"

Danny whirled, then stalked out of the kitchen and down the hallway toward the front door. He was tired and wanted to go to bed but he couldn't stay now, not after the way his father had disrespected him. He strode to his car, got in and slammed the door. Who the hell was his dad to try and make him apologize?

The coupe roared to life and Danny jammed it in reverse and dropped the clutch. The tires smoked as he backed off the driveway and onto the manicured lawn. He hit the brakes and locked the tires. The coupe was still sliding backward over the grass when he ground the transmission into first gear and dropped the clutch again. The rear wheels churned a pair of furrows that led back to the brick paving and turned into a long set of black tire marks as Danny gunned the coupe down the drive and turned onto the highway. He knew what he was going to do. He was going to get Rachel and go somewhere private. He didn't have to worry about keeping Rachel's respect and admiration. All he had to do was show up and look handsome.

As he turned off the highway toward Rachel's house, Danny was going too fast and almost missed the corner completely. Luckily on Saturday morning there wasn't much traffic. The coupe was nearly in the opposite ditch when it straightened out. He would have ploughed into anything coming in the other direction. He swerved back into the proper lane and hit the accelerator, speeding down the road until he reached the entrance to the parking lot of a small white church. At the last second he slammed on the brakes and turned into the parsonage driveway, sliding to a halt less than a foot from the garage door.

Danny laid on the horn. Rachel didn't know he was coming so he had to let her know he was here.

In the church study, Reverend Pratt looked up from his work. "What is that infernal racket?" He needed peace and quiet when composing his Sunday sermon. He got up to investigate.

In the parsonage Rachel and her mother were eating breakfast. Rachel knew the sound of Danny's car horn. "Goodness, I wonder what he's doing here at this hour," she said.

"Who?" demanded Mrs. Pratt.

"Danny."

"That ruffian?" Alice Pratt spoke angrily. "We told you not to see him anymore!"

"I like him, Mom. I like him a lot." Rachel got up from the table.

"Don't you dare go out there child! Your father will take care of this."

Reverend Pratt was already on his way, stomping across the parking lot with every intention of throwing Danny off church property. Inside the house Rachel ignored her mother's warning and went to get her coat.

"Rachel, you come back here!" Mrs. Pratt stood and pushed her chair back angrily. "That boy is just plain bad, and will come to a bad end."

"Mother, how do you know that? Daddy says faith can work miracles. God can change him."

"Then you can see him when God is finished."

Rachel was putting her coat on. "Maybe God is using me to do His work. Did you ever think of that? I have to see him, Mom. I'm sorry, but I just have to."

When he saw the preacher coming, Danny got out of the car. He stood with his elbow resting on the coupe's roof, a cocky smirk on his face.

Pratt arrived in a huff. "What are you doing here, young man?" he demanded.

Danny knew he wasn't welcome at the Pratt house and he reveled in it, going out of his way to annoy the Reverend and Mrs. Pratt at every opportunity. Before answering he reached into his pocket for a cigarette and lit it, casually blowing the smoke upward. Then he leaned back and said, "Hiya, Rev. How they hangin'?"

The Reverend Pratt harbored nothing but hatred in his soul for Danny Long. As far as he was concerned all teenage boys were spawn of the Devil, and Danny Long was among the worst. He suspected Rachel was sleeping with Danny, but he couldn't prove it and he'd already tried everything including temporary physical restraint to keep her from seeing him, but there seemed to be no permanent solution. He was embarrassed and angered by the situation, convinced that people were already talking behind his back, even though there was no evidence at all that this was true.

Rachel opened the front door and ran to the car. "Hi, Danny," she said breathlessly.

Danny gazed at her mildly, his eyes half closed. "Hey there, pretty ones."

Pratt bristled every time he heard Danny say that. He was not so unworldly as to fail to recognize which part of his daughter's anatomy Danny was referring to. The first time he heard it he was aghast that Rachel would allow such unseemly familiarity. It made him even angrier that she seemed to like it when Danny called her that.

"Get back in the house, young lady. I'll deal with…"

Danny pushed himself away from the coupe and looked at the preacher. "You'll deal with what, Pops?"

For the moment Reverend Pratt lost his voice. The preacher was a big man with a powerful booming voice, but he was not by nature a courageous man, and Danny intimidated him. It was one of the reasons he hated the boy.

Danny stared at Pratt for a moment and then turned to Rachel. "Its short notice, but I wanted to see you, Baby. Let's go for a ride."

This was unheard-of behavior for Danny. Usually she had to contact him. But here he was, asking her to go with him on what seemed to be a whim. It was so romantic and exciting. Maybe this was the breakthrough she was hoping for.

"Okay," she nodded.

"No!" The voice that was lost was suddenly found.

Rachel turned to her father. "I'm sorry Daddy. I have to."

"You'll do what I say, girl. Go back inside now."

"No, I'm going with him."

Reverend Pratt started toward his daughter, and Danny stepped between them. "Let her go," he said. "I don't want to have to hurt you. Just let her go. I'll take care of her."

"Are you threatening me?"

"Just a little friendly advice. Don't get in the way. People get hurt when they get in my way."

"Danny!" Rachel was shocked, "Don't talk to him like that. He's my dad."

"Sorry. Poor choice of words. Are you coming or not?"

She answered him by opening the passenger door and getting in. Danny waited until her door closed and she couldn't hear him. Then, smiling contemptuously, he leaned close and spoke. "You gonna do something, sky-pilot, or just stand there with your thumbs up your ass?" He waited briefly for a response. The preacher clenched his fists but said nothing.

"That's what I thought." Danny opened the car door and got in. He rolled down the window and looked up at the preacher, the contemptuous smile still in place. "Don't wait up for us, Rev. We'll be gone all night."

Danny backed rapidly out of the driveway. The tires screeched as he stopped abruptly in the middle of the road and sat still, the coupe's chassis throbbing with the rolling rhythm of the engine's high-performance idle. He shoved the transmission into low gear. Danny grinned to himself. Reverend Pratt hadn't moved. He was still watching from the driveway. Danny looked over at him and offered a mocking salute, index finger to his forehead. Then he gunned the engine twice and dropped the clutch. The coupe roared out of sight in a cloud of tire smoke.

"Why did you come?" Rachel asked.

"Because I was thinking about you."

"What were you thinking?"

He reached over and ran a finger lightly over the inside of her thigh. "I was thinking about how incredibly gorgeous you look naked on white sheets."

She delighted in hearing that kind of talk from him. It was the only tenderness she knew. "Do you want me naked now?" she asked.

"You know it, cupcake. Anytime, anyplace."

"You think you can just waltz in and take me to bed any time you want?"

"You think I can't?"

She laughed. "I know you can."

His eyes hardened with lust. "There's a hotel I know near the river. The manager's a friend of mine. We're going there now."

She answered him by nodding her head yes. She would do anything Danny wanted her to do.

The Reverend Pratt turned and walked toward the house trying to think of what to do, but no thoughts penetrated his anger. Rachel was eighteen and of legal age, but in the eyes of her parents she was still a child, unable to determine God's will for her life without their guidance. Her defiance was intolerable.

"We must pray about this, Alice," Pratt said as he entered the house. "God will tell us what to do."

So they knelt together in the living room, and the Reverend Pratt asked God to give them an answer. When he rose to his feet he felt calmer. Suddenly a thought popped into his head unbidden. There *was* a way to get her back. He would call the police. He couldn't tell them that she left willingly. Legally she could do what she wanted, but if he told them that Danny forced her into his car, the police would have to find her and bring her back. The police would believe him without question. He was a man of God.

Gideon and Alice almost never argued. Alice usually let Gideon make all the important decisions, but there had been times, especially of late and especially when the subject was Rachel, when she aggressively opposed him. This time she was absolutely and adamantly against what her husband planned.

"This is wrong, Gideon," she said. "It is wrong to lie, no matter what the reason. You ought to know that better than anyone."

"What would you have me do, Alice? How are we to deal with this? I have a reputation to uphold, a standing in the community. Don't you see that once our reputation is gone we are finished here? We cannot sit idly by while our own daughter and this…this creature…destroy us. We must fight fire with fire."

"There is a better way, Gideon. Let God help us find a better way. What you plan is immoral and I have no doubt it is also illegal."

"Then tell me what to do."

"Let us pray again."

"There is no more time for prayer. The police must be informed at once or this will not work. I am calling the police and I am going to tell them Danny Long has kidnapped our daughter. We have to get her back here. This has gone far enough."

He picked up the phone and prepared to lie to the police.

15 - WHAT THE HEART KNOWETH NOT

The sixteen days that Dan Long spent at the side of his unconscious son were the most difficult days of his life. In war, he faced death many times without flinching. In a hospital room in North Dakota sitting beside his gravely injured son, death terrified him. Knowing that he was responsible for his son's condition was not the worst of it. The worst was knowing that there was nothing he could do to make it right. The damage was done, and whatever happened now was up to Michael and his doctors.

Against all odds his son survived, but Dan was still just a spectator. He often felt the desire to have the last fourteen years back again, to have another chance at the things he'd done so poorly the first time around. It was a deep regret, a gnawing, persistent wish to wipe out the past and start over. It was a stupid wish, he knew, but he could not let it go. I have cheated us both out of so much, he thought. So much is gone forever. I wonder if there is any future left to be had. I wonder if I have the right to reach for it.

He glanced back at Michael and Megan, walking behind him on the path toward the house. Megan was laughing at something Michael had said, and his son was smiling back at her. Like normal teenagers… but that wasn't right. It wasn't normal for Michael to act so normal after all that had happened. He seems so…happy? Was that the word? It seemed almost ludicrous to apply that term to Michael given the events of the recent past, but it seemed to fit. He looked happy.

The tables have turned, Dan thought. Now I'm the one who needs him, and he doesn't seem to notice that I am here, and I have no right to ask that he notice. The thought was a tearing pain, and Dan embraced it as a just penance, and a tiny payment on a debt that could never be satisfied in full.

Megan was laughing again as the three entered the house. From her reading chair in the sun room Edith heard the laughter and looked up from her Bible. "Who's there?" she demanded.

"Just me and a friend," Michael called. "Go back to your reading."

"Come in here, I want to meet this friend of yours."

"We're busy."

"Michael, I want to meet her," Megan said.

"Yes, bring the child in here. She wants to meet me." Edith's voice was filled with the kind of blustering friendliness she affected when welcoming new members to her church.

Michael turned to Megan. "You don't want to meet my mother."

"Yes I do."

"What for?"

"Come on, I just want to meet her."

Megan took his hand and pulled him toward the sun room door. Michael followed with a reluctance born of a desire not to waste his time. There was no point in listening to Edith's threats and criticisms, but perhaps no harm in letting Megan find out for herself what his mother was about. Michael let Megan pull him forward. Dan continued a few feet down the hall and stopped out of sight on the other side of the sun room door. He could not help smiling to himself. The girl spoke her mind fearlessly, and he had the feeling his wife was not going to enjoy this conversation.

Edith's reading lamp illuminated the Bible in her lap and the floor in front of her. Edith, herself, was mostly in shadows, her face an outline, her eyes two spots of gray that vanished and popped back into existence every time she blinked.

"Step into the light. I want to see you," said Edith as she tilted the lamp upward.

Megan stepped forward into the circle of light. How's this?"

"Well, aren't you just cute as a button," Edith cooed. "Michael wherever did you find her?"

"That's not important."

"Can't you answer a simple question?"

"Mother, what do you want?"

"I just wanted to see your new friend, Michael," her voice took on a whining quality. "I think a mother has the right to know what's going on in her son's life."

"No, you don't have the right, no, she isn't new, and you've seen her long enough." Michael started to turn away, pulling Megan with him.

"What's your name, dear?" Edith asked.

Megan turned back to face her. "Megan Sullivan."

"Megan. What a pretty name. I suppose you think I'm quite an ogre."

"Why?"

"Oh, I imagine Michael has filled you with all sorts of lies about me."

"No, he hasn't done that at all."

"I find that hard to believe, not after all the battles we've had."

"The war is over, Mrs. Long. You lost."

"Don't be so sure of that child. God has a way of making things turn out for the best in the end."

"I know. That's why you lost."

"Megan, this is pointless," said Michael. "Let her believe what she wants."

Megan gazed blandly at Edith's shadowed face. "You really are quite pathetic, you know," she said.

"You find soul-saving pathetic?"

"Did you actually believe beating Michael would save his soul?"

"That is a vicious lie. He was never beaten." Edith declared emphatically.

Megan laughed out loud.

"And you should not believe everything you hear," Edith continued.

"Amen and halleluiah!" Megan intoned sarcastically.

"You are an undisciplined and offensive child," Edith's voice became hard. "It is Michael's willful disobedience and his lack of respect that led to his punishment, things your parents seem to have neglected to teach you, young lady. Disobedience must be punished. Every soul needs saving, and the Lord provides the means required. I did not enjoy punishing my son, but I always do what God commands."

"And you think God wanted you to beat him?"

"I do as God wills. Have you not heard what I said, child?"

"You speak as though you only made Michael stand in a corner for being naughty!"

"Whatever I have done it was in my son's best interests, and God will be my judge, not you."

"Can God even find you? You should open a few windows, let in some light and air. This room is terribly stale."

The last of Edith's calm veneer evaporated. "Do not use that tone with me, young lady," she snapped. "I will have my proper respect!"

"Do you think parents who beat their children deserve respect?"

Edith pushed forward in her chair threateningly. "Get out of here," she said, her voice filled with menace.

"Oh, don't you want to talk anymore?"

"Get out!"

"Are those the sticks you used?" Megan pointed innocently at the sticks propped in the corner behind Edith's chair. "Do they still have Michael's blood on them or have you scrubbed it off?"

Edith's glance shifted quickly toward the sticks standing in the corner and then back to focus on Megan. She planted her feet and rose from the chair like a boxer answering the bell. "Get out of here!" she roared again.

Megan stood her ground, observing the outburst with a look of mild surprise. She spoke to Michael out of the corner of her mouth in a stage-whisper voice. "I don't think she likes me. What should I do now?"

"Whatever you do, don't turn your back," Michael answered dryly.

Edith, who now stood less than five feet from them, looked as if she could not decide whether to scream or attack. Her cheeks were flushed to a dark crimson, her eyes wide with rage.

She's going to have a stroke, Michael thought, either that or explode. He put his hand on Megan's shoulder and guided her out of the room. "Well," he said, "I'm glad you two have finally had a chance to get acquainted. What do you think so far?"

"A little high-strung, I think." Megan looked at Michael. "Seriously, I think she's on the edge of a nervous breakdown."

"Could be," Michael said, his face looking as though he had said, "So, what?"

Dan knew his wife had a temper but he was disturbed by the violence of her reaction to Megan's questions. When he and his wife fought it was as equals. She could not use her physical presence to intimidate him, and she had never tried. This was something new to his direct experience, and it was either a calculated viciousness, or Edith was actually losing control. Either way it was a side of her he had not really believed until Dr. Graham told him of Michael's many old injuries, and seeing it for himself was a revelation.

As Dan followed Michael and Megan into the kitchen, Michael turned to his father with mild annoyance. "Dad, Megan and I are going to find a place to talk in private for awhile."

Dan didn't hear the dismissal. The thought that kept nagging him had returned with renewed urgency. "Michael, how often?" he said.

"What?"

"How often did she beat you?"

"Dad, just stop asking that question. It's too late to worry about it now."

"But..."

"I'm not going to talk about it."

Dan paused, wanting to take the subject further, but knowing Michael would not answer him. "Okay," he said finally, "I'll be in my study if you need me for anything." He turned and walked away.

"Why don't you just tell him?" Megan asked.

"He already knows the answer. He wants me to tell him he's wrong and everything is fine and I'm not going to do that."

"Don't be so sure," Megan said gazing speculatively down the hall. "I think he wants to know the truth. He wants to take the blame for all of it."

"Here's what I think, Megan. The number of times she did it doesn't matter in the least. The fact that she did it even once, and Dad let her get away with it, is enough. That's all the knowledge anyone needs, and Dad knows it."

Megan spoke again as Michael opened the door to the carriage house. "I didn't really have to meet her. I just wanted her to know what I thought of her. I hate what she did to you."

"It's over. Forget it."

"But what she did was horrible!"

"How do you know that? I never said how bad it was."

"From the scars, stupid."

"How do you know about the scars?"

"Remember the time we went swimming last summer and you refused to take off your tee shirt? When it got wet I could see them through the cloth."

"So you knew. Why didn't you mention it before?"

"I told your dad the day after you left."

"You told my dad, but you didn't mention it to me?"

"I knew you didn't want to talk about it, but your dad needed to know. Didn't he say something to you?"

"I think maybe he tried a couple of times. I wasn't interested."

The leather chair in the carriage house by the upstairs window was big enough for both of them. They squeezed into it.

"She's still going to be a problem isn't she?" Megan asked.

"My mother? I don't know and I don't care. I can always leave again."

"Would you really do that?"

"If things went bad, I'd go in a second. But she hasn't been a problem so far."

"You can always come and live with us if you need to."

"Oh, I'm sure your dad would approve of that," Michael said mockingly.

"No, I think he'd really like to have you. He knows you can't help how you feel."

Michael's head jerked toward her. "What's that supposed to mean?" he demanded.

Megan hesitated. She didn't want to sound condescending, but Michael couldn't possibly understand real faith. He'd never been exposed to it.

"I mean your mother. She's such a terrible role-model. No wonder you've rejected God. I think Dad understands that now."

"Is that what you think? You think my mother actually succeeded in beating beliefs into me, just not the ones she intended? He's a poor little victim who just can't help believing what he believes because his mother hit him too hard and addled his brain?"

"No, it's not like that."

"Then what the hell is it?"

"Michael, why are you angry? You've never explained yourself to me, so I took what I thought was a reasonable guess. It seems like a good explanation, and it satisfied Dad."

"I don't give a damn who it satisfied. Your explanation assumes I don't have a mind. It's insulting and obviously untrue. I'm not the first kid who grew up like this. Do you think everyone who gets religion shoved down his throat automatically decides he doesn't believe in God? The world should be full of atheists by now."

"I'm sorry. I didn't mean to insult you."

"Well, you did. Don't do it again."

"All right, then tell me why you believe the way you do."

"I don't *believe* anything, not in the sense you mean it. I observe and reach conclusions from my observations. I believe what I can prove."

"But most people reach different conclusions."

"From observation? I don't think so."

"Of course they do."

"What observations do they make that leads them to believe in God?"

"God is inside them and in the many wonders in the world around them. They feel God in everything."

"Megan, don't be such a child. This isn't a subject that calls for poetic drivel. It is a precise question requiring an exact answer. Does God exist or not, and if he does, how do you know it?"

"Not everybody is as cynical as you are, Michael, and they can see as well as you can. I can see God in everything."

"So now we've gone from feeling to seeing. Do you feel God or see him? Do you observe facts and trace those facts back to the Lord of the Universe, or do you just have a random feeling and stick a convenient label on it? My guess would be that you haven't traced anything back to anything."

"Well, just maybe I'm right and you're wrong."

"All right, convince me."

"How can I convince you? You don't believe in God or the Bible or anything."

"So I have to believe it before I believe it? You've got it backwards, Megan. Facts come first, then the conclusion. It's called *thinking*. You can convince me if you show me convincing evidence for God."

"But God is beyond that kind of evidence."

"How many *kinds* of evidence are there?"

"You can't point to something and say *This* is God. You can't really see God, but you can point to lots of things that can't exist without God."

"Like what?"

"Well, I can point to the wind, and the grass, and the birds in the trees. I can point to the song in my heart, and the love in my soul."

"Yes, those actually are things you can see and experience. They are evidence for air, grass, birds, trees, music and love. But how do you get from that to God?"

"But all of that comes from God."

"Really? Imagine that."

"Don't be sarcastic. Somebody must have made it."

"How do you know that?"

"There has to be a God behind it. It can't have happened by accident."

"What can't have happened?"

"Existence. The world."

"What makes you think a god had to *make* existence, and what does that mean anyway? What is *existence* if it doesn't include what *exists*? Did God not exist before he made existence?"

"But how else could it have gotten here? Somebody had to make it."

"Think about what you're saying, Megan. If you need a God to explain what *is*, how do you explain the God who made it? You're right back in the same place all over again. Is there a Super God to explain God…and a Super-Duper God to explain Super God? Where does it end?"

"But it had to start somewhere. *Somebody* had to make it. I just know it."

"In that case I'm a little confused. Would you please explain the difference between just knowing and total ignorance?"

"I know God's love in my heart. I feel it inside me. That can't be wrong."

"So we've gone from seeing back to feeling again. All right, let's explore this in your terms. There's more to life than love and joy, Megan. When you feel pain and suffering does that come from God too?"

"No, that comes from sin."

"Whose sin?"

"Ours. Everybody's."

"I spent four months in the hospital because I sinned?"

She didn't know how to respond. She guessed where the conversation was going, and she sensed she could give no satisfactory answers.

"Do you want to know what really happened in the rail yard?" Michael asked.

"If you want to tell me."

"Hell yes, I want to tell you. The bastards raped me, Megan. I knew there was evil in the world, my mother is evidence enough for that, but this was beyond anything I could have imagined. I didn't even know what they did to me was physically possible. It was a thousand times worse than being beaten, and your loving, benevolent God just sat back and let it happen. Can you explain that?"

This was beyond anything she had guessed. She could think of nothing to say.

"The Bible says that nothing happens without God willing it. Was it God's will, Megan? That's what my mother thinks. She thinks being raped and beaten within an inch of my life was God's will. She thinks I deserved it for leaving home. What do you think?"

"Oh Michael, I'm so sorry. I didn't know!"

"Of course you didn't. I didn't tell you. I don't need your sympathy, Megan. I need you to understand. Tell me what you *think*."

"I can't think right now."

"Yes you can. Is your God the same one my mother prays to?"

"Please don't compare me to her." Tears began to well up in her eyes.

197

"You believe the Bible don't you? My mother doesn't make up what the Bible says. She knows exactly what it says from beginning to end. She spends most of her waking hours reading it."

Megan wiped her eyes and faced him, determined to defend her beliefs. "She might know what it says, but she doesn't really understand it."

"And you do? Exactly what validates that conclusion? The Bible actually says what she says it does. Disobedience is a sin, and the wages of sin is death, and a lot of crap even more stupid and vicious than that. Maybe you think God let me off easy."

"But you're a good person, Michael. You left because of what your parents did to you. God wouldn't punish you for that."

"Then why did *He* let it happen?"

"I don't know."

"Maybe you think God was teaching me some other lesson, you know, for my own good. Maybe you think what happened was really good for me but I'm just too dull to understand why."

"No, no, no! It was your parents' sin, not yours."

"Oh, I see now. God let *me* get raped to teach my parents a lesson."

"You're twisting my words."

"I'm sorry, please clarify."

"Sin came into the world long ago, and it wasn't God's fault. Satan made Eve tempt Adam with fruit from the tree of knowledge."

"Oh, *now* I get it. Way back in the Garden of Eden Adam ate an apple from the wrong tree. It was just a matter of timing, a sort of delayed holy justice. Adam isn't around to get raped for the crime of eating an apple, so God decided I should be the one to pay."

"Michael, I don't know. I'm not smart enough to know."

"Are you sure? The answer is staring you in the face."

"I can't even think right now. It must have been horrible for you, Michael. I'm so sorry."

"Forget that. Why did God let it happen?"

"Satan made it happen."

"So Satan is in charge, not God?"

"I can't answer you the way you want to be answered. I don't understand why God does what he does."

"Of course you don't. Your God makes no sense, and the only possible answer doesn't fit your beliefs. But it did happen. That's a fact, not a feeling, and it proves beyond all doubt that your God is a lie."

"Things happen all the time we can't explain. That doesn't mean God doesn't exist."

"You mean things happen that *you* can't explain given your belief in God. Come on, Megan, for the sake of what you know be honest about what you don't. I think you've figured out that what happened to me was *in fact* not good for me or punishment for my sins or any other silly explanation. You are *not* a stupid person. Do you or do you not agree that what happened to me was evil?"

"Yes, yes, it was evil! I'm sure of that to the very bottom of my soul!"

"Then tell me why your God let it happen. Does he run things around here or not?"

"I don't have an answer."

"You haven't tried to find one."

"But I feel God inside me sometimes. Isn't that evidence?"

"You mean you feel something that somebody told you is God."

"No. It has to be more than that."

"What?"

"I don't know."

"Of course you don't. You can't *know* anything without evidence. You can only *pretend* to know."

"No, it's more than that."

"Then name it."

"Faith. I have faith."

"And you hold onto your faith in the face of facts that directly contradict it? We have a number of more accurate terms for that. "Dishonesty" is one that comes to mind."

"No, it's not dishonest. It just means I don't have all the answers."

"And you'll find the answers by refusing to observe the facts and draw logical conclusions from them?"

"But I'm not smart enough to understand why God does the things he does. All I have is faith. It's all anyone has."

"You mean that's all you have if you refuse to think."

"You can't expect me to understand everything."

"How are you going to understand *anything* if you don't think?"

"And if I do, I'm automatically going to agree with you?"

Michael laughed. "We can talk about that after you start *thinking* about it."

"What does this mean for us, Michael? What if I never accept what you're saying?"

"Then you don't accept it."

"Will we still be friends?"

"You're going to have to answer that question for yourself. You are wrong about this, Megan. Terribly wrong. But I hope you never make a decision about the facts based on whether or not we'll be friends afterward. That's dishonest too."

"How can you say that all that has happened to you doesn't affect how you think about things?"

"It depends on how you mean that. Have my experiences informed my conclusions? Of course they have. How else do we gain direct knowledge?"

"Well, I think your experiences have been so bad that you've reached the wrong conclusion."

"You mean you *feel* I've reached the wrong conclusion."

"Yes, and I know you're wrong. I know the love of God in my heart. I wish I could show you how that feels."

"Learn to recognize the difference between thinking and feeling, Megan. Until then, don't presume to judge my conclusions."

"I said I was sorry. What do you want from me?"

"What I really want is for you to understand what an awful mistake you've made."

"But you can't blame God for what happened to you."

"I don't. There is no God."

She was honestly afraid for him. She believed that God and the prospect of eternal life and the end to all suffering gave life on earth its meaning, and she could not imagine an alternative. She thought she understood him. He had suffered so much injustice, no wonder he was lost. She wanted to take back what she said, not because she agreed with him, but because what she said raised a barrier between them, and she wanted no barriers. She wanted to comfort him, but she knew he would refuse to be comforted. She knew he would tell her that no comfort was possible, and that none was necessary.

"Michael, what's going to happen to you?" she asked.

"I'm going to live my life and gain all the happiness I can from it," he replied seriously. "I'm going to concentrate on where I'm going, and not on where I've been, and after awhile my mother and the rail yard will be so far in the past they won't matter anymore."

16 - THE JUST AND THE UNJUST

From long experience Detective Anderson could tell Joey Lonneman knew something about the Baker murders. It wasn't what he said, but how he reacted physically to the questions he was being asked. To a student of body language as adept as Anderson, it was clear that Lonneman knew who did the killings, and that he was afraid to talk about it. Anderson did not suspect that Joey had anything to do with the murders. This nervous little twitch was not capable of killing anyone. But Anderson was convinced Lonneman had seen or heard something that would help the investigation, and he was determined to drag it out of him.

When Boyd and his partner found out that Joey lived in an apartment overlooking the crime scene they immediately began to look for him. Unfortunately for Joey, they found him just after he had robbed a laundromat cigarette machine of 33 dollars in change. It was a small-time charge, but enough to make a small-time crook like Joey sweat. When they told him they would drop the charge if he talked about the Baker murders he began to sweat a lot more. In Joey's world, talking could get you killed. He'd seen it happen, and he didn't want it to happen to him.

"Come on detective," said Joey. "You've asked that question at least ten times already. I told you I didn't hear nuthin' an' I don't know nuthin.' How many times I gotta tell you that?"

For the last fifteen minutes Joey's responses had taken on a whining quality that was beginning to get on Anderson's nerves. "When I asked that question the first time you said you didn't *see* anything," said Anderson. "What were you looking at that you didn't see?"

"Nuthin'. I didn't see nuthin' neither."

"You're lying to me, Joey."

"No it's the truth, detective. Until you told me about it I didn't even know the Baker's were shot."

"Who said anything about a shooting? I didn't tell you they were shot. I said they were dead."

"How else could they get it?"

"They could have been stabbed, Joey. They could have been run over by a truck. They could have fallen off a log and broke their necks. What makes you think they were shot?"

"I don't know. I don't know nuthin'."

"You know, I'm sick of hearing that Lonneman. I think I'm going put you in jail and let you cool off for a couple of days."

"You can't do that. Charge me, or let me go!"

"Oh, I'll let you go all right, right after I put out the word on the street that you're a snitch. What do you think will happen next, Joey?"

"You can't do that!"

"If you don't come clean with me that's exactly what I'm going to do."

"All right, all right! What if I pointed you in the right direction?"

"I want a name, Joey."

"I don't have no name."

"That's too bad, because that's your only way out. Give me his name!"

"I can't give you what I don't have."

Anderson got up and went to the door. "Hanson," he called. "Get in here and get this piece of garbage out of my sight."

"I can't give you what I don't have," Joey whined again.

Anderson was turning away. "I don't care anymore, Joey. I'm going to spread the word that you're a snitch and then I'm cutting you loose."

"No, wait!" Joey cried. "I think I might remember something."

"Well, good for you Joey. Is it a name?"

"If I tell you, you gotta protect me."

"Just give me a name, Joey."

"Danny Long. I think his name is Danny Long. He's a punk from out of town that's been hangin' around with them. The Baker boys, I mean. I saw him shoot 'em. Saw it plain as day from my window."

"When?"

"Friday. Maybe two o'clock in the afternoon."

"What sort of weapon did he use?"

"Short barrel revolver. .38 I think. I was too far away to see for sure."

"All right, Joey. I think you told the truth this time."

"So you're not going to tell anybody it was me who told you?"

"No, your secret is safe with me, Joey, at least until the next time I need a rat."

Anderson opened the door to the interrogation room and stepped outside. "Hanson, will you find Mr. Lonneman here a nice warm cell to rest in? He's going to be our star witness, and we don't want anything bad to happen to him until after he testifies."

Lonneman's head jerked around. "Wait! I gotta testify?"

"Of course you *gotta* testify. What the hell did you think?" Anderson turned away. "Where's Boyd?"

"Right here, detective," Boyd was sitting at a small desk in one corner of the room banging out an arrest report one letter at a time.

"Boyd, I want you to find out everything you can about a kid named Danny Long. He's probably from out of town. Lonneman fingered him for the Baker killings."

"I'm on it," said Boyd.

*   *   *

Harvey Reed knew there was something wrong with the story, but he was not prepared to call Reverend Pratt a liar without evidence. Danny Long kidnapping Rachel Pratt seemed wrong. It just didn't fit the picture. Danny was a liar, a troublemaker, and an emotional loose cannon, but a kidnaper? Reed didn't think so, not unless he'd very recently crossed over to truly criminal behavior. That was possible, he supposed, maybe even likely given the right circumstances, but what was the motive? It was well known that

Danny and Rachel were an item, yet Pratt claimed the boy forced Rachel into his car when she refused to go with him. Why? Why had she refused and why had he forced her?

But what really bothered him was the way the Pratt's reacted when he questioned them. Mrs. Pratt claimed there was no previous history of Danny being violent with Rachel, but when she said it, her husband became visibly angry and immediately contradicted her. Mrs. Pratt had glanced at her husband and then down at her feet for a moment. After that Reverend Pratt did all the talking.

Reed was going to issue the APB. They had to track the boy down and find out what was going on, despite his misgivings. The kid had a history of running from the law, but it shouldn't take long to find him. That jacked-up, muscle-bound coupe would be about as difficult to spot as an elephant in an empty parking lot.

He rose to go to the radio room just as his phone rang. He picked it up and answered, "Reed."

"Reed, this is Detective Sergeant Anderson, Minneapolis police. You know a kid named Danny Long?"

*   *   *

Danny barreled through the little burg of Harrelson, Minnesota like it was open country. He knew the chance that the town's single cop would be around at this hour was pretty slim. Danny could have robbed the city bank and got away with it, except the bank didn't open until ten a.m. on Saturdays.

From Rachel's house this was the fastest way to Minneapolis and he was in a bit of a rush to get where he was going. As he reached the main highway he slowed just enough to glance quickly in both directions, blew through the stop sign and turned left. The tires squealed in protest, but Rachel said nothing. She was used to Danny driving like a maniac. The car accelerated rapidly toward the east edge of town, and Rachel sat back in the seat to wait out what she knew was going to be a very quick trip into the city.

Her mind could not let go of the fact that Danny came to her. It was so much out of character that it had to be a sign. She was sure of it.

She wanted so badly for him to love her. She knew the Bible said sex was a sin outside of marriage, and she wanted to be a good and virtuous woman, but she also wanted Danny. God only knew how much she needed him, and she hoped the Lord would forgive her for using the only means she knew to keep him.

Spontaneously she reached out to touch him on the shoulder.

"What?" he said, glancing out of the corner of his eye.

"I love you," she answered, her hand caressing his arm.

Danny smiled broadly. The smile held a mixture of lust and contempt, and as usual Rachel misread it completely. She knew he liked to be with her and love wasn't something that happened overnight, at least not always. Love could grow. It could start small and grow into something much bigger, something greater than what it was in the beginning. Love was growing inside Danny. She was sure of it. Just like his baby was growing inside her.

"Danny, let's get married," she said impulsively.

He looked at her incredulously. "What?"

"Let's get married," she repeated.

"Why?"

"Well, we love each other don't we? That's what people do when they're in love."

"What makes you think I love you?"

"I know you love me."

"Jeez girl, get a grip on yourself."

"If you don't love me, why are we together?"

"Because you always give me what I want."

She knew what he meant. "That can't be the only reason," she said.

"Why not? You're the hottest piece of ass I know."

"Don't say that!"

"Rachel, I meant it as a complement, but I don't love you, and we're not going to get married. Not ever."

"*Not ever* is a long time."

"Exactly. So forget it."

She removed her hand from his arm and looked out the side window. "You don't know your own heart," she said.

"This is crazy." He hated it when she got this way.

"I *know* you love me."

"Really? How? How do you know it?"

"I just know it."

Danny snorted contemptuously. "Think with your brain, sugar tits, not your hormones."

She fell silent for a moment, then she said, "You can't make me believe you feel nothing for me. I know better."

"Oh, I feel something all right, right between my legs."

"Why are you being so crude?"

"Why are you being so stupid?"

"You love me."

"You are really beginning to piss me off."

"If it isn't love, what is it?"

"Haven't you been listening to me?"

"You love me. You have to love me. It's what God wants."

"Of all the stupid… Rachel, I itch and you scratch. You scratch real good. If you want to call that love, be my guest."

"You don't mean that. I don't believe you. I know you love me." She said it as though she still believed it, but her stiff posture betrayed a hurt and an uncertainty she couldn't hide. "God wants us to be together. I know He wants it. Everything happens for a reason."

"Rachel, you are so right. If I stopped the car and slapped your ears off, would you have the brains to figure out the reason I did it, or would I be wasting my time?"

"Don't talk like that."

"Then shut the hell up!"

She did what he told her to, still unwilling to let herself believe him but afraid of his anger.

He gripped the steering wheel and drove faster.

They were cruising at nearly ninety mph down a long, straight stretch of road when they heard the siren. Rachel sat up straight in her seat. "What's that?" she asked.

"Shit. What do you think it is?" Danny glanced at the rear-view mirror. The cop was about a quarter-mile behind them and closing. It might just be a speed trap, but what if the cops suspected. What if they had some shit piece of evidence that he killed the Baker boys? Danny mashed the accelerator to the floor, and the car leaped forward. Rachel grabbed the seat cushion reflexively. "What are you doing? Aren't you going to stop?"

"What fun would that be?"

"But it's the police!"

"Yeah, it's the police. If they get close enough they can kiss my ass."

Danny glanced at the speedometer needle as it passed one hundred and kept going. He knew a dirt road that cut across to another highway about ten miles up, but he wanted more distance between himself and the cop before he got there. The tachometer wound out to the red line, and then beyond it. The car swayed dangerously. He could feel the vibrations of the road and the power of the engine pulsing through his grip on the steering wheel. The feeling was exhilarating. He wanted more speed. He pushed down harder on the accelerator, trying with all his might to shove it right through the floorboards, but the coupe had nothing more to give. The cop was farther back now but still in sight.

"Danny please! Stop the car and let me out. You're scaring me!" Rachel had to shout to be heard over the noise of the wind and the roaring engine.

"No time," he shouted back.

"You're going to kill us!"

"Shut up." He glanced up at the rear-view mirror again. The cop was almost too far back to see now. The road led into a stand of pine trees, and a series of sharp curves followed. They were almost to the turn-off. He was going to ditch the cop right here! The trees would mask the turn, and the fool would never know he was chasing down an empty highway. Danny glanced in the mirror again and put the coupe into a sideways drift around the last curve. They were almost home free.

He saw the roadblock and heard Rachel's scream simultaneously. A phalanx of police cars sealed off the road ahead. The turn was less than two-hundred yards away, but he was never going to make it. Danny slammed on the brakes and the tires locked. The car was going too fast. They were going to hit.

The police cars were parked in a shallow "V", the formation blocking the road from ditch to ditch except for a small opening on the right shoulder. The opening looked too small to get through, but Danny took his foot off the brake and steered for it anyway. He would just have to make a bigger hole.

His foot was back on the gas, the car accelerating again. Now, if he could just get straight and hit the opening... Get it straight! The coupe was only slightly out of line when he hit the hole. The rear bumper caught the inside police cruiser and something ripped loose as they went by. The coupe skidded and slammed against the outside patrol car. The second impact pushed the outside cruiser a few inches toward the ditch, the coupe scrapped through the opening, and he was free on the other side. Yes!

Danny's elation lasted only for a split second. When he tried to pull back onto the highway, the car wouldn't come out of the ditch. He fought desperately for control as the rear end slid deeper and deeper. The car was almost sideways, bucking wildly over the uneven ground. If the wheels caught, he'd flip before he knew what happened. He had to get it out of there! Ease off on the gas a little. Steer into it. Steer into it. Not too far! Suddenly the right rear wheel caught on a rock, and the left side of the car came off the ground. Danny jerked the steering wheel to the right, the wheels crashed down hard, and the car popped back onto the highway. No time to wonder how he got out of that. Get on the gas and go!

The coupe streaked down the road, accelerating rapidly. He heard sirens again. The cops were after him like a pack of wolves, but the coupe was already a half-mile in front and running hard. The undercarriage rattled and shook as though the car was about to come apart and something was dragging on the road, but the roar of the engine still rang hot and sweet in Danny's ears. They'd never catch him. The coupe was just too goddamn fast!

"Danny you have to stop!"

He'd forgotten Rachel was still in the seat beside him. "No." he snapped.

"You have to!"

"Shut up."

The speedometer needle was dancing on the peg above the one-twenty mark. The rattle was louder and the shaking more pronounced, but the cops were falling back. He was getting away. No way in hell he was going to stop now.

"I don't want to die, Danny. Stop the car!"

"Not fucking likely."

"Danny, I'm pregnant. You have to stop!"

"What?"

"I'm going to have your baby."

"For Christ's sake, so what?"

"It's our baby! You're putting our baby in danger."

"Jesus Christ. You sound like a fucking soap opera."

"It's *your* baby!"

"It's *your* problem. Now shut up."

They came to another series of sharp curves, and the cops inched closer. Danny could still outrun them on the straight-aways, but he'd lost his advantage on the corners. The car wasn't handling like it should. The road didn't straighten out for another five miles, and the bastards were getting closer. He began to push harder in the corners, trying to stay ahead. Another curve. Danny slid into it, foot on the gas, tires screaming. The rear wheels caught the outside shoulder and he almost lost it. Rachel began to sob and the cops inched closer. Why didn't the bastards just give it up? He had to shake them! A road-block. A goddamn road-block! They had to know what he did. They had to! It didn't make any sense otherwise.

The coupe slid around another curve. For the moment the cops were out of sight. Danny saw an approach and a small dirt path to the left that led off into the trees. He slammed on the brakes and prepared to turn. The car wasn't equipped with seatbelts and Rachel braced herself with one hand on the dash and another on the door. As the car swerved toward the shoulder, her hand inadvertently pushed the latch. It happened in an instant. The door flew open, and she was thrown out by the force of the turn. Her skull hit the pavement with a violent crack, and her body tumbled into the ditch and slammed against a fallen tree.

The coupe completed the turn and slowed for just an instant. Too bad about Rachel, but the cops were all over him. Danny couldn't stop now. He just couldn't. They knew what he did and he had to get away. Foot back on the gas, he reached over and pulled the door shut as the coupe rocketed over a hill and disappeared into the trees.

Mercifully the first impact with the pavement knocked Rachel unconscious. She didn't feel her bones breaking, and her skin scrapping off, and her insides turning to mush as her body careened across the pavement and into the ditch. She was dead before she hit the tree.

Danny's turn didn't fool the cops. A set of black tire marks and the battered, lifeless body of Rachel Pratt marked the spot decisively. But they couldn't find Danny. Somewhere in the maze of woods and lakes and back country roads he gave them the slip.

17 - CRISIS OF FAITH

Edith Long sometimes regretted her anger, but rarely tried to suppress it anymore. There were so many pressures, so many things that did not go her way, so many injustices in her life, so much to be angry about. Even the act of reading her Bible, once a source serenity and peace, now enflamed her heart with rage. It was so obvious that the Bible spoke the Truth. How could they be so stupid as to deny it?

She wanted to make them see, and they refused to see. She wanted to force them to do God's bidding, but she could not force anyone. It was not only their refusal that made her angry. It was her weakness, and the self-loathing that came with it.

Several times in her youth, in those moments when the feeling of weakness was especially strong, she had considered suicide. She was thinking about killing herself on that fateful afternoon eight years ago when Christ entered her life. But God had cleansed the darkness from her soul and for a long time she was sure that this terrible demon was gone forever. God empowered her. God made her strong! But she no longer felt His presence.

Despite everything she tried, evil still grew in the hearts of those around her and she could not stop it. Her greatest disappointment was in her son. Michael was to be an example of Godliness. She had dedicated his life to The Lord, and God had promised that her wish would be fulfilled. Yet The Devil maintained an unshakable grip on his heart. She knew the fault for that lay somewhere in her own soul. That was the only place such a failure could reside.

She remembered the sermon on her first day in her new church, and how profoundly it affected her. She remembered the feeling of peace that washed over her soul as Pastor Pratt read from the book of Isaiah, "though your sins be as scarlet, they shall be as white as snow." These were the words that set the course for the rest of her life, and she still believed them. She had to believe them. Without those words her conversion was meaningless, and so was her faith. She fervently wished she could recapture the sense of unblemished joy she felt when she heard the words for the first time.

Edith knew that faith was one requirement for eternal life. But faith was nothing if not lived fully. Was she *living* her faith? Was she really doing God's will?

She remembered being told once that finding Christ meant she would never have to fear death again. She had believed it then. She did not believe it any longer. Often she awakened late at night from dreams filled with the horrors of hell-fire, and the awful certainty that God knew the thoughts she kept hidden in her heart, and she felt terror as only the true believer can feel it. In a few rare moments of clarity she saw, as clearly as she permitted herself to see anything, the source of that terror. God had provided her with an excuse, not a reason to live. She was not really the selfless sycophant she claimed to be, mindlessly awaiting the Lord's pleasure to give her life purpose. No human being could be and remain human in any sense that held meaning. There had to be an actual personal motive to go on living, and Edith's motive was not holy.

In order to feel secure, she needed to control the thoughts and actions of others, but she controlled nothing. She took this not as a sign that her faith had failed, but that she had failed her faith. She did not know how she had failed, but she knew this terrible fear was part of her punishment.

The pressures of uncertainty seemed to grow with each passing day, and gradually Edith began to yearn once again for her life to be over. She did not wish for the temporary reprieve of the New Testament death followed by the Second Coming and Final Judgment. She yearned to avoid judgment. She yearned for the blessed peace of eternal non-existence. She did not want to let herself think of it, it was a mortal sin to want it, and her faith told her there was no permanent escape, but she could not help wishing for it anyway.

Edith's eyes stared sightlessly at the wall opposite her chair. She was thinking it was time to pray again. She had always made it her practice to pray for her family daily, but now she prayed for herself, for enlightenment, for relief from the terrible self-doubt that dominated her waking hours. She placed the Bible on the reading stand, fell to her knees, and folded her hands.

"Oh, Lord, I am thy unworthy servant," she began. "Please tell me what to do. The task you have set before me is so difficult and I am helpless before it. I fear I have failed in my mission. Michael has hardened his heart against me. I cannot reach him, my precious Lord. I know I have done something wrong but I do not know what it is. Please give me a sign. I have followed your Holy Word as best I knew how yet I have failed. I am only a woman. Please forgive me, Lord. Without Your guidance I am lost. Your precious Will be done. Amen."

Her eyes remained closed for a long moment, awaiting some inner sign of blessing and support. Sometimes she felt better after praying, but today there was nothing. She rose despondently from her knees and sat down again. Her eyes strayed to the Bible lying on the stand beside her. She took it up and opened it. The pages fell apart to the book of Isaiah and she found herself reading: "Behold, the day of the Lord cometh, cruel both with wrath and fierce anger, to lay the land desolate: and he shall destroy the sinners thereof out of it." Was this a message meant for her? Was it a warning of her own destruction, a call to arms, or merely the meaningless random turn of a page? There was a time when answers to questions like these came easily for her. Now she could not decide.

A loud, demanding knock on the front door interrupted her reverie. She rose to her feet wondering who it could be. The knock came again, louder and more incessant. "Open up in there, this is the police," a voice demanded.

Edith walked quickly to the front door and opened it. There were four policemen standing on the porch with weapons drawn. Several more were scattered about the buildings and grounds. A plainclothes detective stood with his weapon in one hand and his badge in the other. "What is going on here," said Edith.

"Edith Long?" said the detective.

"Yes."

"I'm detective Harvey Reed, Mansfield police. We have a warrant for the arrest of your stepson, Danny. Please step aside."

"But he isn't here."

"We'll be the judge of that, ma'am. Please step aside. We have a warrant to search the premises."

Edith numbly stepped away from the door and allowed the police to enter as Dan walked into the hallway. "What is the meaning of this, detective?" he said angrily. "You can't just come barging into a man's home any time you feel like it."

"Mr. Long," said Reed, "we have a warrant for Danny's arrest."

"On what charge?"

"Kidnapping and murder."

"What? That can't be true!"

"I'm afraid it is Mr. Long. Where is Danny?"

"I have no idea. He left the house early this morning. He hasn't been back since. Who is he supposed to have killed?"

"Three men in Minneapolis yesterday. Rachel Pratt this morning."

"Ridiculous!" Dan's exclamation of disbelief was accompanied by Edith's gasp at Rachel's name.

"Do either of you know anything about this?" Reed asked.

"No, of course not," Dan responded, "and I find this very hard to believe. Rachel is Danny's girlfriend."

"*Was* his girlfriend," Reed corrected. "I have a job to do, Dan. Let me do it."

"Yes, yes, I'll cooperate of course, but you are wrong about this. You have to be. It doesn't make any sense."

"The courts will determine what makes sense," said Reed. "Would you and Mrs. Long please go into the living room and sit down while we conduct our search? Simpson, go with them."

"So we are to be guarded while you turn my house upside down?"

"Its procedure, Mr. Long. Can't be helped," Reed said shortly. "Now tell me who else is on the premises. I don't want anyone hurt unnecessarily."

Dan's eyes widened. "Michael and his friend are around here somewhere. If you hurt either one of them I will personally see your end, detective."

"They won't be harmed," said Reed, ignoring the threat. A few minutes later Michael and Megan were escorted into the living room by a policeman.

"What's going on, Dad?" asked Michael.

"They want Danny. They say he's killed some people, but I don't believe it. I just don't believe it." The words belied the thought running through his mind. God! Would Danny do something this stupid? He picked up the phone to call his lawyer.

Edith sat in a chair across the room while Dan made his call and then spoke as he hung up the receiver. "Well, are you satisfied?" she asked.

"What are you talking about?"

"It should be clear even to you, Daniel. This is what you have brought your son to. You once accused me of turning Michael into a criminal. Well, Danny is a murderer and the guilt for that belongs to you. I have attempted to bring God into this family. I have tried to serve as a righteous example and you have fought me every step of the way. This is what you get for it."

Dan stared at Edith for a long moment and then said, "You know Edith, maybe you're right."

"What?" She could not believe he was admitting it.

"Yes, I think you're right. Everything that has happened is my fault. When Danny began to make some very bad choices I should have nipped it in the bud. I should have let him pay for his mistakes. Instead I ignored them or covered them up. When Danny told me what you were doing to Michael I should have believed him. I should have at least investigated. Then I should have divorced you and thrown you out on your worthless ass, or killed you on the spot. Instead, I let it continue. I let you go right on beating him because I wasn't interested enough in my son's welfare to find out what you were doing. I should have believed Danny but I didn't. I should have stood up for Michael but I didn't. When I think of how completely I have failed as a father I wonder if I can ever redeem myself. So you are correct. But we're both guilty, Edith, so let's have the decency to share the blame. We both know Michael has suffered greatly for our sins, but who knows how much Danny has been damaged by living in this house."

"You can't think that I had anything to do with any of this."

"We were supposed to build a family, Edith. We created a perversion instead."

"I have always done what I thought was best with the Lord's guidance."

215

"Shut up, Edith. I am tired of hearing that lie, and I am sick to death of you. I want you out of this house by the end of the month. I am going to end this grotesque marriage once and for all."

"You can't do this to me. God will not permit it!"

"Then let God stop it."

Michael sat still.

"I should have investigated…I stood by and let you go right on beating him…" There was pitiless self-judgment and open contrition in Dan's words. His father fully understood what he had allowed to happen, and in this moment of crisis, Michael realized that he no longer wanted to make his dad pay for mistakes that lay in the past. Dan Long was indeed a changed man. His words and actions over the past several months had proven that beyond doubt.

"This wasn't your fault, Dad." Michael spoke gently.

"All of it was my fault."

"How are you responsible for this? Danny's eighteen. He's old enough to tell the different between right and wrong. He made his own mistakes, and if he's guilty he will pay for them, just as you have paid for yours."

Dan paused, trying to follow Michael's thinking and apply it to this situation. He couldn't do it. "No, Michael, you're wrong. This is *my* fault."

Michael did not respond. There was a sense of profound relief in the knowledge that he could let himself admit that his father was deeply sorry for what he had done, and that he was trying to make amends. There was a sense of sadness that Dan was taking on more blame than he deserved. The emotions expressed themselves in the desire to reach out and ease his father's pain, but now was not the time.

When the police finished, every room in the house had been thoroughly searched and so had every building on the premises. "Here's my card, Dan," said Reed walking into the living room. "I want you to call me if Danny shows up or tries to contact you. The only thing you can do to help him now is turn him in. Any other course will only make it worse."

"All right, detective. If he contacts me I will call you."

Dan followed the police to the front door and closed it after them then returned to the living room and addressed Phil Whitcomb, who had just arrived. "Phil, did your contact at the police department know anything?" he asked.

"It doesn't look good, Dan. They have a witness to three of the killings and a motive for the forth. The girl's father phoned the police at about nine yesterday and said Danny forced her into his car and took off. The police think she knew about the killings and didn't want to go with him. The police put out an APB and set up a roadblock after Danny went through a speed trap doing 90 mph and heading east toward the city. Danny ran and the police chased him into the roadblock but he got through it and escaped somehow. The girl fell out of the car, or was thrown out during the chase."

"Any chance it was somebody else and not Danny?"

"None. Both the police at the roadblock and Reverend Pratt gave a positive identification. The witness to the other shootings is not very solid, so we may have a chance there, but there is no doubt it was Danny at the roadblock."

"So, what do we do now?"

"Hope he turns himself in. Then we'll see."

"This whole thing stinks, Phil. Danny might have run when he was chased, but I can't bring myself to believe the rest of it."

"It isn't going to be easy, Dan. The boy is in deep this time."

"Well, I guess you have your work cut out for you, don't you Phil. Don't make me regret the retainer I've been paying you all these years."

"Dad," said Michael.

Dan was about to show Whitcomb to the door, but stopped when Michael spoke. "What is it, son."

"You need to be very careful right now. I think Danny is dangerous."

"Not to me."

"Just be careful."

"He's my son, Michael. Don't you think I know my own son?"

"I'm telling you that he is capable of hurting you if you don't give him what he wants. I think he's capable of killing."

"Michael, you are completely wrong about this. Danny will not hurt me. I think he will call me, but I will convince him to turn himself in."

"Just be careful, Dad."

217

"Why are you saying this?" Dan's face was attentive, his gaze underlining the obvious and awaiting whatever response Michael might care to give.

"Because it matters to me," said Michael. "Don't give him the chance to hurt you."

Edith Long rose quietly from her seat and left the living room.

"Then let God stop it," her husband had said. The long wait for The Master's signal was over. Her faith was restored. She returned to her chair in the sun room and sat down, picking up her Bible as she did so. She did not open it. There was no need to consult the Holy Scriptures. She would have to choose the correct time but she knew exactly what God wanted her to do. She was conflicted no longer.

She knew her husband hated her, and just as it did for everything else, the Bible told her why. John 15:19 said, "If ye were of the world, the world would love his own: but because ye are not of the world, but I have chosen you out of the world, therefore the world hateth you."

She had once accepted this burden, even as Christ accepted the burden of the Cross, in the knowledge that God saw and would reward her sacrifice with eternal life. But her husband's stubborn refusal to see God's Truth, even as she struggled and sacrificed to help him see, was almost more than a mortal human being could bear. He had threatened divorce many times, but this time she knew he meant it. He dared to deny the Word even in God's Holy Sacrament of marriage. As surely as the sun rose in the east and set in the west, retribution would be swift and sure. God had commanded that she see to it personally.

*   *   *

There was an empty building on the corner of Lowry Avenue and Johnson Street in Northeast Minneapolis. Danny and his friends often used the place to drink and get high, and he remembered the hang-out in his hour of need. The building had no electricity, no heat and no plumbing, but the ground floor was still marginally habitable if one's only desire was shelter.

The light from a street lamp on the corner filtered through

the grimy shards of glass that remained in the frames of broken windows, illuminating a floor littered with trash and rat droppings. Danny sat with his back to the wall in the only corner of the room that wasn't damp, and pondered the events of the past several hours. It was one a.m.. He hadn't slept in thirty six hours, but at the moment he wasn't sleepy.

There was concern and caution, but no real fear in Danny, even now. In spite of all that had happened, his mind still automatically assumed his personal immunity from every consequence. No matter what they knew, the cops were not going to get him. He was too smart to let that happen. He still had wheels, and the gun lay on the floor beside him, loaded and ready. The coupe was gone, ditched in a wooded ravine, and replaced by an old Dodge sedan he'd stolen from a farmer. The Dodge was parked behind a storage shed in the back of the building, safely hidden from the street. He had stripped off a few hundred dollars from the ten grand roll he took back from the Bakers. It was too bulky to carry the whole thing around in his pocket for any length of time. The rest of the money was stuffed in a crack in the building's foundation near the car.

Everything was going to be fine. If he was going to make a getaway and find a place to live in comfort he would need more money, but his dad was good for it. He had no real worries.

The cops were buzzing around town like busy little worker bees. He'd find a phone and make the call to his dad later, when the hive settled down. There was nothing to do now but relax. He yawned and stretched. He really did need to get some sleep. He had a dusty blanket he'd found in the trunk of the Dodge. There was a dirty mattress in the corner. He laid down upon it, wadded up his jacket for a pillow and fell asleep in minutes, secure in the unshakable belief that every box had an exit, and he would find one when needed.

An hour later Danny awakened with a start. *Somebody was in the building.* He could hear footsteps. He picked up the gun and stood, peering into the gloom. Some kind of light was shining through a broken window pane facing the alley. He crept to the window to investigate. Crouching beneath the window sill he slowly raised his head to peer over the edge. The light came from a pair of police cruisers parked in the alley beside the building. They'd found his car!

The sedan's doors were open and seat cushions were scattered on the ground. They were tearing the car apart, looking for evidence. They must know the car was stolen, maybe that *he* had stolen it. This avenue of escape was cut off.

Shit! The money! He rose higher to get a look at the crack in the foundation where he put it. He'd taken the precaution of pushing a rock in after the money so it wouldn't be found. But the place was crawling with cops. He'd never get to it.

"Police! Put your hands up and turn around." Danny froze. He knew he was visible in the light from the alley. The cop could see him but he couldn't see the cop. Suddenly he ducked beneath the window sill and whirled, pumping two wild shots in the direction of the voice. Answering shots rang out. Danny heard the thud of a bullet hitting the wall near his head and the whine of another as it ricocheted away. He was on his feet and running.

He dashed down a long hallway and slammed open the door at the end. There was a large room with several boarded windows to his left. He could see the streetlight shining through the cracks. He darted toward the windows intending to break out of the building, but he tripped on something and hit the floor on his stomach, the gun flying from his hand. He jumped to his feet. *Where was the gun?* It had to be here somewhere. He'd heard it slide away, but it was too dark to see where. It had to be here somewhere! Somebody was coming. He could hear running footsteps. Many footsteps. *God damn it, where was that gun?* He would have to leave it. There wasn't time to look. He had to get away. He ran for the nearest window and leaped. His feet cleared the bottom sill by a foot. His shoulder crashed through the boarding and he fell to the sidewalk. In a heartbeat he was up, searching wildly for the best avenue of escape. A narrow crack between two buildings beckoned from across the street. He dashed for the opening and disappeared.

*   *   *

Dan was sleeping, his head propped on his hands in front of the phone on his desk, but he picked up the receiver before the first ring was over.

"Hello…Danny?"

"Dad?"

"Danny, where are you?"

"Dad, I need help."

"Danny, where are you? Tell me where you are, and I'll come for you."

"I need money, a lot of it. I have to go away for awhile."

"Danny, did you kill those people?"

"What people."

"The three men in Minneapolis, and the girl."

"I don't know about anybody in Minneapolis. I haven't been there in months. What girl?"

"Rachel Pratt."

"What? Hell no! The stupid bitch hit the door lever on a corner and fell out. So she's dead, huh?"

"Yes, she's dead, and you will be charged with killing her."

"Oh for Christ sake, she did it herself. I didn't do anything."

"Danny, her father says you kidnapped her. Is that true?"

"That stupid prick! She got in the car willingly, Dad, I swear. The old bastard tried to stop her but she wanted to go. If the police hadn't chased us she'd be alive. The cops killed her, not me."

"You ran, Danny. If you're innocent, why did you run?"

"Hell, so what if I ran? That doesn't prove anything."

"Danny, I will help you, but you have to do exactly as I say. I want you to tell me where you are, and I will come for you. The police will be with me and…"

"No," Danny interrupted angrily, "not the goddamn cops. I'm not going to spend a minute in jail. Get me the money."

"Danny this is the only chance you have. Turn yourself in, and I will face this with you. You will have jail time but if you come in voluntarily, it will help a lot."

"No."

"Think about what you're doing, son. This is going to ruin your entire life if you don't face it."

"Fuck that shit. I need money, not your stupid advice."

"This isn't stupid. They have a witness in the Minneapolis killings who says it's you, but he's weak. Maybe Phil can negotiate something for you."

"And you want me take a chance on that?"

"You ran from the cops and somebody died, son. You're implicated in other killings. You have to face this."

221

"God damn it! None of this was my fault! If somebody comes at you, you do 'em!"

"What does that mean, "you do 'em?"

"Nothing."

"Nobody made you run, Danny."

"But you don't understand, Dad. There is more to this than you think."

Dan paused. "Danny, is there something else you need to tell me?"

"No it isn't like that. It's just...complicated."

"No son, it's really very simple. If you turn yourself in I will support you all the way. If you decide to run you're on your own."

"You don't mean that."

"I will not finance a fugitive."

"You're serious? You won't give me any money?"

"Dead serious. I will not help you unless you turn yourself in. Now where are you?"

"You can go to hell, you son-of-a-bitch!" The loud click Dan heard was the sound of Danny slamming the receiver into its cradle.

18 - THIRTY PIECES OF SILVER

Danny glanced in the rear-view mirror. The car following him was turning off the road. He breathed a deep sigh and rubbed his hands on the wheel trying to relax his grip. His arms and legs ached almost unbearably from long hours of tension and the pressure inside his head threatened to pop his eyeballs out. It was like this all the time now, like swimming in a clear glass bowl naked, in front of eyes that watched his every move—huge, grim, accusing eyes that followed him wherever he went and never blinked, and never looked away. He needed a gun. He needed money. He needed a cigarette. But more than anything, he needed a place to rest.

The car was a piece of crap, but at least it ran, and there had been no time to be choosy. The area around the abandoned building on Lowry Avenue had been crawling with cops and he was lucky to have gotten away at all. Now every badge in the Midwest was after him, even the FBI. A newspaper somewhere in Iowa called him armed and dangerous. He wasn't armed, and he sure as hell didn't feel dangerous. He was just moving, he had no idea where to. No road was safe, every random stranger a potential enemy with the power to put him in chains if he was recognized.

They almost had him yesterday. Somebody at a rest stop recognized him from the police description and he just barely got away. What little cash he had left was running out of his pockets like water. The gas tank was almost empty. It was always almost empty. The damn car seemed to drink gas even when the engine wasn't running.

A rusty sign at the edge of the road said "Chalmers—pop. 47." He thought maybe this was Nebraska but he couldn't be sure.

He turned off on the first side street he came to at the edge of town and then circled around to park facing the county road that served as the town's main street. He turned off the engine, leaned back against the seat cushion and rubbed his eyes. Suddenly he slammed his hands on the dash and swore bitterly. He was tired of running. Nobody had the right to force him to do anything he didn't want to do. Nobody had the right to take away his freedom and they wouldn't if he had a gun. He wouldn't be running if he had a gun, he'd be coming after them!

He sat for several minutes, trying to calm himself. The business district was less than two blocks long and Danny could see all of it from where he sat. There was a grocery store, a liquor store, a general store, three bars and a gas station that consisted of a tiny office and a shop in back. No cops were in sight and there probably were none. The town was too small to have even a part-time cop.

He had to have gas, even if getting it meant being recognized. Danny started the car and pulled up to the single pump in front of the gas station. He got out and tried to activate it, but it didn't seem to be working. He waited for a few seconds for the attendant to show up, and then walked inside.

The office was tiny and the furnishings very Spartan. There was a little roll-top desk near the bathroom door and a cash register sitting on a small glass counter facing the entrance. The counter display was stocked with several different kinds of candy bars. Danny walked around to the back of the counter and began to poke around, looking for things he could use. He grabbed a candy bar, tore the wrapper off with his teeth and began to eat it as he shoved several more into his pockets. The roll-top was locked but he jimmied it open with a paper clip he found lying on the floor. The inside of the desk was piled high with papers—bills, receipts, old newspapers. A pack of cigarettes lay open next to a book of matches. Danny picked up the pack and lit up, drawing the smoke deep into his lungs. The nicotine hit steadied him. He stuffed the pack into his shirt pocket and took another drag. He felt better.

He went to work on the top drawer and had it open in seconds—more paper and a few food crumbs. In the second drawer he hit the mother lode. A Remington semi-automatic service pistol lay in the drawer beside a box of .45 caliber shells. It wasn't especially unusual to find a gun like this in a locked drawer. It was U.S. military

224

standard issue, carried by soldiers through two world wars, Korea and now Vietnam, and smuggled home as souvenirs by many a returning veteran. Danny brought it up to his eyes to examine more closely. It was a thing of beauty, solid, cool and heavy in his hands. The clip was full, lying in the drawer beside the gun. The chamber was empty, the safety on. Whoever owned the gun knew how to take care of firearms. It was clean and well oiled. Danny's dad had one like this, a Korean War model that he carried ashore with him at Inchon. This one looked older but it was essentially the same gun.

His dad kept his gun locked in a safe in the study at home. Danny only shot it once under his dad's close supervision when he was 12 years-old. He remembered the heft of it, and the god-awful kick of the weapon when it discharged, the deafening noise and the dead numbness in his palm from the recoil. He remembered the story of how his dad stopped a North Korean staff car with it once. The bullet went right through the radiator, broke the water pump, and cracked the engine block. The thing was a cannon compared to the .38 he'd used on the Baker boys.

Danny heard somebody moving around in the shop. He slammed the clip home, jacked a shell into the chamber, and stuffed the gun into the back of his waistband under his jacket. Extra shells went into his pockets. He closed the roll-top, straightened up and squared his shoulders. It was amazing how much better the gun made him feel. With a gun like this no flatfooted cop was going to get him! He took one last look around the office and opened the door to the shop.

A '53 Chevy was parked over the service pit. A white-haired man dressed in the uniform of a service station attendant whistled tunelessly to himself as he went about the task of changing the oil.

"Hey, how about a little service, Grandpa?" said Danny.

The attendant, who was pouring new oil into the engine, looked up and smiled "Oh, howdy, friend. Didn't hear you pull up. Let me get this last quart in and I'll be right with you."

The attendant drained the rest of the oil into the engine, carefully closed the hood and polished his hand print from the chrome hood ornament with the clean rag he held in his hand.

"What can I do for you?" he asked.

Danny pointed over his shoulder with his thumb toward the gas pump on the other side of the building. "The goddamn pump doesn't work."

"I guess it's still off. You're the first person to buy gas today."

"Well, turn it on. I need a fill."

"Hang on a minute." The man walked over to a switch on the wall and flipped it on. He motioned for Danny to follow him as he walked out the open overhead garage door and around to the pumps.

The attendant examined Danny's car as he filled it. "Boy, this baby's a classic," he said. "They don't make 'em like this anymore."

"It's a piece of shit."

"The '53 in the shop is mine. You should have seen her before I started work on her."

"Nice paint job," Danny admitted. "Is there an engine under the hood?"

"You bet. Mechanically she's solid. I went through her myself." The attendant finished pumping gas and placed the nozzle in its receptacle. "That'll be seven dollars and forty-two cents."

"Okay. Can you break a twenty?"

"I think so. Come on inside."

Inside the office Danny reached back as though to get out his billfold then stopped. "Tell you what," he said thoughtfully. "I'll trade you even-up."

"What?"

"For the Chevy. I'll trade you even-up."

The attendant laughed. "That's crazy. Mine's worth three or four-hundred bucks easy. You'd be lucky to get seventy-five for yours."

Danny chuckled. He found the situation hilarious. Somehow the world didn't look nearly as bleak as it had an hour ago. "What's the matter? Not your day to make a deal?"

"I would never make a deal like that."

Danny pulled out the .45 and pointed it at the bridge of the old man's nose. "How about now?" he asked.

It was different when you had a good set of wheels and a weapon. It gave you a whole new perspective on your place in the universe. Before he clubbed the attendant over the head with the barrel of the .45 Danny asked which state he was in. Now he knew exactly where he was and what he was going to do. As he thought again about that last conversation with his dad his cheek muscles bulged in anger. Danny didn't like the word 'no' when it was directed toward him. In fact, it really pissed him off. To hell with the cops and their eyewitness! To hell with running! He was going back to Minnesota to get what he had coming to him and he was going to kill anyone who got in his way!

*   *   *

In the days immediately following Danny's disappearance, Dan spent most of his time in his study with the door closed. He neither worked nor came out to eat. After the third day Michael began to bring him food from the kitchen but Dan rarely ate more than a few bites and the two said little to each other. Their longest conversation came when Dan suddenly looked up as Michael was about to leave the study and asked, "Michael, why are you doing this?"

"Because you do not deserve what you are putting yourself through over Danny," Michael answered.

"Is it pity?"

"No, it's not pity. It's justice. You think it's your fault, but it isn't. Danny is where he is because of what *he* did. This did not happen overnight. He was a long time in coming to the trouble he's in, and he had to make a lot of bad choices to get there. You didn't make his choices for him, Dad."

"I could have helped him. I could have changed what happened."

"Maybe you could have seen what Danny was turning into, but I don't think it would have made a difference in the long run. You think you know Danny, but you don't. I'm not surprised at all that this happened."

"If you saw it coming, why didn't you tell me?"

"Would you have listened?"

Edith was making no preparations to leave the house but Dan didn't care. When the papers were served he would have her carried out the door if she wouldn't leave under her own power. He warned her once, he would not do so again. She'd had fourteen years to get ready for what was going to happen. He called Phil Whitcomb and told him to hurry it up.

Edith received the papers from the courier several days later and as soon as she realized what it was, she threw the package down angrily. So it was done. Very well then, it was time to act. God would not allow this. Daniel Long was going to be punished for his evil ways. He had no right to divorce her. The Bible said divorce was a sin, and she would not stand still for it, especially not now, not when Michael and Danny needed her guidance more than ever.

She heard Michael, Megan and Dan talking in the kitchen. In the past several days Dan had come out of his study and was spending more and more time with Michael. Edith didn't like it. And that little hussy Megan Sullivan was spending entirely too much time with Michael. They would all go outside before long. They did the same thing yesterday.

She heard the outside door close. She rose to her feet and walked across the room to the shuttered window third from the end. She knew they would have to walk past it to reach the garden. There was a crack in the shutter that would allow her to see them if she stood very close and put her eye up to the opening. A moment later they walked by together. Michael was laughing. Never, not in all the years of his childhood, had Michael ever laughed with Edith. Yet he was laughing out loud now. He was enjoying himself. Her eyes narrowed with jealousy. *This was not right!*

Edith appeared to the casual observer to be functional, but her current state of being, arrived at not through accident, or disease, or mental defect, but by choice and through long practice, was certainly not rational. She believed herself to be a champion of the good against the evil, but did not recognize the monstrous evil in her own soul. Her ability to reason from observation, and to recognize her own motives, had been willfully and systematically suppressed. In the self-created chaos that had once been the intellect of Edith Long, her rage was fear for the welfare of her son's eternal soul, her jealousy was unrequited love, and the evil act she was about to commit was the inexorable Will of All-Mighty God.

Edith went to the phone and dialed a number. "I want you to do it now," she said into the receiver. "They are in the garden."

It would take him about twenty minutes to get here but they would still be in the garden. Yesterday they spent half the afternoon out there. She sat down to wait, hardly able to contain her anticipation.

She felt the spirit of the Lord upon her stronger than ever before. Daniel was going to be punished! Her precious Michael would not be allowed to fall under Dan's influence. Michael was consecrated to the Almighty. His life belonged in God's hands to be directed through her as He saw fit. No other outcome could be permitted. No other outcome was Holy.

She waited impatiently for several minutes, and then got up and walked to the crack in the shutters again. The three of them sat together on a bench near the fountain at the center of the garden. She checked her watch. It was time. She turned from the window, grabbed her Bible and marched out of the house holding it before her as though it was a shield of righteousness.

They saw her coming and together they rose to face her. When she grabbed a short length of iron sprinkler pipe that had been left on the lawn by the gardener, Michael stiffened. He knew the look on his mother's face. Edith was close to losing control or had already lost it. Dan thought little of it. It was obvious that she was angry, but he wasn't afraid of Edith. It was impossible for him to take her seriously. Megan's assessment was based mostly on what Michael had communicated to her about his mother. She knew the situation was potentially dangerous. She did not know how dangerous.

As Edith neared she raised the Bible higher. She walked up to Dan and shook it in his face. "Stay away from my son!" she screamed at him. "You have no right. Michael is mine. The Lord gave him to me to train, and you are contaminating him! God is going to punish you for this. He will destroy you!"

"Give it a rest, Edith," said Dan. "We are having a quiet, enjoyable conversation. You were not invited, and you are not welcome. Now, get that Bible out of my face."

"No, I will not leave. I am a vessel of God's will. You may not stand against me!"

"Dad, watch the pipe," Michael warned.

Dan heard, but did not heed, his son's warning. Instead he stepped closer to Edith with the intent of physically compelling her to leave.

"Hello, Dad."

Dan whirled around in shocked surprise. "Danny?" he said with disbelief.

"Yes, Danny!" Edith crowed triumphantly. "When you rejected him, he came to me for help. I gave him what I could but he needs more, and I am going to see that he gets it. He has promised to forsake his evil ways for me. I have brought him back to the fold, Daniel."

"Danny, is this true?" Dan looked at his son incredulously.

"You seem surprised, Dad."

"Yes, I am," said Dan. "But I am glad you came back, whatever your reason. Are you ready to turn yourself in, son?"

"No, I'm here for my money. Mom promised me the money I need."

"You have no money here and neither does your mother."

"I want my money. The money you owe me. The money you refused me when I needed it."

"There is no such money, Danny. You are speaking of *my* money, and I told you before I would support you only if you turned yourself in. I am not going to give you anything until you do that."

"Dad, don't make me hurt you."

"Hurt me? Son, what you did has practically destroyed me. You can't hurt me any more than you already have."

"Don't be so sure about that." Danny produced the .45 from his waistband.

"Do you think you can threaten me with that?" said Dan. "You don't know me very well."

"But Dad, I'm not threatening you. Not directly. You are going to go to the bank and withdraw fifty thousand dollars in cash. You are going to bring it back here to me within an hour. If you don't do it, I will kill Michael."

Edith gasped, her head jerking toward Danny. "That's not what we agreed," she exclaimed.

"Stuff it, bitch" said Danny.

"No! You said you were going to do it, and I would give you the money you needed afterward."

"Edith?" Dan turned to look at his wife.

Danny laughed. "Edith, you are such a goddamn fool. Did you think I would kill the goose *before* he lays the egg?"

Michael stood slightly apart from the group, having backed away a step to keep both Edith and Danny in his range of vision. He caught Megan's eye and got her to move back as well. The time to act was approaching. Danny would kill if he was opposed and his mother, a killer of the spirit all her life, and prone to irrational fits of physical violence, could not be trusted either. Michael knew there was a chance they could all die in the next few minutes but he was not going to let death take them unopposed. He was going to act. The choice to prevail or go down fighting was not a snap decision arrived at in the heat of the moment, it had been made long ago, and now it was as much a part of Michael's character as breathing was. He did not think of what he was going to do as courageous. It was simply the only course of action worth considering. The boy who wondered once where courage came from had no need to wonder any longer.

Dan turned back to Danny again. "Son, you need to think about what you're doing. You can't win this way. Turn yourself in."

"Don't be stupid, Dad. It's too late for that."

"Do it Danny!" Edith's voice was urgent. "You promised, and it must be done."

"Do what?" Danny was looking at his father when he said it.

"He is evil. You must destroy him."

"Did you hear that, Dad? The bitch wants you dead. She's paying me to kill you."

"I heard it," said Dan. "Nothing Edith says or does surprises me anymore. But you have chosen to do her bidding, Danny. That surprises me a great deal."

"Do you call this doing her bidding, Dad?" Danny looked at Edith and said contemptuously, "I would kill him, step-mommy dear. But that would make me entirely dependent on you, wouldn't it? I don't think I'm going to let that happen."

Edith had no plan to use the pipe. A plan presupposes a thinking mind. She wasn't even fully aware that she had the pipe in her hand. She saw it and picked it up because she was angry, and when she was angry she found things to hit with. She would not have dared strike her husband under normal circumstances. He was much too strong and quick for her. But Dan was turned away from her at the moment, looking at Danny, and the desire to destroy the object of her greatest hatred took over. She lowered the Bible and raised the pipe.

Danny and Michael both knew exactly what she intended to do with the pipe, but in that moment Danny froze in fear. He knew that his father was no good to him dead or disabled. He needed money now, and he needed Dan to get it for him. He couldn't shoot Edith because he was afraid of hitting his father who stood between them, so he watched helplessly as the pipe rose into the air and began to move forward. In the split second before the pipe began its downward arc, Michael yelled a warning and leaped at his mother.

Dan began to turn in response, and in the instant the weapon found its mark Michael's forearm deflected it's path just enough to keep it from striking his father directly. The tip of the pipe dealt a glancing blow to the side of Dan's head, knocking him out and tearing a long, bloody gash behind his ear. Dan crumpled to the ground as Michael's rush forced his mother back. Her heal caught on uneven ground and she fell backward with Michael on top of her.

For a frozen moment nobody moved. Edith was moaning, the wind knocked out of her. Michael still lay on top of her, but he and Danny were both looking at their father. The wound was bleeding profusely and to the medically untrained eye it looked as though Dan Long was gravely injured. He wasn't moving at all and there seemed to be blood everywhere.

Suddenly Michael grabbed the pipe and tore it out of his mothers grasp as he leaped to his father's side. Megan joined him a second later. Danny didn't move except to lower the gun. He seemed to be unable to comprehend what had just happened. All of his plans were destroyed. Even if his father was alive the bastard was in no condition to get Danny any money, and money was what he came back for.

"Megan, go call for an ambulance," said Michael.

"No!" The voice was Danny's.

"Dad needs help. Let Megan go for help."

Danny glanced at his brother but did not respond. He could not believe this. It was over. The money was out of reach, his escape plan ruined.

"Danny, let her go for help." Michael was on his feet now, his eyes observing Danny's actions carefully.

"*No!* Both of you stay right where you are," Danny commanded.

"He's going to die if we don't get him to the hospital."

"Goddamnit, fuck him! Fuck that worthless bastard! He's no good to me this way."

"I think he's dead already." It was Edith speaking. She had risen up on one elbow to look at her husband lying on the ground a few feet away. Danny turned slowly toward his stepmother and Edith realized in a shocking moment of clarity that she should not have called attention to herself. There was rage in her stepson's stare, the same kind of reasonless fury she had experienced herself no more than a minute ago, and the shock came from the realization that it was directed toward her.

Suddenly, under the pressure of the moment and through the medium of Danny's countenance alone, she saw what she had spent a lifetime trying to keep hidden from herself: the contents of her soul stripped naked of any pretense and reflected back upon her in the person of her stepson. In this moment, she knew what she would have done with the power that Danny held in his hand. She would have used it.

Cold fear squeezed her lungs until she could not breathe. Danny walked toward her, the gun swinging at his side with an easy negligence that seemed to emphasize rather than belie his intent. He made no immediate effort to raise the weapon, but she knew he would. She knew it with the certainty of a soul recognizing its own.

She looked again at her husband on the ground, this time hoping to see some sign of life, anything to deflect Danny from his purpose. There was none. She tore her eyes away from the sight of what she had done.

Danny loomed over her, his lips curled ugly with fury. "You worthless bitch." His voice was in shocking contrast to the way he looked, a slow, expressionless monotone.

"No Danny, please. You don't realize it right now, but I have saved you." She knew any attempt to convince Danny of this was futile. She didn't believe it herself anymore. But these were the only words she could think of to forestall the terrible purpose she recognized in her stepson's eyes.

"Bitch," said Danny, his voice becoming thick with rage. *"What have you done?"*

Suddenly Danny kicked Edith viciously in the side. She cried out in pain and tried futilely to crawl away. He followed and kicked her again, this time in the face. She was stunned and blinded, her nose broken by the blow. When she could see again Danny's gun was pointed at her chest.

"Please Danny, you can't kill me," she whimpered. "I am your mother."

"My stepmother, bitch."

She watched as Danny's hand tightened around the grip of the .45.

"Thou shalt not kill—Thou shalt not kill." Her frenzied whisper was almost inaudible. The words were more than a desperate plea to Danny, they were self-damnation. Then came a frantic appeal to God's pity and compassion, couched in the same lie that had fueled the last eight years of her life. "I only did what I thought You wanted Lord. God have mercy! I only did what I thought You wanted." Even now, as death stared her in the face, she could not be honest. She knew her plea was a lie. She knew God would see right through it. But the lie was all she had to offer.

Danny was squeezing the trigger. She knew he was going to kill her, and she believed with every fiber of her being that she was going to Hell. She no longer had the will not to believe it. "No!" she cried. "Oh God, forgive me!" The exclamation was driven by neither hope nor remorse, but by an emotion whose name was terror.

"No! Danny, don't! You can't! Oh God, please forgive…"

The explosion of the gun cut off the last sentence before she could finish it. The bullet ripped through her stomach, its path a white-hot, searing agony. The gun fired again and another bullet struck, puncturing a lung on the way in and breaking her spine on the way out. Her chest began to fill with fluid. She gasped for air, trying desperately to finish her plea, but she managed only a faint gurgling sound. She wanted desperately to beg the Lord's forgiveness again, she wanted to scream, to *force* God to hear her prayer before it was too late. But it was already too late. God had withdrawn His countenance, and snatched the breath from her lungs in the hour of her greatest need.

Her peripheral vision began to fade. Her eyes found Danny again, still standing over her, gun back at his side. The rage was gone from his eyes, supplanted by a look of satisfaction that was more terrible than the emotion it replaced. She felt her heart skip a beat, then contract three more times in rhythm and pause again. A second passed. She felt another beat, but it was weaker than the last, and she knew as the terror rose to engulf the remains of her conscious mind that these were the very last moments of her life on earth. A second later her heart stopped, the last spark of awareness disappeared, and her body relaxed into death. The self-made hell that was the mind, the soul, and the life of Edith Long became a bag of flesh and chemicals corrupting in the afternoon sun.

Danny waited for a moment, satisfying himself that his stepmother did not require another bullet. He should have killed her a long time ago, he thought. He did not know, and would not have cared, that Edith Long had just received a human kindness she did not deserve.

19 - IN EVERY END, A BEGINNING

When phone rang at the desk of Detective Harvey Reed, he looked at it with disgust. He was only here because he had extra paperwork to finish. This was his day off, and he wanted to go home. He considered for a second what would happen if he ignored the call and just walked out, but it was only a momentary fantasy. When the phone rang he always answered. He grabbed the receiver and said, "Reed."

It was dispatch on the line. "Glad you're in Detective. We have a report of shots fired out at the Long place. I thought you'd like to know."

Reed sprang into action, grabbing his gun and badge as he spoke into the receiver. "I want all available units responding. Cover the intersections we talked about. I want everyone in position *now!* And call me when it's done. I'll be in my car."

Three weeks ago Michael, came to visit Detective Reed in the station house. The boy told the detective of his brother's rage when Dan would not give him the money he asked for. Dan had already spoken to Reed about the call, but Michael had detailed information about his brother's behavior, and Reed found the boy's insights to be compelling. Michael told the detective of Danny's absolute refusal to accept any constraint on his behavior, his narcissism, his blindness to the results of his actions, his vindictiveness toward anyone who got in his way. Michael believed his brother was perfectly capable of doing what he was accused of doing, and that he might come back to try and punish his father for his refusal to give Danny what he wanted. That's when Reed began to make plans.

In the past several days there had been a number of reports that someone fitting Danny's description was in the area, two of them had him driving an older model Chevrolet. The reports could not been verified, but there were enough of them to make Reed suspicious. There was a possibility the shots meant Danny really was back in town. It was the height of foolhardiness to return to Mansfield with the police looking for him, but Michael had convinced him this was just the thing Danny might try, and Reed was prepared for it. He checked his gun as he walked rapidly out the front door of the station house. He had his own post to man.

When all was set, Reed was going to send one car in with siren blaring. If Danny was back, the noise would put pressure on him. The boy liked to run. Let him run away from those he wished to harm and into the arms of the police. He did not want to face the boy. He knew there was a chance he would have to shoot him if they ever met again, and he wanted to avoid that almost as much as he wanted to see Danny punished for his crimes, but he would do his duty no matter what that required.

*   *   *

Danny looked up from his stepmother's body. "She finally got what she had coming," he said to no one in particular.

"You need to get out of here, Danny." Michael said carefully.

Danny's face suddenly distorted with petulant rage. *"Damn it, I want my money!"*

"Dad can't give it to you now," said Michael.

"I need money! Why didn't you stop her?"

"I tried, Danny. Why didn't you?"

"Shut up. You got any money on you?"

"No."

"Then you're no good to me. I might as well shoot the both of you."

"You can't do that. How will you get your hands on Dad's money if you kill me?"

"What are you talking about?"

Michael was talking, not so much to convince Danny, as to buy time. He knew Detective Reed had made plans for Danny's return. If the shots had been heard and reported to the police, Reed would be on the way, but he was not going to assume anything not in evidence.

"Who gets the money now?" said Michael. "If Dad dies they won't give it to you. You need me to keep it for you. It's the only chance you have to get what you want. You need to get out of here and find a place to hide. Wait for things to settle down. I'll keep half the money for you. We can split it fifty-fifty later when you can come back."

"Yeah, right, good idea, fifty-fifty, right down the middle." The sneer was back on Danny's face again. "Maybe I'll take the girl to make sure I get what's coming to me."

"You take Megan and I promise you will never see a cent of that money. You don't need her anyway. You need me. Come on, Danny, have I ever lied to you? I'm always straight with you even when you don't like what I say."

"What kind of fool do you think I am, kid? What if he doesn't die?"

In addition to remaining alive himself, Michael had two main goals: to keep Megan safe and to get his father to a doctor. Danny would talk only so long, then he would act. Michael had to find a way to neutralize his brother, and he could think of only one way to do it. It was very dangerous, and carried with it a high probability that he would be shot, but it was certainly no worse than the situation they were in now, and time was running out. He still had the pipe in his hand. If no other option presented itself he was going to attack Danny with it, gun or no gun. He would have to choose the right moment, and he would have to act quickly in order to have a chance of succeeding, but it was better than waiting for Danny to decide to shoot them.

Michael started to put his plan into action by moving about a bit, letting himself wander closer to his brother. The closer he was when he attacked the better his chances would be. But before he could act, Megan suddenly went to her knees and began to sob, holding her hands over her face as she did so. "Please don't kill me," she wailed. "I'll do anything you say, but don't kill me."

"Megan, I'll handle this," Michael warned. Megan ignored him and began to crawl toward Danny, still on her knees and sobbing. She reached him and grabbed his arm. "You don't need to kill me. I won't say anything. I promise."

"Megan, get out of the way!" Michael knew she was trying to distract his brother, but she was taking a terrible chance.

Danny was enjoying it. She was a little young, but cute in an adolescent sort of way, and he liked hearing her beg for mercy. The fact that she was Michael's girlfriend made it even more enjoyable. Danny tried half-heartedly to free his arm, but Megan wouldn't let go. Then she switched her grip to Danny's gun hand, wailing that she didn't want to die. Danny looked down at her and laughed, trying again to pull his hand away. Megan tightened her grip and sobbed louder, hiding her forehead against Danny's arm as she held on with ferocious determination.

Danny seemed to see no danger in Megan holding onto him. He was still amused. "Damn it girl, let go of my arm." He laughed and slapped her across the top of the head with his free hand in a half-hearted attempt to get her to let go.

Suddenly Danny's head jerked up. A siren had just begun to wail only a few blocks away and it was coming closer. He turned toward the sound, violently pushing Megan away from him as he did so.

In that moment, Michael charged. He had two free steps before Danny saw him coming. The gun was coming level as Michael leaped over Megan and crashed into Danny's chest. The gun went off with a roar as Danny staggered backward from the momentum of Michael's attack.

Michael brought the pipe down as hard as he could on his brother's gun hand. Danny grunted in pain and dropped the weapon as the attack pushed him backward. The gun lay in the grass behind them. They both tried for it, but Michael got there first. He grasped the weapon and started to rise, but Danny planted a brutal kick in Michael's side and he went down, the gun and the pipe both flying from his hands. Danny scrambled for the gun, but just as he reached it the pipe struck him on the shoulder. Megan was on his back with the pipe in her hands trying desperately to hit Danny on the head with it.

Danny threw Megan off just as Michael rejoined the battle. They both went down again, and the gun went off a second time. Megan's head hit the ground hard, and she was momentarily stunned. Michael was trying everything he could to keep Danny occupied and avoid the gun, but he knew that Danny was too much for him to handle.

"Run Megan," he yelled, "Get out of here!"

Megan ignored the warning. She was up and on Danny again, beating on him with the pipe wherever she could find an opening while Michael attacked with his fists. The fury of their assault held Danny at bay. They kept him on the defensive, forcing him to concentrate on protecting himself and the gun. At close quarters the .45 was a hindrance. He could use it as a club but he could not aim it while he had to protect the hand that held it.

Suddenly Danny threw them both off with an enormous effort and struggled to his feet with the gun still in his hand. The gun was raising to shoot, and Michael crouched to charge at Danny's legs when a voice spoke.

"Police! Drop the weapon," the voice commanded.

Danny froze. The cop was somewhere off to the right, out of the range of his vision. The voice sounded vaguely familiar but Danny didn't care who it was. He wanted so badly to shoot Michael and Megan right now. He wanted to kill them both for what they tried to do to him, but the cop… *the goddamn cop was in his way!* He spread his hands, raised them to shoulder level, and began to turn around. He did not drop the gun.

"I *will* shot you if I have to, Danny," said the voice. "Drop the gun. Now!" Danny froze again. He was not afraid. There wasn't a cop alive who could take him. Hadn't he proven that time and again?

Detective Reed was an old hand at this kind of game, and his next move was made with the assumption that Danny would not go easily. Immediately after he spoke he quietly took three rapid steps to his left. The act removed Michael and Megan further from his field of fire, increased the distance that Danny would have to turn to bring his gun to bear, and put him in a place where Danny would not expect him to be.

Danny chuckled to himself at the cop's stupidity. He was just going to have to teach this brainless flatfoot a lesson he would not survive. Suddenly he whirled, brought the gun down in front of him, and triggered three rapid shots toward the location of the voice. The act was carried out with athletic precision, in one blinding, fluid motion. But the boy began to fire before he had his target, and the shots sailed through empty air as two bullets from Reed's police issue .38 tattooed the center of Danny's chest no more than an inch apart.

The gun fell from Danny's hand and he looked down at himself in surprise. There was blood on his shirt and he couldn't figure out where it came from. There hadn't been any blood a second ago. His knees felt weak. It was a curious sensation, physical weakness was completely new to him, and now his head was a block of iron and the earth was a giant magnet, pulling him down. He resisted for a moment, then decided it wasn't worth the effort. His legs buckled. He fell face forward in the grass and died.

Detective Reed ran over to the boy with his gun still drawn. He checked for a pulse but there was none. "Damn you, Danny Long," he said. "God damn you to hell! I didn't want to do that." He looked down at Danny for a moment longer, and then rose to his feet and holstered his weapon. A quick glance at Edith told him she was dead too.

With his brother no longer a threat, Michael was back at Dan's side. "Mr. Reed, my dad is alive." He was busy checking Dan's pulse again. "I think he's hurt bad."

Reed yelled at one of the uniformed officers to get the ambulance into the yard.

"Michael, look at your sleeve. You've been hit!" Megan pointed at Michael's arm. There was a hole in his shirt near the shoulder and his shirt sleeve was already soaked with blood to the elbow.

Michael glanced down at his arm. "Yes, he got me when I jumped him. I'll be ok."

"You need to sit down, boy." Reed walked toward Michael. "That looks pretty serious."

Michael ignored the detective and turned to Megan. "And what the hell were you doing? You could have been killed!"

"I was trying to keep *you* alive, stupid," Megan shot back. "I knew what you were going to do. I could see it in your eyes. Only you would have tried that with nothing but a lousy piece of pipe in your hand."

"You should have run when I told you to."

"Did you think I was going to let you fight him alone? Now sit down."

"I had to do something. He would have killed us."

"I know that. Sit down, Michael!"

"I need to help Dad."

"The ambulance is coming. Sit down before you fall over."

Finally realizing he felt dizzy and weak, Michael took Megan's advice and sat down on the garden bench. Megan and Detective Reed helped him get his shirt off. It appeared to be a flesh wound, but a nasty one. The bullet had gone through Michael's upper arm leaving a half inch hole going in and a larger one coming out. They tore his shirt and tied it around his arm to stop the bleeding.

An ambulance pulled up in front of the garage and two paramedics got out. "Over here," Reed called, motioning toward them. The paramedics gathered up their gear and came running. "Him, and him." Reed instructed, pointing at Dan, then at Michael. "The others are dead."

One of the paramedics went to Dan. The other knelt beside Michael, and began to examine him.

"Not me, you idiot," said Michael. "My dad! Take care of my dad."

"That isn't tomato sauce on your arm, son."

"This is nothing, damn it. Take care of my dad!"

Dan Long opened his eyes and realized after a moment that he was in a hospital room. Michael sat in the chair beside him and Megan Sullivan stood by the window.

"Hello," said Dan.

Michael looked up and smiled. "Hi Dad."

"Well, isn't this ironic."

Michael chuckled. "A little."

"What happened?"

"Do you remember where we were, in the garden? Danny was back and he wanted money, and you wouldn't give it to him."

"Yes, I remember."

Megan moved over to the side of the bed and put her hand on Dan's arm.

"How are you feeling," she said.

"Wonderful. Tell me when they find my head. What happened?"

"Mom hit you with the pipe when you were looking at Danny," said Michael.

"Where is she now? In jail I hope."

"Dad, she's dead. Danny shot her."

"Oh god, why?"

The sinking sensation in Dan's chest was not from a sense of loss over the news that his wife was dead, but from renewed fear for Danny. The boy refused to learn. He just kept digging himself a deeper hole.

"He couldn't get at your money with you knocked out cold. That made him mad, and he shot her," said Michael. "She just got in his way, Dad, and he shot her for it."

"What's wrong with your arm?" said Dan, pointing toward the bandage and the sling his son was wearing.

"Danny's gun went off when we were trying to get it away from him. I'll be fine."

"He shot you too? Where is he now? Has he been caught?"

Michael paused. He knew that what he was about to say was going to hurt his father, perhaps more than he had ever been hurt before, and if Dan Long was going to survive, it would be up to Michael to help him find the will to live through the coming moment, and a reason to live the next.

"He's dead too, Dad. Detective Reed had to shoot him when he wouldn't give up."

Dan's eyes squeezed shut and his mouth opened in agony. The slow, ragged intake of his breath was the sound of a soul stricken with a crushing sense of loss.

"How long ago?" Dan said finally.

"Not long. Only a few hours. Dad, tell me what you're thinking."

"I can't. I must not put this on you."

"I want to hear it."

"No you don't."

"You have to tell me Dad. I can help you."

"There is nothing left to help."

"Dad you need to stop this. It's not your fault."

"Then whose is it? Who else is to blame for this?"

"Your mistakes did not turn Danny into a killer. Danny did that all by himself."

"Michael, how can you say that? What about what I did to you? I do not deserve to be forgiven for either of you, and I cannot forget what I did, even if you can."

"Dad, this isn't forgiveness and I promise you I will not forget either. I am simply acknowledging that you are not the man who forced me to leave home. You are different. I think you can be the father I used to imagine you were, and I don't want to lose that. You are going to get better, and then you are going to come home."

"Come home to what? I've destroyed my family."

"I'm still alive. You haven't destroyed me."

"Everything else then. There's nothing left for me."

"Damn it, I don't want to hear that! If you think you have no reason to live, I'll give you one you can understand. You owe me. You owe me the father I never had. You owe me all the things a father is supposed to give his son. Do I need to tell you what that is? You tried to give it to Danny and he rejected it. Now you owe it to me."

"You're wrong son, I gave him nothing."

"Then I'm your second chance."

"Danny is dead, and you're better off without me."

"Well I'm still here. I'm not going away. Don't dismiss that as though it means nothing to you."

Dan looked at his son and smiled sadly. "Yes I get that, and for the life of me I can't figure out why."

"Listen to him, Mr. Long," said Megan. "Just listen and think about what he's saying. He says he isn't forgiving what you did, and I believe him. I've never heard it put this way before, but it makes sense. It's what you are now that matters to him, not what you did or thought you did in the past, and it's what should matter to you, too. Michael wants you alive and happy because *that* is important to him."

"What am I that is worth what you are trying to do?"

"You don't know what you are, because you won't let yourself know it," Michael answered, "and you suffer under a burden of guilt that isn't justified. Not anymore. You made mistakes. Learn from them and move on."

"I don't understand any of this," said Dan.

"Well don't be so quick to condemn yourself until you do," said Michael.

The doctors let Dan out of the hospital long enough to attend the funeral of Edith and Danny Long, held in the chapel of a local funeral home. Michael went to be at his father's side and Megan went because Michael did and she wanted to support them both. Dan did not appear to grieve but spoke very little and did not seem to listen to the service. He stared straight ahead, motionless until Michael took him by the arm to lead him out after it was over. As the three were walking away from the graves after the burial they were stopped by Detective Reed.

"I wish I could express how sorry I am about this, Dan," said Reed.

"You don't need to. You did what you had to do," Dan replied.

"I tried to disarm him without a fight. He wouldn't listen. I did not want this to happen."

"I know that. It's all right Harv, you knew it was going to end this way before I did. You tried to warn me."

"I've seen boys go this way before, Dan. Sometimes it's hard for a parent to recognize when it's happening, and after a certain point it just can't be stopped." Detective Reed turned to Michael. "You take care of your father, son. He's a good man."

"I know," said Michael.

*   *   *

It was a frosty morning in mid-September. The leaves were already nearing the peak of color and in the low spots it was cold enough for Michael's breath to become visible. The sun was about to clear the horizon as he pushed through the tall grass to his old vantage point on top of the hill. He sat down and settled in for a wait.

His dream came again last night, the dream that he was back in the rail yard fighting for his life. It happened much less frequently now, and with less intensity, so it took him only a moment when he awakened to realize it wasn't real. But as he lay waiting to fall asleep again he heard a freight train rumble by on the tracks near the highway, and that made him think of the passenger train.

The train always came very early in the morning, but when the weather was good and school was not in session, he was often on the hill to watch it go by. It occurred to Michael as he lay thinking, that in all the months since his return from the hospital he had not been back to the lookout even once. He wondered why. It took him a while to figure it out, but when he finally did he set his alarm and fell asleep immediately. There was something he wanted to do early in the morning.

Dawn broke in the east and the world began to brighten. Michael heard the warning blast of a diesel locomotive echo far in the distance and lifted his head. He knew that sound. It was different in a very subtle way from the sound made by a freight train, and to Michael it was as indelible as a fingerprint. The noise came from the Empire Builder, on the last leg of its long reach from Seattle to St. Paul. He squinted at the western horizon trying to catch a glimpse but it was still too dark, and the train was too far away.

He remembered when he saw it for the first time at the age of nine, racing toward him across the countryside in the morning light. He thought then it was the most beautiful sight on the face of the earth. He had always understood the malevolence of the world he grew up in, but never why the sight of this train always lifted his spirits. This morning for the first time he understood, at least as an emotion he was at last beginning to find the words for. The beauty lay in the sight of form and function married superbly to a human purpose, the uplift in seeing that purpose unchained and running free. That is what the train helped him to imagine as possible, and in the dark hours of his childhood, that is what he needed so desperately to see.

Again the sound of the horn echoed across the rolling prairie, and again his eyes squinted, trying to make out the source. He saw it first as nothing more than a headlight appearing suddenly around a far-off bend. Then there was the brief glint of light on the engine's windshield, and a minute later another flash as the windows of the passenger train's iconic domed observation cars reflected back the rays of the rising sun. Michael rose to his feet to watch as the train hurtled toward him, a long, low, orange and black arrow dashing across the countryside so fast he could imagine at this distance that it was flying rather than rolling upon rails of steel.

The engineer noticed Michael standing on the hill, his form backlit by the morning sky, and when the train was still a half-mile off its horn blew again. Year after year the engineer had watched that figure grow taller. He knew that one day the boy would never come back again, and when he disappeared for almost a year the engineer thought he would never see him again. The engineer did not know who the lad was or exactly why he missed seeing him, but in the instant before he blew the horn he realized how happy he was that the boy was back.

When he was a young child, Michael was always the one to signal first, waving in order to coax a response. The engineer's preemptive blast was a greeting to the unexpected, and an acknowledgement of a sense of values and emotions both he and the boy knew they shared. As the train approached, Michael slowly raised his hand in answer to the engineer's greeting. The gesture looked like farewell—farewell and benediction—and the engineer realized suddenly that he would never again see the boy standing on the hill.

The train reached the curve that rounded the hill, heralding its arrival with another blast from its horn and a roaring avalanche of sound. The hillside shook with the channeled force of its passing and then it was gone.

Michael stood motionless for a minute, replaying the last few seconds in his mind, fixing it in his memory for all time. Last night as he laid thinking of the train and what it meant to him he came to realize that all the old barriers to achieving what was possible were gone. He did not need to imagine the possible in order to endure the actual. The possible was his to be earned any time he wished to begin.

So Michael Long was here on a bright September morn to say goodbye to the train and this place on the hill. He did not need them anymore, not as he once needed them. They would live on in the sense that all memories live, as mileposts upon which to gauge the progress of one's soul. But the possible was to be made real by doing, not by dreaming, and there was so much to be done.

The End

www.ingramcontent.com/pod-product-compliance
Lightning Source LLC
Chambersburg PA
CBHW071142170626
46809CB00002B/734